# FATAL GAMBLE

## A GALLAGHER NOVEL

**JP O'DONNELL**

Author of Deadly Codes: A Gallagher Novel
and
Pulse of My Heart: A Gallagher Novel

**FATAL GAMBLE**
**A GALLAGHER NOVEL**



*iUniverse books may be ordered through booksellers or by contacting:*

*iUniverse*
*1663 Liberty Drive*
*Bloomington, IN 47403*
*www.iuniverse.com*
*1-800-Authors (1-800-288-4677)*



*ISBN: 978-1-5320-6994-9 (sc)*
*ISBN: 978-1-5320-6995-6 (e)*

*Print information available on the last page.*

*iUniverse rev. date: 03/04/2019*

To Ronney: my wife, my editor, always my best friend

# Chapter 1

At six-thirty in the morning, Dr. Jonathan Becker reached over and turned off the alarm clock for the last time in his life.

He got up, and then, on an impulse, bent over and kissed his wife, Suzanne, who was still sleeping.

"Bye, Sweetheart. I'll be in the office all day. See you for dinner," he said softly.

She rolled her head slightly upward and partially opened her eyes. She nodded and smiled. Then she snuggled her head into her pillow and went back to sleep.

Dr. Becker quietly closed the bedroom door and walked down the winding staircase to the foyer of their Country-French home. He disarmed the alarm system by entering the four-digit security code into the keypad at the side entry to the house, stepped out, and picked up the morning edition of the *Boston Globe* from the driveway. It was a beautiful October morning in New England. He sat down at the kitchen table for his favorite breakfast combination—the newspaper and a bowl of triple-berry Cheerios.

He left the house at seven-thirty in plenty of time to make it to his office in West Castle for his first patient at eight-thirty.

To avoid the traffic on Routes 3 and 95, he always drove on the back roads to West Castle and listened to the sports radio station, WEEI. Between 7:40 and 8:00, the two co-hosts did a segment called "Headlines" in which they satirized and spoofed the leading stories of the day or discussed some whacky news item. It was funny and irreverent—a great way to enjoy the ride.

Dr. Becker reached West Castle after the usual twenty-minute drive and turned into the large parking lot of his medical building. Looking at the six-story, multi-shaded brick building in the morning sunshine, surrounded by its manicured landscaping, always gave him a warm sense of satisfaction. He was part of the six-man partnership that bought the land, designed, and built the Parker Hill Medical Building, which was the foundation of his financial assets and the place where he had established one of the most successful pediatric practices in Massachusetts.

He drove to the rear of the parking lot. "Headlines" was almost over, so he lowered his window slightly and sat in his Lexus with the motor running to listen to the final portion of the show while he looked over his appointment book for the week.

A black vehicle pulled into the space immediately to his left. The front passenger window rolled down. An arm extended out of the window. The motion caught Dr. Becker's attention, and he slowly turned his head toward the black car.

*What's happening here?*

A .357 Magnum revolver equipped with a silencer at the end of the barrel was pointed directly at him.

*My God—not like this!*

Before he could react, the glass window of his car shattered with a loud "pop." A powerful force struck his neck and lower jaw, driving him violently to his right. His body recoiled. Still leaning on his right side, he offered an easy target for the second bullet that screamed along the top his head. Blood and particles of bone splattered all over the interior of the car.

The black car slowly backed out of its space and drove away. Dr. Jonathan Becker slumped forward. His body gradually settled to the right of the steering wheel. The motor of his car kept running.

It was eight o'clock.

"Headlines" was over.

# Chapter 2

Corin Albrecht always parked her car in the rear of the parking lot so she could admire the flower beds as she walked toward the building. Today, the hearty mums and marigolds were gorgeous, and she was totally focused on them until she felt the crunch of glass under her shoes as she passed by a car.

*"Oh, my god! Glass! Did someone break into this car?"* she thought as she lifted her foot quickly and stepped back.

Her eyes followed the glass trail toward Dr. Becker's car, then up to the blown-out window. She walked back and leaned down to look in the car. The sight of a man's body slouched over the front seat horrified her. The color red was everywhere.

Blood!

She screamed, feeling as if her knees were buckling under her. With tears streaming down her face, she reached for her cell phone. Her hands shook so badly it took three tries to dial 911.

"West Castle Police. Is this an emergency?"

"Yes! Someone's been shot. I think he's dead! I just saw him!" she yelled.

"Try to calm down ma'am. Can you tell me your name and your location?"

"My name?"

"Yes, tell me your name and where you're located."

She looked back toward the medical building as if she had never seen the place before.

Finally, she answered, "Parker Hill Medical Building."

"Where in the building are you, Ma'm?"

"In? Uh … no … I'm outside … in the parking lot."

"Okay, Ma'am. Help is on the way. Stay on the line with me. Are you injured? Is anyone else hurt?"

Corin was unable to respond.

The operator continued. "Did you see what happened? Can you tell me your name?" Is there anybody else with you?"

Corin Albrecht remained silent and swallowed hard. She put her cell phone into her bag and backed away from the gruesome scene, feeling weak and nauseous. She clutched her forehead with her hand and tried to keep herself from fainting.

Within seconds the sound of sirens blared from a distance and grew louder. Three police cruisers, followed closely by an ambulance, entered the south entrance to the parking lot. The flashing red and blue lights reflected off the glass windows of the building. The scene had become eerily electric.

Three police officers—guns drawn—emerged from the cruisers. They crouched down—eyes scanning all around the parking lot for any signs of the shooter. Seeing none, they approached Corin who was standing in the rear of the parking lot holding her head in her hands.

"Are you alright, lady?" shouted one of the officers.

Corin looked up. Her face had become ashen. She took a wobbly step and pointed to Dr. Becker's car.

"He's in there," she screamed.

As Corin began to lose her balance, one of the officers placed his arm around her shoulders and gently guided her to the back seat of his nearby cruiser. Now confident that no imminent threat existed, the other officers sprinted toward the car and waved the ambulance forward. The ambulance sped toward the back of the parking lot and came to a screeching halt. Three uniformed men emerged from the ambulance and rushed over toward the officer who was tending to Corin.

The first officer to reach the car winced as he looked at the victim's gaping, bloody wounds. He leaned in and placed his hand on Dr. Becker's neck.

"I think I've got a pulse here," he yelled.

Two of the EMTs quickly responded to his call. Working carefully as a team, they placed an oxygen mask over his mouth and nose and applied manual traction to stabilize the doctor's spine as they up-righted him in his seat. They dressed his wounds with trauma pads and slid him out of the vehicle onto a backboard and into the ambulance.

"Oh my god, it's Dr. Becker," one of the men called out.

"Dr. Becker?" said the officer.

"He's a pediatrician in this medical building."

"Jesus!" the officer said, as he looked skyward and shook his head in disbelief.

One of the police officers hopped into the back of the ambulance with one of the EMTs and barked to no one in particular, "Hold that vehicle until the crime scene guys get here and process it." With that, the ambulance sped out of the parking lot toward West Castle Hospital.

The third EMT remained on the scene and spread a light blanket over Corin who had begun to shiver in the morning air.

"She's in shock," he said to the police officers as he offered her a bottle of water and encouraged her to lie down.

"No—no—I'm okay," she murmured as she sat in the car.

Shock and anguish spread throughout the small crowd of onlookers that had gathered a short distance from the car. Most were employees in the building; others were patients who had arrived for their appointments. They stood in disbelief as the emergency vehicle, with its sirens blaring, drove away carrying the pediatrician who had been loved and respected by the entire community.

The police officers moved quickly and cordoned off the rear section of the parking lot, including Dr. Becker's car, with yellow crime-scene tape. Even the police officers seemed unnerved by the entire situation; after all—West Castle?—shootings just didn't happen in this town.

Detective Jack Hoskins pulled up in a dark blue, unmarked car and left it parked diagonally with the front door open. As he got out of his car, all of the police action seemed to stop and focus on him. The uniformed police officers deferred to him as he peered into Dr. Becker's car and started asking questions. Hoskins, a burly, barrel-chested man, was no stranger to crime scenes. He had been a Boston cop and police detective for more than thirty years before taking the job in West Castle, a place with little stimulation for someone used to solving big-city crimes. But now, in just his second year on this road-to-retirement job, he felt a familiar rush of excitement as he looked at a scene that bore all the markings of a mob hit.

"What've we got here?" asked Hoskins, his eyes riveted on the blood- splattered interior of the car.

"No one saw or heard anything, Jack," said one of the officers. "The vic is Dr. Jonathan Becker—pediatrician in this building. Appeared to be shot at least twice. Once in the neck; once in the head."

"Is he gonna make it?"

"Doubtful. Looked pretty bad."

"Where's the woman who made the call? Did she see anything?"

"She's sitting over there—in my cruiser," said the other officer, a young guy who looked like he had just graduated from high school, let alone the police academy.

Hoskins made his way over to Corin.

"Excuse me, ma'am. Detective Jack Hoskins—West Castle Police Department. I know you're upset, but I need to ask you a few questions."

Corin looked up at him. Her skin was flushed, and her face wet with tears.

"Did you see anyone near the car or driving away when you came in today?"

"No," she said softly.

The response hardly left her mouth when Hoskins barked, "Did you see a car leaving the entrance to the lot when you came in?"

"No. It was pretty quiet when I got here," said Corin, trying to cope with the barrage of questions from her intimidating inquisitor.

"Did you hear any loud noises? Popping sounds? Tires screeching? Anything unusual?"

"No—nothing until I stepped on the broken glass and looked into the window of that car," she replied with a shrug but still shaking from her jarring discovery.

Hoskins recognized that she had nothing to offer and brusquely turned away, barely acknowledging her willingness to help. He walked back to Dr. Becker's car and studied it intently. He looked past the gore. Instead, he tried to visualize the path the bullets must have taken as they smashed through the glass, penetrated his head and neck, and then passed into the leather fabric of the passenger door. The size of the holes and their location near the door handle indicated a large caliber weapon fired in a downward direction. Hoskins, unfazed by the blood all around him, studied the floor mats and seat cushions, looking for possible clues or bullet fragments. The crime scene did not repel him—it made him salivate.

Hoskins called over to the two police officers who were taking notes from people in the crowd.

"I want every employee in the building interviewed. Find out what they heard, what they saw, anything unusual that happened here in the past few weeks. Did they see any strangers hanging around? Talk to all of Becker's employees, especially those who took his phone calls and messages. Did he owe anyone a lot of money?

Any patient or family who had a problem with him? Was he running around on his wife? Ask if he got any threatening phone calls."

The officers nodded, scribbling his orders on their notepads as they tried to keep up with his ranting. Hoskins flashed a look of disdain and then mumbled a final condescending jab.

"You guys got it all? You better not forget anything."

Hoskins slowly got into his car, using his left hand on the edge of the roof for support as he settled into his seat. His eyes winced—a sign that his back problems had become more than just a minor annoyance. Just as he was about to drive out of the parking lot, Hoskins' two-way sounded.

"Detective Hoskins?"

Hoskins held his two-way closer with an annoyed look. "What is it?"

"Just got a call from the ER. Dr. Becker—DOA at the hospital."

Hoskins didn't respond. He merely drove out of the parking lot and turned right toward West Castle Hospital where he hoped to see Dr. Becker's wife.

*By this time, someone must have called her about the attack on her husband.*

Hoskins wanted to be one of the first to judge her reaction to the news.

*The random act of some nut job or the work of a professional hit man? Either way, I'm gonna take a look at the spouse first.*

# Chapter 3

A woman sat on a bench in the waiting area of the Emergency Room at West Castle Hospital with her head down, sobbing uncontrollably. She had short, silver-gray hair and wore a black leather, waist-length jacket and black pants. Her face was pale and drawn—no make-up. It appeared that she had just thrown herself together before getting to the hospital. Another woman, looking shocked herself, had one arm around her shoulders trying to offer comfort while simultaneously looking all around the room as if searching for help.

Hoskins walked in to the Emergency Room. The police officer who had accompanied the EMTs to the hospital immediately came over to him.

"Which one's the wife," asked Hoskins.

"The lady on the left with the gray hair," said the officer.

"Do you know who notified her?"

"Not for sure, but I believe it was someone from the medical staff who told her to come over as soon as possible. She's only been here for a few minutes."

Hoskins nodded. "Okay, let's go," he said as he motioned the officer to follow him to the bench where the two women were sitting.

"Excuse me, Mrs. Becker," said the officer. "This is Detective Hoskins. If it's alright, he'd like to have a few words with you."

The woman with the gray hair slowly looked up. Then she merely nodded her head as she dabbed her eyes with a tissue.

"I know this is an extremely difficult time for you Mrs. Becker," said Hoskins. "I'm sorry about your husband, but could you answer a few questions for me?"

"Yes, I'll try," she replied.

"Do you have any idea who could have done this to Dr. Becker?"

"No—I still can't believe it," she said, her voice trembling.

"Did he give you any signs of trouble or that anyone was causing him problems?"

"No—nothing unusual. He never said a word about any problems. I would have known."

Her voice cracked with emotion, and her head leaned onto the shoulder of the other woman. She began crying again.

Hoskins crouched down beside her, and took her quivering hands into his. This was not easy for Hoskins, a man who could never be accused of having a soft touch.

"Mrs. Becker," he said with a reassuring voice, "I want you to know that we will do everything possible to find out who did this."

His words were full of conviction—not just a casual promise, but a vow that he would devote all his time and energy to solving this crime.

Hoskins nodded to both women and said, "If you'll excuse me ladies…" He trailed off without finishing and walked over to the registration desk of the emergency room.

He turned to the charge nurse, a pretty brunette sitting behind the desk.

"Who's the doctor on duty?" he asked.

"Dr. Kendrick."

"I need to speak to him."

She pushed a button at her desk that opened a set of automatic doors, allowing Hoskins to enter the main area of the emergency room. A few minutes later, another set of automatic doors opened, and a young man emerged, wearing hospital scrubs and a surgeon's cap that was off-center and tied loosely around his head.

"I'm Dr. Kendrick. How can I help you?" the young man asked.

He placed his hands on his hips and quizzically eyed the intimidating person standing in front of him.

"Jack Hoskins, West Castle PD. Just want to make sure that nothing is disturbed until the medical examiner performs the autopsy."

"No problem. We've already contacted the ME's office. They'll be doing the 'post' within the next two hours."

"What was the time?"

"He was pronounced at 8:25 AM," said the doctor with a matter-of-fact tone.

A few seconds passed. Hoskins did not respond. Kendrick's shoulders sagged as he seemed to relax into an "off the record" demeanor.

Kendrick sighed.

"We haven't had a murder victim brought into this hospital in more than ten years. And then today—it happens to be one of the doctors on the staff. How do you figure that?"

He hesitated for a second as his question hung in the air. He looked around to the rear door of the ER, and then turned back to Hoskins.

"This is really a tough one," he said, "I knew Jonathan Becker very well."

"Yeah, this is tough for all of us, Doc," said Hoskins.

No expression; no emotion. Then he asked, "You knew Dr. Becker pretty well?"

"Yes,"

"Anything you can tell me about him—any issues in his life—personal matters that might cause someone to harm him?"

"Not Jonathan Becker … no one ever had a bad word to say about him."

Hoskins shrugged, almost ignoring the response, then turned and coldly walked out to the waiting area. He paused for a brief moment and stared across the room toward the two women. Suzanne

Becker continued to sit on the bench; the other woman held her a little more tightly and talked to her quietly.

Hoskins just nodded as he walked by. He had already eliminated Suzanne Becker as a suspect in his book. He had held her hands and seen the pain and total devastation in her face. As a veteran of dozens of murder investigations, he had learned to read people—to look into their eyes and know when they were faking, trying to throw the police off track. He knew Mrs. Becker's reactions were genuine and that she had nothing to do with her husband's murder.

Hoskins had just one problem—until the ballistics tests and the report from the medical examiner came back, he didn't have a single clue to tell him where to begin.

# Chapter 4

Daniel Cormac Gallagher Jr. rolled over in bed, opened one eye, and looked at his clock radio—eight forty-five in the morning. He had planned to get up by seven thirty but just couldn't get his body moving.

Definitely not a morning person, he had pressed the snooze button five times before finally turning the clock off sometime after eight o'clock. When he eventually did get out of bed, he always needed several cups of coffee and a long shower to get his molecules mobilized; then, usually by about ten-thirty or eleven, he was up to full steam.

But lazy mornings suited him just fine. As a private investigator, the scoundrels he secretly followed didn't cause too much mischief in the mornings, and the people he interviewed never seemed to be available until later in the day.

He finally got into the bathroom and looked at himself in the mirror.

"Oooh, you look pretty scary today," he said, bending over the sink and splashing some cool water on his face and stubbly beard.

His black hair was infiltrated with ever-increasing amounts of gray at the temples and the crown.

*Is that what they call distinguished? Well, at least I've still got a full head of hair.*

His hair was trimmed short, hardly requiring a comb to make it look presentable. He reached for his toothbrush and applied a generous amount of toothpaste. Brushing and flossing his teeth were true compulsions—no cavities or gum disease for this guy—his teeth were perfect, and he worked at keeping them that way.

At age forty-five, Gallagher had reached a certain level of peace and comfort with his life. He had recovered emotionally from his divorce and the painful circumstances that caused him to leave the Boston police. He had started his business as a private investigator seven years ago. By now, his reputation had spread so well that each new case that came through the door seemed to bring two others. A dogged investigator, he had a clever, but natural way of getting information out of people. Strangers felt comfortable around Gallagher and were willing to talk to him. Somehow people would actually tell him things that they might not tell to the police. Whether it was the front-desk clerk at a motel or a hooker on the street, Gallagher could convince them to provide the facts he needed to help solve a case.

Most of his cases had a similar theme: looking for a missing teenager who had left the suburbs for the wild life of the city; trying to locate a deadbeat father; tracking the escapades of a cheating husband; or running background checks for suspicious fathers whose daughters were intent on marrying a gold digger. No matter what the assignment, he had an amazing record of success and generally produced the results his clients wanted.

In some ways, however, this success merely underscored a flaw that he actually recognized in himself—he simply couldn't let go. Gallagher was relentless. He had to follow a job through to its end, never accepting defeat or letting circumstances get the best of him. He would become consumed with a case and dissecting the evidence, the details of which would stay with him morning, noon, and night, until he came up with an answer that tied everything together into one neat, plausible package.

This singular, unwavering approach had been a problem for him as a police officer and eventually led to an impasse with his supervisors, who felt that he refused to follow departmental orders and protocol. He still bristled at the unfair accusations that had been leveled at him. He had to admit, when he left the police force, most of his superiors had been glad to see him go. This left a blemish on his record, but more importantly, a scar on his psyche.

Except for his personal secretary, Diane, no one ever called him anything but "Gallagher." As far back as he could remember, that was his name to his friends, teachers, teammates, even his first wife, and now, Kate, the latest woman in his life. In fact, his business card simply read, "Gallagher, Private Investigator." This fit perfectly with the way he conducted himself—nothing fancy, get to the point, no wasted words, just Gallagher.

He turned the knob in the shower counterclockwise to the three o'clock position to let the water warm up. While he waited, he pushed the message button on his answering machine and listened as Diane gave him his "heads up" for the day.

"Good morning, Dan. Just wanted to remind you that this is the night Mr. Cunningham has a late meeting at the office and then has to drive down to Hartford for an all-day conference tomorrow. I'll be in the office. Call me if you need anything."

*Thank God for Diane! Without her I wouldn't know where to go every day.*

Mr. Cunningham's wife was one of Gallagher's newest clients and had come into his office a few weeks ago with suspicions that her husband was having an affair. She was convinced that he used his late meetings and days out of town as cover-ups for romps with his latest mistress. Mrs. Cunningham had reached her limit, and she was ready to take the old boy for everything he was worth. It was the same story that Gallagher had heard dozens of times before but really one of the easiest mysteries to solve. He had told her to keep him informed of the next "late meeting."

Tonight was the night.

Gallagher stepped into the shower and ducked his head under the invigorating, pulsating stream of hot water.

*I hope Mr. Cunningham has a good time tonight; this is going to be the most expensive piece of ass he's ever had.*

# CHAPTER 5

6:20 AM

Dr. Richard Evans stepped out of his forest-green Dodge Ram truck and walked across the upper level of the parking lot and then down the sloping asphalt toward the ground-floor entrance of the Parker Hill Medical Building. It had been three weeks since the murder of his friend and real-estate partner, Dr. Jonathan Becker. Still, the shock had not worn off. The West Castle police had questioned virtually every employee in the building and interviewed all the neighbors but had yet to come up with one witness—and neither a suspect nor a motive. As he walked toward the building on this quiet Tuesday morning, Dick Evans considered his own theory.

*Some lunatic with a vendetta against the medical profession. Who else could it be? And just Jonathan's luck to run into him!*

At this time in the morning, it was still dark, as Daylight Saving Time had a few more days to run before the clocks would be adjusted on the weekend. Dr. Evans, an internist who had practiced in West Castle for more than thirty years, was one of the first to arrive at the building. He liked to sit in his office with a cup of coffee or catch up on some dictation before his first patient arrived.

He was one of the six partners who had built the building, sold most of the units as office condominiums, and now shared ownership in more than 20,000 square feet of rented medical space. With Jonathan Becker's death, the responsibility for putting together the documents necessary for the remaining partners to buy Becker's share of the partnership from his estate had fallen on Dick Evans' shoulders. It was a painful process—not just a result of the paperwork involved, but mostly because of the constant and eerie reminder of the words "in the event of a partner's death." When they drew up the buyout agreements, Dick never expected that Jonathan, the youngest member of the group, would be the first to die.

Dr. Evans entered the building and walked into the atrium, past the Japanese flower garden in the outer lobby. He usually walked up the stairs to his second-floor office, but his knee had been giving him increasing trouble. He decided to take the elevator. He pressed the "Up" arrow, and the elevator door opened immediately.

As he got inside the elevator he thought that it was good to take the elevator once in a while so he could check to see if the management company maintained it in proper condition. They had painted it a few years ago with a yellowish-brown color that was so atrocious that one of the doctors demanded that it be repainted. Now, it was a soft shade of blue, and things appeared to be in pretty good repair.

At the second floor, the door opened, and Dr. Evans stepped to the edge of the doorway. An imposing figure standing directly in front of him blocked his path. The person wore a Red-Sox cap, a dark jacket, jeans, and a pair of running shoes. Dr. Evans started to move past this obstruction. Suddenly, a .357 Magnum revolver was pointed straight at him.

Dr. Evans froze.

*Who is this?*

His thoughts flashed to his partner, Jonathan Becker.

*Oh, my god, I'm going to die the same way!*

Three shots were fired in rapid succession. Two bullets struck his chest, and as his body absorbed the tremendous shock of the bullets' impact, he sprawled to the back of the elevator. A third shot struck the center of his forehead. Blood splattered all over the interior walls, floor, and ceiling. Dr. Evans sagged toward the floor as the life in his muscles and bullet-riddled body evaporated. Blood trickled down from his half-open mouth as a widening red stain appeared on his shirt.

The shooter calmly placed the gun into the right pocket of the jacket, turned to the left, walked quickly down the hallway, and then down the south stairwell. The shooter exited the building through the side entrance; then walked out to a lone car in the lower parking lot, just a few spaces from the door.

Within minutes, the car was gone.

# Chapter 6

Gallagher positioned himself in the lobby of 600 Washington Street in downtown Boston around five in the afternoon.

He read the *Boston Herald* and sipped a cup of coffee while he waited for Mr. Cunningham to walk out of the elevator. Mrs. Cunningham had supplied Gallagher with photographs of her husband so he could easily identify the little rascal. Gallagher had visited this lobby twice before to verify Cunningham's identity and get an idea of his usual routine at the end of the day. When Mr. Cunningham stepped out of the elevator, Gallagher had his man pegged. Using his high-speed digital camera without a flash, he snapped several pictures of Cunningham as he walked through the lobby on his way to the parking garage.

Pulling out of the garage in his own car, Gallagher followed Cunningham's car at a safe distance as the quarry drove down Essex Street and across to the entrance of the Expressway North. Once on the Expressway, he drove out of Boston, north on Route 93 to Route 95 South and exited in Burlington, Massachusetts, where he took a short drive down Cambridge Street and turned in to the parking lot of the Café Escadrille. Because of rush-hour traffic, the trip from Boston had taken fifty-five minutes.

Gallagher knew the Café Escadrille well and had eaten there with Kate about six months earlier during one of their first dinners together. He watched as Cunningham gave his car keys to the valet and walked up the small staircase and into the restaurant.

Gallagher parked his own car, waited for a few minutes, and then walked into the restaurant.

The hostess greeted him at the top of the landing with a wide smile, "Good evening and welcome to the Café Escadrille. How many in your party?"

"I'm supposed to meet some friends here, and I'm a little late, so they may be seated already. Okay if I just take a quick look around?" asked Gallagher in a nonchalant tone.

"Sure," she replied. "The bar is on the upper level in case you don't see them at a table."

Gallagher took a few steps into the restaurant and looked over to his right. At the first window table in the corner, he spotted a very attractive woman with shoulder length, brown hair wearing a lace-patterned, high-necked, white blouse. She appeared to be in her late forties, but had a face and figure that would make even young men stop for a second look. She smiled and laughed as she held hands with the older man sitting across from her at the table—none other than Mr. Matthew Cunningham.

*How lucky can I get? Sitting right at a window table!*

Gallagher turned around and walked past the young hostess who was so busy studying her reservation list that she didn't even see him go by. Outside the restaurant, he walked down Cambridge Street, trying to look casual. He held the small digital camera in his right hand and snapped several time-dated pictures of the happy couple—so engrossed in each other and their wine that they failed to notice any activity on the street outside their window.

After a leisurely dinner, they drove their separate cars several blocks north and turned left onto Burlington Mall Road, where they arrived at their final destination of the evening: the Burlington Marriott Hotel. Gallagher kept a healthy distance behind them but stayed close enough to capture pictures as they walked into the hotel, arm in arm.

He followed then into the lobby and photographed them as they checked in at the desk. He tried to fade into the background, looking detached from the scene as he browsed through the brochures near the entrance while carefully recording every detail of their actions with cool precision. Cunningham remained busy with the clerk at the desk while his beautiful companion glanced idly around the lobby.

Suddenly, she looked over at Gallagher and began walking toward him.

*Dammit! I've blown my cover!* he thought.

"Excuse me," she said, smiling as she reached over and plucked from the rack a brochure advertising The Samoset Resort in Rockport, Maine.

"No problem," he said, backing away and casually returning her smile.

She walked back to the registration desk and put one arm in Cunningham's while showing him the front of the brochure.

"Someday you'll have to take me to this place," she suggested as they walked toward the elevator.

As the elevator doors closed, Gallagher knew that, in the soon-to-be-declared war of Cunningham vs. Cunningham, he had just provided Mrs. Cunningham with all the ammunition she needed.

# CHAPTER 7

"Good morning, Dan, looks like you were busy last night."

Diane greeted him as he walked into his Commercial Street office just after eleven o'clock in the morning. She was wearing her usual bubbly smile that made him know she was genuinely happy to see him. A woman in her mid-fifties, Diane Beane had the remarkable gift of seeming to always be in a happy mood.

"Guess you can tell from the pictures in the camera I left for you last night that I was on the trail of the adulterous Mr. Cunningham." He winked at her and smiled. "Are the reports ready?"

"They're all on your desk," she said.

Like everything else in her life, Diane did her job with an efficient, attention-to-detail approach that made the word "conscientious" seem inadequate. She had already downloaded all the images from Gallagher's camera, printed out the pictures, and created a time-sequenced portfolio and descriptive narrative of the evidence. Gallagher would be the first to admit it—he'd be lost without her.

"Thanks, Diane. Could you set up a time with Mrs. Cunningham? I'd like to go over everything with her."

He poured a cup of coffee—his fourth of the morning— from the Mr. Coffee carafe in the corner of the reception room.

"No problem. I'll call her today," she said. She glanced at the coffee cup in his hand. "Still trying to get your engine running this morning?"

"Every morning," he said.

Diane smiled.

"There was also a message from another woman who wants to schedule an appointment. I left a note on your desk near the telephone."

"Thanks, I'll check it."

Gallagher walked into his small private office and plopped his six-foot frame down behind the dark mahogany desk. His office was decorated handsomely but in conservative taste. His desk was positioned to the right of the room with large windows that angled behind and to the right, allowing him to look outside at the weather and the harbor below. Two leather-upholstered arm chairs were located in front of the desk. The wall to the left of the desk bore only two pictures—a black-and-white photograph of Larry Bird with a choke hold on "Dr. J," Julius Erving, during a Celtics-76ers basketball game in the 1980s and a color photograph of Red Sox catcher Jason Varitek putting a similar strangle hold on "A-Rod," Alex Rodriguez, during the Red Sox-Yankees playoff in 2004. Both photographs were Boston sports classics. Gallagher loved their emotion and intensity.

Other than the reports Diane had left for him, the top of the desk was basically bare with only a telephone, a flat-screen computer monitor mounted on a small pedestal, and a box of tissues located near the leather arm chair on the left. Gallagher had learned to keep the tissues handy since some of his clients got quite emotional.

Gallagher sipped his coffee as he looked over the material Diane had organized. He had very clear, time-dated photographs of Mr. Cunningham leaving his office, sitting at dinner in the restaurant with the other woman, and then checking in at the hotel while the woman stood behind him.

*Mrs. Cunningham and her lawyer should have no trouble winning this divorce case.*

Usually when he turned over evidence that was this damning, the husband and his lawyer recognized their hopeless position and tried to settle the case before a judge issued a judgment that wiped the guy out financially.

He put down the portfolio and glanced over to his telephone where Diane had left a lined, yellow, Post-It note with his messages. He peeled off the sticky paper and held it up and slightly away from his face to bring the writing into better focus.

*Man, I've got to see an eye doctor. I need a pair of reading glasses.*

The note read, "A woman called for an appointment—said the nature of the consultation was very private—would discuss it with you personally. She sounded very nice. Let me know if I should call her back."

Gallagher usually preferred to know what was coming through the door so he could pre-screen cases that had no interest to him. Locating a runaway or missing teenager was one thing, but trailing a sixteen-year-old girl and her boyfriend to see if they were having sex in a parked car was something he'd rather avoid.

Gallagher hesitated and then reached forward to push the office intercom.

"Diane, it's all right to schedule an appointment with that woman who called. I can see her any time at the beginning of next week. What was her name anyway?"

Diane's voice came back across the intercom, "Her name is Suzanne Becker."

Gallagher paused, thinking that he had heard that name somewhere— *Becker—Becker?* Nothing clicked.

"Okay," he said, "Give her a call."

# CHAPTER 8

The shooting of Dr. Richard Evans, coming just weeks on the heels of the murder of Dr. Jonathan Becker, had caused hysteria in the town of West Castle. The community buzzed with unconfirmed reports, rumors, and wild speculation about who had committed the murders and what should be done to protect the citizenry from further acts of violence. To say that everyone had overreacted was putting it mildly—this included the police.

The physicians, staff, and employees of the Parker Hill Medical Building feared for their lives and were afraid to return to the building unless steps were taken to guarantee their safety. Because the Parker Hill Medical Building played such a vital role in the medical health of the community, the West Castle chief of police took drastic measures to reassure the public that it was safe to return to the building.

Two police cars were assigned to monitor the upper and lower parking lots. A police officer was stationed on each floor of the building twenty-four hours a day. In addition, two plain-clothes officers frequented the building throughout the day—visiting various offices, labs, and waiting rooms— walking through the hallways hoping to spot a suspicious person or pick up a clue that would lead them to the killer who had wreaked havoc on this quiet little town.

Security cameras were installed in the corridors, the elevator, and parking areas around the building. Persons entering the building were asked to state their destination to a security officer. Appointments were then verified with the medical office. None of the employees dared to enter or leave the building alone, and a "buddy" system was established, especially when walking out to the parking lots in the evening. Despite these precautions, the tension surrounding the building was undeniable.

The police had interrogated every employee, including all the doctors, nurses, and staff. All delivery men who worked for UPS, FedEx, W. B. Mason, and the like were interviewed to determine if they had ever seen a suspicious person hanging out around the building. The same questions were asked at the sub shop across the street and the pizza place on the corner. The neighbors were questioned: Had anyone seen a car leaving the parking lot on the morning of either doctor's murder?

Despite all these efforts, not one credible witness to the crimes was produced. More than three weeks since Dr. Becker's murder, the police still had no leads to pursue—the investigation was at a standstill.

In his office at the West Castle Police Station, Detective Jack Hoskins put down a stack of reports and looked across his desk at Dr. Michael Ferraro from the Medical Examiner's Office.

"I don't have time to read all of this now. Just tell me—what've we got, Mike?"

Ferraro leaned back in his chair and smiled.

"We've known each other for a lot of years, Jack. Looks like nothing's changed. You still prefer the Cliff Notes version, don't you?"

Hoskins flashed a defensive smile at the gray-haired man.

"Don't worry, I'll read it eventually. Just give me the details so I can get started here. The whole town is going crazy, and they're looking to me for answers."

Ferraro laughed.

"I know, I know. Just busting your chops a little, Jack."

Then, Ferraro quickly dropped the banter and turned serious.

"I've read the report from the crime lab. Dr. Becker and Dr.

Evans were both shot with the same .357 Magnum revolver from very close range. Hard to tell for sure, but the tests suggest that the gun was equipped with a silencer, thus accounting for the fact that no one claimed to have heard any noises at the time the doctors were shot."

Hoskins listened intently as he rocked back and forth in his chair. "Same gun, huh?"

"Yes. Unmistakable."

"I studied the photos from forensics. Looks like he was shot just as he was getting out of the elevator."

"Yes. The blood marks at the entrance to the elevator and heavier blood stains at the back indicated that Dr. Evans was shot just as he exited the elevator. He probably stumbled backward until he hit the rear wall of the elevator and then fell to the floor."

Hoskins nodded and looked down at the papers on his desk.

"Well," said Hoskins, "Forensics says his wallet was still on him."

"Right."

"Same for Dr. Becker. So we can rule out robbery as a motive."

"Yes," said Ferraro.

"Any prints?"

"Nothing on the body. Fingerprints obtained from the south stairwell door and the side entrance doors of the building were matched to employees in the building."

"Yeah, we interviewed all of them," said Hoskins, "and none are considered as suspects."

"So, where do you go from here, Jack?"

"Wish I knew. We've looked at dozens of reports listing patients from both offices that had either a bad debt on file or some dispute with the billing department. None of these reports produced anyone who could even remotely be considered a suspect."

"Any malpractice issues?"

"Checked that possibility, too. Neither doctor had a malpractice claim pending. No complaints were filed at the Board of Medicine."

"What about some common enemy?"

"Not that we can find. These guys were clean—respected members of the professional community."

Hoskins exhaled loudly, leaned back in his chair, put his feet up on the desk and looked up to the ceiling. He put his hands behind his head and stared upward, his level of frustration clearly out in the open.

A few seconds went by. Hoskins seemed oblivious to the presence of Ferraro, who politely waited for Hoskins to continue.

Finally, Ferraro asked, "So—is that all you need from me, Jack?"

Hoskins ignored the question and simply muttered to himself, "How could someone come into this town, kill two doctors, and get away without leaving one single clue?"

Ferraro stood up and lifted his sport coat from the back of his chair. He slipped it on and smiled knowingly at Hoskins who continued to stare up at the ceiling.

"See you around, Jack," said Ferraro as he opened the door and walked out of the office.

# Chapter 9

Gallagher's half-opened eyes with bags beneath them betrayed the fact that he had stayed up too late and needed more sleep. At least he had managed to be on time for his eleven o'clock consultation with the new client. As he opened the door, he saw a very well-dressed, middle-aged woman with silver gray hair sitting in the waiting area. She held a clip board on her lap while she filled out an informational history form.

The form was rather simple— the usual "name, address, telephone number," etc. It also had a section that asked if there was a history of criminal arrests, driver's license suspension, or drug use. In addition, a question asked if the client had ever used the services of another private investigator. Gallagher always liked to know if some other private eye had been sent on the same wild-goose chase. He realized that a person could fill out the form with false information but relied upon a brief statement at the bottom to help guarantee honesty: "Providing false information to any question will result in termination of services by Gallagher: Private Investigator." After all, most people would figure that a private investigator was bound to find out if you had lied to him.

Diane came out from behind her desk and announced, "Dan, this is Mrs. Suzanne Becker, your eleven o'clock appointment. She arrived a little early to fill out the paperwork."

Mrs. Becker reached out her hand, smiled, and said, "Mr.

Gallagher, it's a pleasure to meet you. I've heard so many good things about you."

Gallagher grasped her hand, noting that it was soft, yet her grip was warm and confident.

"Just call me Gallagher. How did you hear about me? Who are these people saying good things about me?"

She smiled widely, obviously enjoying his self-deprecating style.

"You helped some friends of ours... Dr. Michael Pollock and his wife, Ellen. Their son was involved in a motorcycle accident last year."

"Oh, yes, the Pollocks—wonderful couple. Glad to help them. And I was glad to find that guy who ran him off the road; thought he could get away with it! How's their son doing now?"

"Much better. He's finished his rehab and is back in college. Thankfully, his injuries were not permanent; he's going to be just fine." she said.

There was a sincerity and warmth about her that made him like her immediately.

"Let's go into my office, and we'll see how I can help you."

He opened the door and showed her to one of the chairs in front of his desk. He gently took the clipboard from her hand.

"Are you finished with this?" he asked. "It helps me to understand where you're from, and it sometimes points to where we're going."

Gallagher sat down behind his desk. He could see that Mrs. Becker's expression had become more serious. She fidgeted in the chair, trying to get comfortable. Her darting eyes betrayed her level of anxiety. Gallagher made a quick study of her face. For a woman of sixty, she had few lines or wrinkles. Her hair was beautiful—silver gray and flattering to her expensive-looking black suit, silver necklace, and diamond earrings.

Definitely a woman of money, class, and culture.

Sensing her sudden uneasiness, Gallagher tried to make her relax. He smiled.

"So what can I do to help you?" he asked.

He opened his hands as if welcoming a ball tossed from her.

"My husband, Dr. Jonathan Becker, was murdered last month," she answered. Her voice cracked as the word "murdered" came out of her mouth.

"I'm so sorry."

"Thank you." She dabbed at her eyes.

Gallagher sat up, as if a bell had just rung in his brain.

"Now I know where I heard your name," he said. "I read the story in the *Boston Globe*. There was another doctor shot a few weeks later in the same building. Last I heard, they were still looking for the person who did it."

He noticed the strained look on her face.

"Oh! Excuse me!" he said, catching himself for rambling on. "I am terribly sorry about your husband. This must be an extremely difficult time for you and your family."

"That's all right. I know it's been all over the news," she said. "But thank you. We're all trying to come to grips with it. It was a shock; no one ever expected anything like that."

Her eyes had become misty with tears, revealing the pain of revisiting the topic of her husband's murder. Gallagher tried to ease her discomfort by moving on.

"But what can I do to help you? Aren't the police handling the investigation?"

"Yes," she said, "but it's going nowhere. They don't have any suspects that I know of."

"These things take time. A killer like that eventually slips up and blows his cover. That's the break the police are waiting for."

"I don't think my husband's murder has anything to do with some lunatic running around killing doctors. I think there was some other reason. And once Dick Evans was killed, I was more convinced than ever that something else was going on."

She had now fully regained her composure and spoke with confidence and authority.

"Have you told this to the police?"

"No."

"Why not?"

"Because I'm afraid of what they might find. I'm not ready for a public scandal."

"Do you think there was another woman involved?" he asked, but the inflection of his voice indicated that he didn't believe the answer would be "yes."

"No—Jonathan and I had a wonderful marriage. It's nothing like that. But for the past few months, he was acting very troubled, almost depressed. Something was going on in the partnership, but he wouldn't talk about it."

"You mean in his medical practice?"

"No—in his real-estate partnership. He was one of six partners who bought the land and built the medical building twenty years ago. Each partner bought his own office condominium. Then, they sold off the remaining units. They kept some of the suites as rental property and leased them to other doctors and some labs. It was a very good deal for the partners," she went on, nodding her head emphatically to make her point.

"Then, what was the problem?" asked Gallagher.

"I'm not sure, but, suddenly, during the past few months, there was an unusual round of partnership meetings. It was almost as bad as when they were putting up the building twenty years ago. The partners met at least once a week, sometimes twice. The meetings were always at night. Jonathan would never discuss the subject of the meetings, but something about them was really bothering him. I tried, but he just wouldn't talk about it."

"I still don't understand exactly what you'd like me to do," said Gallagher.

"I'd like you to find out what was bothering my husband, and if it was at all related to his murder. Listen," she said in a firm voice, "My husband was an honest and respected man and a wonderful father to his children. If he was drawn into some financial problem or scandal, I want to know before it finds its way into the local newspapers. If it was somehow related to the cause of his murder, then we can get the police involved. But, until I know, I'd rather keep your investigation in the background. You know, as the saying goes, under the radar screen."

Gallagher nodded, thinking to himself that he had to give her credit for taking the initiative to protect her husband's reputation and save her kids from embarrassment.

"Who's been your main contact in the West Castle Police Department?" he asked.

"Most of the questions have come from the lead detective on the case, Jack Hoskins"

Gallagher grimaced as if someone had just stuck a needle in his mouth.

*Oh, shit—anybody but Hoskins!*

Mrs. Becker noticed his reaction.

"Are you okay? Is there some issue with Detective Hoskins?"

"Uh—no—not really. We know each other from years ago when I was on the police force. Let's just say we weren't on the best of terms. But don't worry. It won't be a problem for this investigation," replied Gallagher, trying to rebound.

"I will pay your fee and all your expenses. Money is not an issue in this matter," she continued.

"Diane will go over that with you, Mrs. Becker. I'll be happy to help you." He smiled. "I think I have a pretty good handle on why you're here today. And I can understand your concerns. Where I should begin? Is there someone I can talk to?"

"Well," she offered, "you might start out by talking to Randi Stockdale. The partners hired her to coordinate their meetings and handle the books. She may be able to tell you something." She paused for a second. "It's all right if she knows where you got her name. I don't have her number with me, but she lives in West Castle. You can find her in the telephone book."

They both stood up, recognizing that their meeting was over. Mrs. Becker reached out and gently shook Gallagher's hand again, then turned and walked out of his office. She stopped by Diane's desk, but Gallagher could not hear everything she said—nor did he try. Instead, he just looked out the window, thinking about the possible relationship between the secret meetings and the two murders.

Most of the time, he had a pretty good idea when he started where a particular case would take him and what kind of problems he would encounter along the way.

But this time, Gallagher had no idea what to expect.

# Chapter 10

Randi Stockdale put down her morning cup of coffee as she finished reading the "City/Region" section of the *Boston Globe*. The newspapers had carried articles for several weeks about the murders in West Castle, the public's reaction, and the precautions taken by the police. However, the story seemed to have lost its appeal to the media. Today's paper had no mention whatsoever about the situation in West Castle.

At age forty-two, Randi owned a successful condominium management company that had fifteen different complexes under contract. Most of her clients were residential developments, but she also maintained two medical office condominiums, including the Parker Hill Medical Building in West Castle.

She was just about to leave for her office, when the phone rang. *Probably another early morning emergency* she thought as she picked up the handset.

Expecting to hear her secretary's voice, she was surprised when, instead, the voice of a man asked, "Randi Stockdale?"

"Yes—this is Randi."

"My name is Gallagher. I'm a private investigator looking into the West Castle murders."

Randi paused for a few seconds and then replied as if she were speaking to an annoying telemarketer, "I've already told the police everything I know. I don't think I can be of any help to you."

"Actually, I've been retained by Mrs. Suzanne Becker. She thought I should speak to you. Can you meet with me for just a few minutes?"

"Well, as a favor to Suzanne, I'll do it. But I don't think it will do you any good," she sighed.

"Okay, where can we meet?" asked Gallagher. "You name the place."

"I'll be in my office for the rest of the day. I have a few telephone calls to make this morning, but I'm free after lunch. How about one-thirty this afternoon? 38 Church Street, West Castle. Can you make that?"

"No problem. Thanks—I'll see you then."

Randi put the handset down and wondered, *A private detective? If the police can't find the killer, what makes this guy think he can?*

# Chapter 11

Gallagher arrived in West Castle a short time after one o'clock.

*Why not nose around the Parker Hill Medical Building to get an idea where the shootings had occurred and scope out the area?*

Despite its proximity to Boston, he was not well acquainted with the town of West Castle. In fact, the only information he knew about the murders came from reading the newspaper.

He drove into the parking lot and left his car on the upper level in a space facing a stone wall. The parking lot was three-quarters full, and the few people he could see walked to and from the building in a normal manner. A police cruiser idled in a handicapped space near the ground floor entrance to the building. One uniformed cop sat in the cruiser. He appeared to be reading and occasionally looked up at the entrance doors.

*Looks like life goes on at Parker Hill,* Gallagher thought.

Gallagher got out of his car, walked across the parking lot and then down the slope toward the entrance. He wore a pair of black slacks, a blue shirt, and a navy-blue, crew-neck sweater. As he walked past the police cruiser, the officer just looked up at him for a second and went back to his reading. Gallagher assumed that he must not fit the profile of the guy they were looking for.

He walked into the atrium and stood for a moment, admiring the impressive design of the staircase with its shiny, highly polished brass handrail. A beautiful arrangement of potted plants and a single hibiscus tree flanked the base of the staircase. The Japanese garden in the outer lobby contained a colorful array of red and yellow flowers intermixed with green plantings. The people who maintained this building paid close attention to detail.

The names of Dr. Jonathan Becker and Dr. Richard Evans were still listed on the building directory on the left wall of the atrium. Was this an oversight or an indication that no one had the heart to remove the names so soon? He turned left and pushed the "Up" button for the elevator. He remembered that the newspaper accounts stated that Dr. Evans' body was discovered on the elevator by an employee on her way to an office on an upper floor. When the elevator door opened, he stepped in and pushed "5."

As the elevator slowly moved up between floors, he looked around at the interior and noticed that the vinyl floor looked new and that the blue walls and oak railings did not have a scratch on them. Considering the gory scene described in the newspapers, there must have been a major renovation and cleanup project inside the elevator. A security camera was positioned in the upper right corner of the elevator—apparently a recent installation, since no mention had been made of capturing the killer on video in any of the newspaper accounts.

Gallagher also noted the slow speed of the elevator—probably the customary seventy-five feet per minute— the norm for single elevators in a building less than ten stories tall. He had accumulated thousands of little tidbits of trivia like this in his years first at the police academy, then as a Boston cop, and now as a private investigator. Somehow he remembered that kind of stuff. But the slowness of the elevator made him realize that the killer, who had apparently watched Dr. Evans enter the building and then waited for him to come up to the second floor, had plenty of time to position himself in the corridor before the elevator door opened.

As Gallagher took the return ride to the ground floor, he smiled as he revised his chauvinistic thinking.

*I wonder if the newspapers and the police are making the same assumption. Maybe the killer wasn't a man.*

# CHAPTER 12

Gallagher found a parking place a few doors down from 38 Church Street and approached the small brick building with several businesses, including Cosgrove Management, listed on the simple, white sign with black lettering located to the right of the door. He was just about to announce himself to the receptionist when a tall woman with blonde hair stepped around from a door to a back office.

"You must be Gallagher," she said. "Come on in."

Only an inch or two shy of being six feet tall, Randi Stockdale appeared to be a strong, athletic person who was in her early forties. Gallagher easily pictured her as a member of a women's college basketball team or a marathon runner. She had sharp, defined facial features with high cheek bones, but they all blended together with her blue eyes to yield a look that he found appealing. She stared at him suspiciously as she sat down at her desk. The office had a simple decor—a desk, a gray, high-backed swivel chair behind it, and a file cabinet up against a side wall. Gallagher sat in the plastic-molded chair in front of the desk.

"So what can I do to help you, Mr. Gallagher?" she asked. Her expression indicated her uncertainty about discussing anything with him.

"I've been retained to look into Dr. Jonathan Becker's financial background, especially the past six months, to see if there's any link to his murder," he said directly. "His wife hired me and said I should start by talking to you. She obviously trusts you and feels that our conversation and any information you share with me will be confidential."

"I've always liked Suzanne; this whole thing must be unreal for her."

She looked away and paused for a few seconds. Then she heaved a deep sigh of resolve.

"All right, fire away," she said. "I'll try to help in any way I can."

"What can you tell me about the real-estate partnership?" he asked, eager to get right to the point of his visit.

"Well—it was somewhat of an interesting group of guys who got together and built a medical building. Five doctors, all in different specialties and practices, and one guy in the home-construction business. After they bought the land and put up the building, they hired me to manage the building and then, later, to manage their business partnership."

"How did they get together?" asked Gallagher.

Randi dropped her hands to her sides and looked up as if she were a school girl. Her hesitancy to speak was now replaced with a measured, but detailed, account of the facts of the story.

"Three of the doctors, Jonathan Becker, Dan Oblas, and Dick Evans, were all practicing in West Castle and were unhappy with their office space. Phil Lombardo, an orthopedic surgeon, who also dabbled in real estate, was interested in buying some land on the north end of town to put up a medical office building. He needed some cooperation from a few of his colleagues in the medical community to get the project off the ground, so he contacted Becker, Oblas, and Evans. They formed a real-estate partnership and later added Tony Cognetti and Barry Nickerson. Tony is a neurologist—semi-retired now and only works a couple of days a week. Barry is a home builder. They thought Barry would add some expertise to the group since they planned to do a 'design-build' building, and none of the doctors had experience in that area."

Gallagher listened and said nothing, occasionally jotting a few notes on a small pad.

Randi paused for a few seconds and pushed her hair behind her ears. She took a sip from a bottle of water on her desk and continued with her story.

"So, they put together a plan to buy enough land to build an eighty-thousand square foot building with parking for three-hundred cars. It was an ambitious project, full of problems and risks. But they pulled it off and made a bundle of money in the end. It turned out to be the largest and most beautiful medical office building in the area. Twenty years later, it still looks pretty good."

"You seem to like these guys, "said Gallagher, picking up on her enthusiasm. "Did they treat you pretty well?"

"Yes, they were always good to me."

"How long have you worked for them?"

"I was young when I first met them. I had just bought my business from my aunt after my uncle, Dave Cosgrove, passed away. You probably noticed that I kept the name 'Cosgrove Management.'"

"Yes. In fact, I did wonder about that."

She continued.

"They were one of my first big accounts; it helped me to get started. After they saw how I could run the building, they hired me to handle their partnership affairs. I had a good relationship with all of them." Shaking her head sadly, she added, "I can't believe Jonathan and Dick were killed like that."

Her voice faltered. She paused for a few seconds, as if regaining her composure from the troubling thoughts of the recent murders.

"Do you have any ideas about who could have done it?" she asked.

"No, I'm just getting started on this. There's a whole lot more I need to know before I can answer that question. You said there were problems and risks. What kind of problems?"

"Well, first of all, they had to buy three abutting parcels of land owned by three different owners. The first parcel was easy. They bought it from an old trucking company that had moved out of the area. But the second parcel was a different matter."

"How so?"

"An elderly plumber owned it and initially agreed to sell it to the partners. The owner of the third parcel ran a car repair shop. He smelled a big project coming and convinced the plumber to sell the dilapidated old building to him instead. That gave him the entire frontage on Central Street, and he decided to sit back and hold out for a lot of money. As luck would have it, while he waited for the big sale to go through, a fire destroyed the old building, and he collected on the insurance. A real coincidence, huh?" she exclaimed, rolling her eyes to indicate the absurdity of the situation.

"No doubt—a timely catastrophe." Gallagher nodded, hoping she would continue with more details.

She didn't disappoint him.

"Meanwhile, the partners tried to keep their project quiet. But the car-repair owner was a savvy guy, and knew he had the final piece of property they needed." She paused for a second and then said with a smile, "Mickey Ryan was his name; a real character. But, in the end, they outsmarted him."

"How's that?" asked Gallagher, his interest piqued now.

"They waited for quite a while and then let out the word that a lack of financing and problems with a zoning variance had killed the project. Mickey was antsy to get some money in his hands and thought he had lost his chance for a big payday. So, the group sent Barry Nickerson as a 'straw' buyer to Mickey. Mickey didn't know that Barry was a member of the partnership and thought he was just a builder trying to make an investment in local real estate. Barry told him he hoped to acquire the other parcel in a few years and then build some low-cost residential housing units."

"Is Barry a good actor?"

"Apparently good enough. Mickey fell for his story and sold the land to Barry for a lot less than the price he expected to get from the partnership. A year and a half later, when Mickey saw them breaking ground for a huge medical building, he had a fit. He hated those guys and vowed to someday get even with them."

"Have you told this to the police?" asked Gallagher.

He leaned back in the chair and crossed his legs, moving his notepad up near his knee. He stared at her intently, waiting for her response.

"No, it really never came up. They were more interested in finding out if these guys had any girls on the side that might have done them in," she said sarcastically.

Gallagher arched his eyebrows.

"Well—did they?" he asked.

She waved her hand to the side.

"No, they were all family types. None of them would get involved like that. In fact, they were very tight as a group and very loyal to each other. They would debate an issue, vote on it, and then never hold a grudge or bring up a previous disagreement again."

"What about Mickey? Did he ever pursue his vow?"

"Yes. Just after the building was completed, he tried to get more money out of them. Threatened them with a law suit, but he really had no case. Tried to get them to pay him $100,000 to drop the suit. But they were tough and told him to go pound sand. Never heard from him after that. I got the feeling he was a vindictive guy. They never seemed too concerned about it," she said, giving a quick shrug of her shoulders.

"Where's Mickey now?" he asked.

"I don't know. I think he lives in Medford, but it's been quite awhile since I've seen him. Maybe fourteen or fifteen years," she said.

"I stopped over to see the medical building before I came here. It's a pretty impressive place. The people in West Castle must have been glad to see such an improvement in the neighborhood."

"Well," she said, leaning forward, "Not everyone in town was thrilled about that building. Some of the neighbors fought it tooth and nail. They were afraid of all the traffic, noise, and dirt during the construction. You name it, they were against it."

"Not unusual. Any change in the old neighborhood is a bad change. Right?"

"Right, but some of them took it to extremes; one woman campaigned so much against it that she ended up in a mental hospital. Probably crazy to begin with." She laughed. "At times, it got pretty ugly at the town meetings when the zoning issues and the variances came up."

"But the partnership won. It looks like they overcame all the objections," he said.

"Yeah—money talks. The selectmen realized that the building was a financial boon to the town. That area used to pay peanuts in real-estate taxes; now the building coughs up more than $250,000 in real-estate taxes every year. So the town got a necessary medical resource and a whole pile of money to support the school system. And the six partners got rich in the process. Everybody came out a winner, except for a few neighbors who didn't see it that way."

"Do I detect a tinge of bitterness in your voice?" he asked.

"Well, I thought they could have paid me a better bonus after all the work I did for them when they were having a problem with the FDIC and the banks."

"What was that all about?" asked Gallagher, now adding to his notes and sensing a more complicated matter than he originally thought.

"The partnership borrowed money for the project from a local bank and still owed two million dollars on the construction loan when the bank went into receivership—you know, one of those banks that collapsed in the mid '80s when the savings and loan scandals made the news."

Gallagher furrowed his brow.

"Shouldn't have been such a big problem. Didn't the FDIC just take over the loan?"

"Yes, but the bozos in Washington didn't contact the partnership for a payment for more than three years."

"Three years?"

"Amazing, huh? I did try to contact the FDIC to find out where to send the payments, but they were in total disarray. No one could help me. Left some messages but never got a return call."

"So what happened?"

"The partnership voted to sit tight and wait for the FDIC to sort everything out. In the meantime, they completed the construction and sold most of the condominium units. I handled the books. Because they didn't have to pay the high interest rates and carrying costs of the loan, the profits were handsome, to say the least. And then the partnership invested the extra profits to make even more money."

"Sort of like playing with house money."

"Exactly."

"Well—eventually this had to catch up to them, didn't it?"

"Oh, yes. It caught up in a big way. Three and a half years later, a representative from the FDIC contacted the partnership and informed them that full payment on the loan was due within thirty days. Not only did they owe the original principal of two million dollars, but interest and penalties were now applied."

"Whoa! That must have hurt."

"Hurt is not the word. They were shocked when they saw that bill. The Feds hit them with compounded interest and penalties that brought the new total to $3.5 million."

"How did they handle that?"

"They hired a lawyer and wrote several letters of appeal, but nothing seemed to work. The Feds wouldn't budge and threatened to put a lien on the building and their personal assets if they didn't pay the full amount. The partners were obviously worried and met a number of times in executive session."

"You mean in private?"

"Right. That meant I wasn't invited to hear what was going on; I just ordered the food for their dinner," she said with a laugh.

Gallagher sat up in his chair. "How did it all work out? Did they pay the $3.5 million?"

"Somehow, it all got worked out. Jonathan and Dick flew to Washington for a meeting with someone; I arranged their flight—just a day-trip type of thing. When they got back, they told me everything was settled. I did the paperwork for a new loan from the West Castle Cooperative Bank, and that money paid off the FDIC loan," she said.

"How much was the new loan?"

"Two million dollars."

"Sounds like the boys did some fast talking in Washington."

"I don't know; they would never talk about it. That's how they were as a group; when they met in executive session, I never knew what went on. Sometimes, it seemed like they took an oath of silence and loyalty. The White House could take a lesson from them about how to prevent information leaks."

She shrugged.

"I don't think they even discussed this stuff with their wives," she said.

Gallagher smiled, but quickly got back to gathering information.

"So, now that Becker and Evans are dead, what's the status of the other partners? Are they all living in West Castle?"

Randi reached for her bottle of water again and took a few gulps.

"No. Phil Lombardo retired from his practice and divides his time between homes in Vermont and Florida. He was really the driving force behind the partnership and made most of the early decisions and handled all the business transactions. He sold out his interest in the rental property to the other five partners about six years ago. Except for social occasions, he hasn't had anything to do with the group for quite a while. Dan Oblas is also retired and living in Bonita Springs, Florida. He's recovering from some recent surgery. I've been meaning to call him."

She looked off to the side and paused.

"I love Dan—such a great guy," she said as her voice trailed off.

Gallagher waited for a few seconds. When nothing more was forthcoming, he urged her to fill in the rest of the blanks.

"And the other partners—Tony and Barry?"

Randi snapped back to reality.

"Oh, yes—sorry. Tony Cognetti has an office in the building even though he only practices part-time. Barry Nickerson lives right here in town and is still involved in his construction business I have to arrange a meeting with Dan, Tony, and Barry to discuss how they want to handle the real-estate assets they still share in the building. My guess is that they'll want to sell everything and pay out the shares owned by Jonathan and Dick to their widows. There's a lot to be settled and I'm 'it.' No one expected this."

She heaved another sigh.

Gallagher pressed on.

"What about the recent executive session meetings? You must have some inkling about them."

Her eyes narrowed. She looked away and then gave an edgy reply.

"Like I said before when you asked—I was never invited to those meetings. I have no idea what they were talking about."

Gallagher stood up from his chair.

"Thanks. You've given me a pretty good start."

He held his hand out to her as a goodbye gesture.

She stood up and awkwardly extended her hand.

"Sure—glad to be of help," she replied uneasily.

"Hope I haven't over-extended my welcome," he said as he firmly shook her hand.

"No—no—not at all," she said with a forced smile.

"Bye Randi. I'll be in touch if I need anything else."

He flipped his notepad closed and shoved it into his back pocket. He was out the door before she could make any further reply.

As Gallagher walked to his car, so many thoughts raced through his mind.

*No one knows the partners as well as Randi Stockdale. There's a lot more she could be telling me. I've gotta get this information to Diane. And Kate—I have to call her about dinner!*

But this case had already hooked him. Gallagher's thoughts were dominated by a single question: *Where can I find Mr. Mickey Ryan*?

# Chapter 13

"How about dinner and dessert with a desperate man?" he said when she picked up the phone.

"Hey, Mr. Private Eye—I was hoping to hear from you. Just say where and when," replied Kate.

"I've got to make a few calls and finish some dictations. Legal Sea Foods at seven. Does that work for you?"

"You're on, but I've got to rush. Bye."

Typical Kate. Never one to waste time on nonessential matters. This was among the many traits he liked about her.

Gallagher walked into his office. Diane sat at her computer completing the monthly report. She kept track of everything for him— hours spent investigating cases, travel expenses, telephone logs, out of pocket expenses for items such as photo developing or enlarging—so that any client who questioned the fee for handling a case would be able to see the costs incurred. Gallagher simply filled out a log sheet with this information; Diane did all the rest. Interestingly, most clients had no idea of the overhead costs of a private eye. There were also the occasional costs of "buying" information. Gallagher had discovered early on in this business that some people love to sell what they know.

"Good afternoon, Dan, I was hoping I'd get to see you today. You are all set with Mrs. Cunningham; she called to thank you for everything. She paid two thousand dollars. Her account with us is completely up to date now."

"Okay, that's great. But now I'd like to add a few things to the West Castle file; I met with Randi Stockdale. She's the woman who coordinated the business affairs of Dr. Becker's real-estate partnership."

Gallagher sat with Diane for the better part of an hour dictating the information that Randi had given him—a simple exercise, but one that gave him a chance to rethink the facts of a case. When they finished, he checked the internet telephone directory for Mickey Ryan in Medford, Massachusetts.

"Sorry no matches" appeared on the screen.

There were many matches for Michael Ryan, but he thought that cold phone calls to ask if they were nicknamed "Mickey" wouldn't be too productive. He finally picked up the phone and called an old friend, Jack Harte, who he knew from his days at the police academy. Jack now worked as a dispatcher for the Medford Police Department.

"Hey, Jack, how's it going?

"Gallagher! It's been a while, man—thought you got swallowed up."

"No, I've just been busy playing that stealthy, intrepid private-eye game. You know how that goes."

"I hear ya'. Guess if you're callin' me, you're trying to track down some dude in Medford. You're lucky. I was just ready to leave for the day."

"Should have figured you'd know why I called. I'm trying to locate a guy named Mickey Ryan. He was in the car repair business in West Castle about twenty years ago."

"Whoa! That goes way back! Doesn't ring a bell with me, but I'll check around for you. Is this guy in some big trouble?"

"I don't know yet; I just want to talk to him. If you find out anything, call me at the office or try my cell."

"No problem, man. I'll check it out."

Gallagher hung up and leaned back in his chair with his hands behind his head, looking out his window at the harbor below. The water was calm except for a small tanker that slowly moved by on low power.

*How deep would a grudge have to be to make someone want to kill two people?*

# Chapter 14

Legal Sea Foods—one of Gallagher's favorite places—had the best seafood in Boston. He hadn't seen Kate in a few days, and as he walked in to the restaurant, he looked forward to spending the night with her.

They had met about six months ago at the wedding reception for a mutual friend. Kate's name was as Irish as they come: Kathryn McSurdy. Thirty-seven years old, never married, and the co-owner of a placement service in Needham for professional offices and high-tech firms. A brunette with hazel eyes that projected hints of green, depending upon the lighting in the room or what she wore, she was five feet, six inches tall with a radiant smile and a perfect complexion. She was, in simple terms, a knockout.

When Gallagher first met her, he couldn't believe how she had lasted so long without being scooped up. But soon after he got to know her, he discovered that she had lived with a professional football player for four years, until she finally broke off the relationship when his steroid-induced temper tantrums became too frightening to endure. Supremely confident in herself, she did not depend on a man for income or affection. She had her own identity, a very profitable business, and was wary of entering into another long-term relationship.

After the pain of his first marriage and the eventual divorce, Gallagher was also content to let things move along slowly—not sure if he could make the commitment of marriage again. But Kate was truly special. She had a wonderfully upbeat and loving personality; she always seemed to listen carefully to what he said and then would respond in a thoughtful way. She was passionate in her beliefs and emotions but would never offend anyone.

His first wife, Lesley, had been so different—a thrill seeker, more superficial, with a "live for today" approach to life. They had met while Gallagher was training in the police academy and she was a law student. She was a hot woman, to say the least, and there were nights when he still thought of the great sex they had together during the first few years of their marriage. But they were a struggling young couple, still in school with no financial assets. He was forced to take a job as a night-time security guard to help pay the bills—too many nights away and unable to devote time to the home front.

They drifted apart.

She had an affair with another law student.

They divorced.

They kept in touch for a while, but he hadn't seen or talked to her in three years. Now married to a different guy, she worked as an assistant district attorney for Middlesex County.

Gallagher looked up from his seat at the bar as Kate came through the door of the restaurant. The auburn highlights of her thick hair—always sculpted beautifully with the bangs coiffed over her forehead—stood out in the entranceway lights.

*How does she manage to look better every time I see her?*

After they were seated, she looked over at him with a mischievous sparkle in her eyes, "So tell me, Mr. Private Eye, have you kept yourself busy catching bad guys this week?"

"Yes, I caught a few, and I'm hot on the trail for some others," he said.

He smiled, totally disarmed by her presence. She looked so beautiful; he was unable to take his eyes off her. And the thought of tracking down some deadbeat father, a cheating husband, or a killer in West Castle became the farthest thing from his mind.

# Chapter 15

Several days went by. Still no word about Mickey Ryan.

Gallagher went back to the telephone book and checked the listings for "M. Ryan" and "Michael Ryan." None of the calls produced the "Mickey" he wanted. He even checked the tax records at the Medford Town Hall, but no one by the name of Mickey Ryan owned property in Medford. He researched the real-estate records in West Castle and found the 1983 transaction in which Barry Nickerson had purchased a property from Mickey Ryan of 685 High Street, Medford, Massachusetts for $150,000. Since then, however, the apartment building at that address had been razed.

It seemed that this guy had just dropped out of sight.

*What about Becker's partners? Would they reveal why he was so distracted in the weeks before his murder?*

Gallagher reminded himself that Randi Stockdale had told him that the partners would never discuss their business dealings with an outsider. Nevertheless, it was worth taking a shot.

Since Barry Nickerson handled the real-estate deal with Mickey Ryan, Gallagher started with him. Maybe, with a little luck, Barry might give him a clue about finding the elusive Mickey.

Barry Nickerson was easy to find. He was in the phone book and answered the door when Gallagher rang the doorbell. Nickerson was a man in his late sixties, six feet tall with thinning gray hair and a neatly trimmed white beard. His face had the weathered look of a person who spent a good deal of time working outside in the sun; his deeply set blue eyes peered out over the top of his glasses that rested halfway down from the bridge of his nose.

"Hope I'm not catching you at a bad time. My name is Gallagher; I'm a private investigator looking into the murder of your partner, Dr. Jonathan Becker."

Nickerson stood in the doorway looking at him, his mouth somewhat opened in surprise, "A private investigator? Hey, I've already told everything I know to the police. But you can come in if you want. I've got nothing to hide."

Gallagher walked into the house while Nickerson held the door open for him.

"Have a seat over here," offered Nickerson as he pointed to a small, cozy sitting room to the side of the entranceway of this typical New England garrison-colonial home with hardwood floors and beautiful Oriental area rugs. Gallagher sat down in a comfortable arm chair across from Nickerson who folded his legs and let his hands rest quietly on his lap.

"Can I get you a drink or something?" he asked.

"No, thanks," said Gallagher politely, eager to get right to the questions.

"Then, how can I help you, Mr. Gallagher?"

Gallagher reached over and handed him one of his business cards.

"Your partner, Dr. Jonathan Becker, didn't appear to be himself in the weeks before his murder. I'm trying to find out if there's a connection to what eventually happened to him."

"Who said he was acting different?" challenged Nickerson.

"His wife," said Gallagher firmly.

"Suzanne? God—I'll bet this has been really tough for her. Out of the blue, he's gone. And then Dick—a couple of weeks later. Who would have ever expected that?" he asked.

"It must have been quite a shock for you as well."

Nickerson shook his head.

"Yeah. I don't think I'll ever get over it,"

"Did you notice anything different about Dr. Becker's behavior before his murder?" asked Gallagher, trying to get Nickerson to open up to him.

"No. We didn't see each other that often except for an occasional meeting. Once the building was finished, we only had to meet a few times a year."

"Didn't you have a number of meetings during the past few months?" Gallagher asked, sensing that Nickerson had been purposely evasive.

"Oh, yeah—uh—guess we did," Nickerson said, as his voice trailed off. He cleared his throat and coughed twice. "It was really nothing. Just dealing with some new leases. We had to work out a few details," he added.

"That was it?" asked Gallagher, his skepticism creeping into his tone.

"That was it!" Nickerson shot back. His jaw jutted forward, and his facial muscles twitched as he clenched his teeth together.

"You bought a piece of land from Mickey Ryan more than twenty years ago, and then sold it to your partners within a couple of weeks for the same price."

Nickerson leaned forward.

"That's a matter of public record, and there was nothing wrong with that transaction!" he snapped.

"I'm not saying that, but I just wondered if you or any of your partners have heard from Mr. Ryan recently."

"No—I haven't heard from Mickey in a long time. You seem to know a lot, so you're probably aware that he wasn't too happy with us after that deal. But he was holding up our project. We had to do something to get things moving. You know, business is often like a poker game; we made a good bluff and won a good business deal. He still came out with plenty of money for that little piece of land."

Nickerson paused for a moment and then looked up at Gallagher as if startled by a new thought, "You don't think Mickey had anything to do with Jonathan and Dick's murders, do you?"

"I don't know. But I'd sure like to speak to Mickey some time."

"Well, he was pissed at the time, but I don't think he'd go that far. He's had a lot of years to get over this. Life's too short to kill two people over a little bit of money. I think it was some crazy nut that had it in for the doctors in that building. Who knows what makes people do something like that!"

Gallagher nodded, acknowledging the truth in that statement.

"But if you're looking for Mickey—last I heard he was in Medford. Most of his connections are in that area. He was pretty good at repairing cars, and he used to do a little bookmaking on the side as well. Aahh, Mickey!" Nickerson said admiringly, "He knew all the angles."

The phone rang and Nickerson leaned over to pick it up.

"Excuse me for a second," he said.

As he held the phone to his ear, his facial expression turned rigid and his mouth dropped open.

"Oh God—no!" he exclaimed.

Gallagher leaned forward toward Nickerson's chair.

"What happened?" asked Nickerson. He appeared grief stricken, almost gasping from the shock of the words he heard.

There was a long pause. Nickerson's eyes blinked repeatedly as the details were relayed to him by the caller. Certainly not good news. He slowly put down the receiver and slumped back into his chair. He looked stunned—a man whose world had suddenly spun out of control.

"Is everything okay?" asked Gallagher.

Nickerson sunk down further in his chair and could barely get the words out of his mouth.

"Phil Lombardo was just found dead in Vermont."

# Chapter 16

Suzanne Becker's suspicions had been correct: a serious problem existed within her husband's real-estate partnership. The news about Phil Lombardo and the abrupt end it had brought to the meeting with Barry Nickerson had proven it to Gallagher.

Nickerson had hardly been forthright in his answers, and Phil Lombardo's death, coming just weeks after that of his two former partners, had to be more than a coincidence. Unlike Jonathan Becker and Richard Evans, Lombardo, a retired orthopedic surgeon, had no current ties to the Parker Hill Medical Building. However, he had been an active partner in the real-estate group until six years ago, when he sold out his interests and retired. What's more, he had played a major role in getting the entire project started, including the purchase of the three parcels of land necessary to put up the building.

Gallagher couldn't jump to any conclusions until he found out the official cause of Lombardo's death. But this was bizarre—three doctors connected to the Parker Hill Building in the quiet town of West Castle were now dead. Could this be a serial murderer with a local purpose? He had asked Barry Nickerson for the details of the telephone call about Lombardo, but Nickerson was too distraught, and he begged off answering any more questions and showed Gallagher to the door.

Gallagher needed more information about those recent partnership meetings and drove over to Randi Stockdale's office.

No luck—she was out on a maintenance call but would return by three-thirty.

Gallagher looked at his watch—2:45.

"Okay," he said to the receptionist, "Tell her I'll be back. I need to see her today."

He felt a sense of urgency to get more of the facts as soon as possible.

He went back to his car and called Suzanne Becker. If he was going to do the job for which he was hired, he had to risk being the bearer of more bad news.

"Mrs. Becker? This is Gallagher."

He tried to stay calm.

"Oh, yes. I didn't expect to be hearing from you so soon."

"Have you heard about Phil Lombardo?"

"Phil? No, what's happened?" she asked.

"Well, I don't know the details yet, but I was visiting Barry Nickerson when he got a call from someone. Phil Lombardo is dead."

"Oh, my god! What's going on here? This can't be happening."

"I'm afraid it is. And I believe you're right about a major issue within the partnership. Do you have any time to see me later today? I need to ask a few more questions. It's better to do it in person."

"I'll be home for the rest of the day. You can come over anytime."

She seemed frantic but clearly willing to help.

"All right, I have another person to see, and then I'll be over."

Gallagher somehow felt it necessary to avoid telling her he expected to see Randi Stockdale. Sometimes, in matters like this, it was best to make sure that the various parties didn't have time to coordinate their stories.

He grabbed a cup of coffee at the local Starbucks and tried to think of something to occupy his time for a while. After a few sips, he checked his pants pocket for his packet of Tums. Coffee and the turmoil of the recent news were bound to kick up his acid reflux. He hoped the Tums would work—he needed the coffee.

He rubbed his hand across his face as he sat at a small table in the coffee shop. His five o'clock shadow had made its usual early appearance.

*I hate waiting like this,* he thought as he sipped his coffee.

At three-thirty, he walked over to Randi's office and took a seat in the waiting room. He had hardly gotten comfortable when Randi came charging through the door. The somber look on her face told him that she knew why he was there.

"You heard about Phil?" she asked as she showed him to her office in the back.

She walked swiftly, removing her deerskin jacket as she entered the room, and then turned to face Gallagher.

"Yes, I was with Barry Nickerson when he got the call," he said, interested in observing her mannerisms under the stress of this latest news.

"This whole thing is crazy. I don't know what's going on," she blurted out, throwing her bag down onto her desk.

"Well, until we learn the details of Phil's death, we don't know for sure if it's all related. Have you heard how it happened?" he asked.

"I spoke to Mark Wolfe, Phil's lawyer. Phil's wife called him. They apparently found Phil this morning near the bottom of the Quechee Gorge. He went there for his usual morning walk. At this point, they don't know whether he had a heart attack and fell or whether someone pushed him. The medical examiner's report won't be ready for a few days."

Gallagher tried to draw more out of her.

"If this wasn't an accident or the result of a medical problem, it sort of blows away the notion that the two doctors were killed by some maniac with a vendetta against the health professions."

Randi didn't respond. She looked away from him. Gallagher kept pushing.

"In fact, you'd have to say that the other three partners are now in serious danger."

Gallagher let that statement hang there for a few seconds to see her reaction.

She blinked nervously and threw her head back, trying to whisk a few loose strands of hair away from her eyes.

"Yes, I guess you're right," she said. "I better call Tony and Dan to make sure they are aware of the situation."

Gallagher stepped toward her. She backed away trying to get a little more personal space.

"Listen, Randi, this has all become deadly serious, and it's got to be tied to those secret meetings. I could tell by the way Barry refused to talk about them. If you're holding anything back, I need to know it now."

His harsh stare and accusatory edge of his voice brought an immediate reaction.

"You know, Gallagher—you can just get out of my face," she fired back, showing him that his aggressive tactics would not intimidate her. "I've already told you I wasn't invited to those meetings. What do you expect me to do, make something up so you can play Mr. Hot-Shot Detective?"

"Don't make it up; just start telling me everything you know. The lives of the other three partners may depend on it."

They stood practically nose to nose.

She said nothing.

Her resolute stare never moved from his eyes.

*What is she hiding? How could she benefit from these murders?*

He finally yielded some space and turned away.

"You know how to reach me," he said as he left the office.

# CHAPTER 17

The drive to Suzanne Becker's house in Bedford took only twenty minutes and was made easier by the GPS system in Gallagher's car.

*Ah—technology! How did I ever find anything before I had this gizmo?*

Seven Cresthaven Drive was an impressive home, sitting on a slight hill with lush landscaping and plantings all around it. The fieldstone front and interesting roof angles were accented beautifully by the flood lights that had just taken effect in the darkening evening sky.

Seconds after he rang the doorbell, Suzanne Becker opened the front door. She had obviously been waiting for him to arrive.

"Please come in," she said, "I still can't believe the horrible news about Phil. I'm so concerned about his wife, Kristen; I tried to call her, but there was no answer."

"Yes," said Gallagher, "It seems like this whole situation is changing faster than we can react to it."

She ushered him to a sitting room to the right of the foyer. As at their first meeting in his office, she was impeccably dressed. Her make-up highlighted her pretty face, and it appeared as if she were just on her way out to dinner at a fine restaurant. He wondered if she always looked this good, or if she had made special preparations for his arrival.

The room had two love seats separated by a small, rectangular ottoman. Gallagher sat down with his back to the front window. On the wall to his right was a beautiful armoire made of bleached wood that had distress marks all over the exterior to give it an antique appearance. It was a work of real craftsmanship and served as the centerpiece of this cozy room. Looking around, he could see that the house had many pieces of art, including one he recognized by the artist, Hamilton Aguiar.

"I love that guy's work," said Gallagher, pointing to the painting on the wall.

"Yes, Jonathan and I like it very much as well. We met him at an opening on Newbury Street and bought that piece. It's titled 'Blue Solitude' and is done with a technique called silver leaf."

Gallagher couldn't help but notice how she still referred to her husband in the present tense. The reality of his death had apparently not settled in.

"Mrs. Becker," he started, "I need to know more about the real-estate partnership. It seems that people are holding back and not telling me everything they know."

"I wish I could tell you more," she said. "Once the building was finished, Jonathan hardly discussed the partnership. He never talked about their meetings. I think it was the way they decided to handle their business. They kept it all among themselves."

"Did your husband keep any records about his business at home?"

"Yes, Jonathan was meticulous about record-keeping both in his practice and the real-estate holdings. He kept most of his files in his office downstairs."

Gallagher immediately asked, "Could I have access to those files?"

"Of course. Anything that will get us to the bottom of this."

"What about telephone records? Do you have your telephone bills for the past few years? It may help to see who he was calling."

"I don't know if he would have saved the old telephone bills. But if he did, they'll be downstairs also. In fact, I still have his cell phone.

Last week, the police returned the contents of his car, and his cell phone was one of the items. I haven't disconnected the service yet."

"Can I have it? There may be something in the contact list."

"Come with me," she said.

She led him through the hallway and the kitchen and down a staircase to a finished basement where Dr. Becker had his office. It was furnished handsomely with an L-shaped oak desk, a bookshelf, and a computer station. To the right of the slide-out keyboard drawer was a file drawer with papers neatly ordered in a Pendaflex filing system. One of the title tabs read "Parker Hill Partnership." Mrs. Becker pulled out the thick file and handed it to Gallagher.

"This should keep you busy for awhile."

On the corner of the desk was a plastic bag containing personal items that were in Dr. Becker's car at the time of his shooting—a small notepad, several pens, a pack of sugar-free breath mints, his appointment book, his cell phone, and the hands-free speaker setup.

Gallagher opened the bag, removed the cell phone, and slipped it into his jacket pocket.

They walked upstairs and stopped in the kitchen.

"Can I get you a drink or a cup of coffee?" she asked.

"No, thanks. I've had coffee already. Any more caffeine in my system might keep me up all night."

She opened a small cabinet near the sink and produced a large Saks Fifth Avenue shopping bag into which she placed all the papers from the file. The fact that it wasn't a bag from Macy's didn't surprise Gallagher in the least.

"This will make it easier for you to carry those things back to your office," she said.

The shopping bag was so heavy that Gallagher had to hold it from the bottom to keep the handles from tearing. On the drive back to Boston, Gallagher could not get his mind off Suzanne Becker. She was a woman who was obviously used to an expensive lifestyle, but she was also a very thoughtful and considerate person, even about such simple things as how he would carry this large stack of papers to his car. Nothing about her was put on; she was genuine and sincere, and life had suddenly dealt her a terribly unfair hand.

He generally liked his clients, but always tried to keep himself a cool distance away in order to maintain his objectivity. After all, sometimes he was the one who had to give them very bad news—news that could change their lives forever. There were also times when he had to advise them to give up on an investigation that had run its course and had nowhere to go. It was hard enough for him to ever let go of a case, but his professional ethics kept him from wasting a client's money on a fruitless chase.

Gallagher never wanted be drawn into relationships that might affect his judgment and put him in jeopardy. But this woman was different—something about her evoked feelings of loyalty and made him want to help her, to exhaust all of the possibilities and push himself beyond the limit.

Gallagher was determined to get the answers she needed, one way or another, no matter how much time it took.

# Chapter 18

**"Retired Local Businessman Found Dead in Vermont; Was Real-Estate Partner of Doctors Recently Murdered in West Castle"**

The story that followed the headline in the City/Region section of the *Boston Globe* was sketchy, at best—no further details other than those that Gallagher had learned the day before. The medical examiner's report was not scheduled for release for at least two more days. Gallagher knew little about Quechee, Vermont, and decided to drive up there later in the morning, if, for no other reason, than to see how much time it took.

*Could someone have driven up to Vermont, killed Phil Lombardo, and still have had time to get back to the West Castle area the same day?*

He combed through the large pile of papers and notes from Jonathan Becker's file— leases, tenant improvements, budget issues, condominium fees, and minutes of meetings related to the valuation of partnership shares. So far, they appeared to be irrelevant to the question he was trying to answer. All of the meetings were attended by the partners and Randi Stockdale, who compiled the minutes, typed them, and distributed them to the partners. There were no minutes or records of the meetings during the past few months that were not attended by Randi.

*Evidently, whatever the partners were discussing in their executive sessions was not destined for a paper trail.*

Gallagher was still immersed in reading through the paperwork when the phone in the front office rang. He heard Diane answer the call, pause for a moment, and then speak to him on his intercom.

"Dan, there is a Detective Jack Hoskins on the phone for you. Can you speak to him, or would you like me to take a message?"

*Hoskins—I should have figured it wouldn't take long for him to be calling me.*

"No, I'll speak to him, Diane, thanks."

He picked up the handset on the phone and said, "Hello."

"Gallagher? Jack Hoskins, West Castle PD. Remember me? I worked in Roxbury Precinct 14 when you came out of the Police Academy."

"Yeah, Jack, I remember. What can I do for you?" Gallagher remembered this intimidator and pain in the ass all too well but resisted the temptation to let his true feelings be known.

"Was just wondering if you could come out to see me sometime today? I've got a few questions for you."

"Questions about what?"

"Well, let's just say it would be better if we had this conversation in person. It's a police matter."

Gallagher thought about coming up with an excuse to avoid the meeting. But then his rational side prevailed.

*Maybe I can find out where the police are going with their investigation into the murders.*

"Okay, Jack. How about one o'clock?"

"I'll be here. Don't be late, Gallagher, I'm a busy man," Hoskins said as he hung up the phone.

# Chapter 19

At O'Sullivan's Lounge in Somerville a disheveled man, in desperate need of a shower and shave, flipped a sweat-stained Red Sox cap toward the back of his head and hunched forward on the bar stool.

Jimmy Nolan nursed his fourth beer of the lunch hour. The first two had gone down fast and easy; the third somewhat deliberately; but now he was mellowed out and just took occasional sips from the fourth. He picked at his burger and fries, and the half-eaten platter of food had grown cold and unappetizing.

For Jimmy Nolan, an ex-military man with commendations for service in Vietnam and marksmanship, this was his usual liquid lunch. He had gotten to the point in his life where he didn't care if he was wasted for the rest of the afternoon. His had been a downward spiraling career that had him, at his high point, serving as the chief foreman of a crew that worked on major projects for one of the premier companies in Greater Boston, Forgione Brothers Construction. He had been in charge of twenty men, working on medium-rise buildings in the fast-paced world of design-build construction. His bosses at Forgione Brothers specialized in health-care facilities. One of their biggest jobs had been the Parker Hill Medical Building in West Castle. Nolan had supervised the project perfectly from its onset—had the subcontractors under control, all the deadlines had been met, and the project was on-budget.

But at the same time, Jimmy was experiencing some difficult times in his personal life. His gambling had gotten out of control. He was in debt up to his ears. In a moment of weakness, he convinced a subcontractor to falsify an invoice for materials and change it to the retail cost rather than subcontractor's wholesale, discounted price. Then, Jimmy and the subcontractor split the difference. It was only a few thousand dollars, but he desperately needed the money.

With just a month left before the first suite in the building would be occupied, the partners in the group began to audit the expense sheets and check the invoices that had been submitted. Confronted with the evidence, Jimmy confessed and offered to repay all the money. He begged the partners to understand his situation and the pressure he had been under. After all, he had been going through some tough times in his marriage and was faced with losing his house. Until that point, he had done a good job managing the project; he had saved them time and money, and in the end, they were getting a great building.

But the only thing the partners cared about were the reports that he had been drinking on the job, that he was setting a poor example for the other workers, and that he had tried to take advantage of them. So they insisted that Forgione Brothers fire him. They cut him loose: never gave him a second chance, threw him onto the scrap heap, and pinned him with the reputation of being a drunk and a thief.

Since then, his life had been a series of part-time jobs and full-time failure. His wife eventually left him for good; he hardly ever saw his kids; and his only friend became the stuff he drank, hoping to forget all his problems.

As he sat at the bar and looked down at the morning newspaper, his attention was focused on a story in the local news that dealt with the recent murders in West Castle and the suspicious death in Vermont. His eyes stared down at the newspaper, only occasionally looking up at the bartender or the other patrons in the bar.

He slowly rubbed his fingers over the words in the story as he kept repeating to himself, almost mumbling at times, "Three down, three to go—three down, three to go."

# Chapter 20

Gallagher arrived on time for his meeting at the West Castle police station and walked into the main entrance where he was met by a uniformed officer sitting behind a bullet-proof window. The officer looked up and said, "Yes, sir?"

"I'm here to see Jack Hoskins.

"Your name, sir?"

"Gallagher."

"May I see your driver's license for identification purposes? What business do you have with Detective Hoskins?" the officer asked with a dour expression on his face.

Gallagher took out his wallet and flipped it open so that the plastic panel with his license could be seen through the window. He understood what was happening—a routine hassle from this desk cop who knew who he was and why he was there but just wanted to show his authority.

Gallagher decided to comply in the hope that this little charade would play itself out.

"Hoskins called and asked me to come down here. Said it was a police matter," he responded.

After a few seconds, a buzzer sounded as the door to the main office unlocked, and the officer motioned Gallagher to enter.

"It's the second door on the left," he said, pointing down the hallway.

As Gallagher turned into the open doorway, he saw Jack Hoskins sitting at his desk wearing a white shirt and a striped tie that stood out next to his black suspenders. Gallagher hadn't seen him for almost ten years, but his burly physique, the jowls on his cheeks, and his shiny, bald head were the same. And yes, the suspenders—Hoskins always wore suspenders.

He looked up from his desk, over his reading glasses and, with a deadpan expression, said, "Come in, Gallagher, and have a seat."

Gallagher sat down.

"How's it going, Jack? Haven't seen you in a long time."

"I'm doin' alright. Seems like you've been spending a lot of time in our little town lately."

"Yeah, I'm looking into buying a condo in a retirement community. West Castle seems like a good spot to start."

Hoskins took off his reading glasses and darted a harsh stare at him, "Don't be cute with me, Gallagher. We picked you up on a surveillance camera at the Parker Hill Medical Building. What do you like to do in your spare time, go for elevator rides?"

"Well, they sure can be fun."

"All right, let's cut the crap. These murders are police business; what are you doing nosing around here? Who hired you?"

"I'd rather not say, Detective. But I'm not looking for any murderers; I'm really doing a business investigation."

"So I guess that means that one of the widows must have hired you. Time to check up on how the other partners are handling the money, huh? Making sure the proceeds are divided properly?"

"You might say that, but then again, I might not."

"Look, Gallagher, you left the police force because you couldn't cut it. You were a guy who couldn't follow the rules, who wanted to do things your own way. I know all about the time you seized evidence after an improper search. If it wasn't for your incompetence, Bobby Slater would be behind bars now instead of running around Chelsea free as a bird."

"My partner and I had every right to go into Slater's apartment. He was beating up his girlfriend."

"Internal Affairs didn't see it that way," Hoskins snapped. "Don't think you can come around here and start solving homicides. If you mess around in police matters, you're gonna get yourself into serious trouble. I expect that anything you find related to these two murders will be reported to me."

He pointed his finger directly at Gallagher.

"You gotta know that concealing evidence about a homicide could land your ass in the Middlesex County Jail!"

An old wound had been opened, but Gallagher was determined not to let his inner feelings show.

"Look, Hoskins, you're not going to have any problems with me. I'm just checking into some personal matters for a client."

He waited for Hoskins to respond, but all he received was a suspicious glare—a sign that Hoskins wasn't buying his glib attitude.

*What can he do to me? There's no way he can stop me from talking to people related to these murder cases.*

He decided not to even bring up the subject of Phil Lombardo's death in Vermont or to ask Hoskins who had tipped him off about his visits to West Castle.

*Why say anything else to complicate this mini-confrontation?*

Instead, he got up from his chair and said, "OK, Jack—it's been great seeing you after all these years. Keep in touch now."

He walked down the hallway and waited for the officer at the desk to buzz him out of the main office.

Out on the street, he walked slowly to his car thinking about all the facets of this case and how they were beginning to consume his every thought.

*Am I overreacting, or does it seem that some of the actors in this play have their own secret agenda? Randi Stockdale and Barry Nickerson have been evasive for sure. Now Hoskins is chiming in with reminders that I blew the evidence on a case years ago. I need some answers.*

Gallagher would never accept a partial solution—one that pertained only to the partners' collective mindset about a real-estate venture that had somehow turned deadly.

No, the situation had drastically changed. Gallagher wouldn't be satisfied until he knew who committed the murders.

# Chapter 21

Gallagher drove out of Boston, headed north on Route 93, and then followed Route 89 north through New Hampshire to Exit 1 in Vermont. He checked his watch as he arrived at the stop sign at the bottom of the exit ramp. The trip to Quechee, Vermont, had only taken one hour and fifty-five minutes.

He was not a particularly fast driver, but he was no slowpoke either. Five to ten miles over the highway speed limit was about right for him. He thought that someone could have murdered Phil Lombardo and then easily made it back to the Boston area by nine or ten o'clock in the morning without anyone really noticing that he or she was missing from work.

He drove along Route 4 toward the main part of the village. He pulled into the information center to learn a little about the area and to ask where the local police station was located. A friendly woman in her early seventies, wearing a name tag that read, "Mimi," informed him that the Village of Quechee was an historic mill town—famous for the Quechee Gorge, one of Vermont's most spectacular natural wonders. The Gorge was formed during the Ice Age as melting glacier waters slowly cut away the bedrock ridges.

"You just drove over the Gorge, but may not have gotten a good look at it from your car. It's really quite a sight," she said proudly.

"Yes, I plan to go back for a better look later. But I do need some information. Where can I find the local police station?"

"Quechee is governed by the Town of Hartford, Vermont. We

don't have our own police force. You'll have to drive over to White River Junction."

Fifteen minutes later, he arrived at the Hartford Police station. As Gallagher walked in, one officer was sitting at the reception desk talking on the telephone. Gallagher looked around the office and waited until he hung up.

"Morning. My name is Gallagher; I'm a private investigator from Boston. Is your chief around?"

The young officer looked surprised, but said, "Yes, sir, he's in his office; you can go in."

Gallagher walked back to a small office directly behind the front desk where a middle-aged, uniformed man was standing, adjusting his coat as if he were preparing to leave. The badge on his coat jacket read "Town of Hartford, Police Department, Chief."

He glanced at Gallagher and said, "Yes—what can I do for you?"

Gallagher opened his wallet to show the chief his identification.

"Gallagher. I'm a private investigator from Boston looking into the business dealings of a real-estate partnership in West Castle, Massachusetts. One of the former members of that partnership was found dead in Quechee a couple of days ago."

The chief held out his hand like he was stopping traffic, "Hold it right there; we don't deal with private detectives up here. This is a police matter that's still under a non-public investigation."

"Do you know when the ME's report will be released?" asked Gallagher, trying to keep him engaged in a conversation and hoping to get something out of him.

"Not for a couple of more days. We'll make a public statement when the time is right. Until then, we have nothing to say to you or anyone from the media," barked the chief with finality.

He brushed past Gallagher and out to the officer at the desk. He glared at the officer.

"From now on, you better remember that I don't appreciate unannounced visitors being allowed to enter my office."

"Okay, Chief. Sorry," the officer replied meekly.

Gallagher stood in the hallway for a moment and then slowly made his way back to the front desk.

"Is he always so friendly?" Gallagher asked the young officer.

"Well, consider yourself lucky that you're not bleeding anywhere."

"I guess so; maybe this death down by the Gorge has put him in a foul mood," replied Gallagher, sensing a sympathetic ear in the young man.

"Could be. We don't have too many homicides up this way."

"Homicide? Do you think someone killed this guy?" he said.

"Well, as the chief said, we don't have the medical examiner's report yet. But if that guy had a stroke or something, I don't think he would have fallen that far and smashed his head on a rock. Someone had to help him get there."

With a mock Southern drawl he added, "But then again, you ain't heard nothun' from me."

Gallagher gave him a knowing smile and walked out to his car. He was becoming increasingly certain that the three deaths were all linked and that someone was determined to kill all the partners.

*But why? What could these doctors have done to make someone want to murder them?*

He went back to Quechee and drove around for a while trying to get a better handle on the area.

Despite the fact that the foliage had passed its peak and most of the leaves had come down, leaving a color scheme that was essentially brown, it was still a beautiful and restful little town that seemed far away from the hassles of a big city. The two golf courses at the Quechee Club were still perfectly manicured, though the hint of winter in the air told him that the golf season there was probably about to end.

It was almost noon and a sign reading "Quechee Village Deli" caught his attention. He parked his car and walked into the deli where an old man wearing a smudged white apron stood behind the counter. He had a sad sack look about him and a name tag on his shirt that read "Sam."

Gallagher looked up at the billboard behind the deli case and read the menu of some great-sounding specialty sandwiches with all the ingredients listed—The Big Balloon, The Quechee Adventure, Granny Smith, Goin' Postal, and several others.

"What's good here, Sam? I need a sandwich to go."

"Everything's good. Where you headed?"

"Thought I'd take a hike down the Quechee Gorge trail."

"You better be careful down there. They found a guy dead on a pile of rocks at the base of the Gorge the other day."

"Really? What happened to him?"

Sam picked up a damp cloth from the side of the counter and began wiping off the sandwich board.

"Well, a lot of people think it was an accident and that he just slipped and fell, but I doubt it. That's a long way to fall without being pushed," he said.

"Is the area open to hikers now?"

"Oh, yeah. The cops had it roped off for a few hours, but it's open again. I'd just be on guard if you walk down there."

"Thanks, I'll do that. How about the 'Goin' Postal' sandwich on rye?' asked Gallagher, switching to the business at hand.

As Sam fussed behind the counter, adding all the ingredients to the sandwich—roast beef, turkey, Vermont cheddar cheese, tomato, sprouts, and garlic mayonnaise— Gallagher tried to use his cell phone to call his office.

"If it's Verizon, you won't have too much luck with that up here," said Sam. "You'll have to wait until you get back onto 89 South in New Hampshire."

"You're right; I'm getting no reception," replied Gallagher, impressed by the fact that the man making his sandwich had guessed correctly that he'd be heading home in that direction. He wondered if his intuition about the fate of Phil Lombardo was equally as good.

Gallagher took his sandwich and a can of iced tea and drove over to the Quechee Gorge. He sat in his car for a while, eating lunch, enjoying the scenery, and noticing how few people were in the area at this time of the year. It was between seasons—the golfers and leaf peepers had left, and the snow season hadn't begun to attract the skiers. He walked down a small set of steps to the side of the bridge and started making his way down the packed-dirt trail. More than a hundred yards below he could see the Ottauquechee River rushing through the Gorge, splashing against dozens of large rocks, creating a foaming and noisy, but beautiful, waterfall.

He noted that the grade of the hiking trail was steep but certainly not treacherous. About half way down to the base, the right side of the trail sloped sharply off toward the river. The trail was bordered by a large pile of rocks. Someone walking past Phil Lombardo at this point or, emerging suddenly from the trees on the left, could have attacked him and then pushed his body down the embankment to the rocks bordering the river. The attack could have happened so early in the morning that no one was present to witness it.

Gallagher returned to his car and began driving back to Boston. As he crossed the New Hampshire border on Route 89 South, his cell phone began blinking with the message, "Voice Mail Received."

He pressed the "OK" button, entered his PIN, and listened to the voice of Jack Harte, "Hey Gallagher, where've you been, man? I've located your boy for you—Mr. Mickey Ryan. Give me a call when you can."

Gallagher stepped on the gas pedal. His BMW 530i took off like a rocket.

*No time for a leisurely drive. I've got a ton of questions for Mickey Ryan!*

# CHAPTER 22

"Hey, Jack. Got your message."

"It's about time. Where the hell you been?"

"Vermont."

"Whaddya doin' up there?"

"Oh, just checking on a few things. I'll give you the details some other time. Tell me what you've got on Mickey Ryan."

"Well, I spoke to a few guys on the force—veterans—cops who have been around for a while. This Mickey is a real character."

"How so?"

"He's no longer in Medford. Moved to Everett. He's selling used cars at Imperial Motors on Route 16."

"I know the place—driven past it many times."

"Yeah, but there's more to the story. Word is the used-car job is just a front for a bookmaking operation. He sells football cards from September through the Super Bowl. Makes real money—cash only—completely off the books."

"Nice deal for Mickey, huh?"

"Oh, yeah. Shows very little income on his tax forms. Lives in a house owned by his long-time girlfriend; drives a car registered in her name. You know the formula: no credit cards, no tax bills, no government audits, no tracing Mickey Ryan."

"What a country."

"Right," said Jack.

"How does he manage to keep from being busted?"

"The usual way. He makes frequent donations to the local cops. They've developed a series of neck strains from looking the other way."

"I get it."

"Hey, look—most of the cops figure it's a victimless crime. You know—just a few guys enjoying a little action while they watch the weekend games."

"I guess. Anything else for me?"

"Oh, yeah. Plenty more. This guy's a real piece of work. There are rumors that Mickey received a substantial insurance payment from a suspicious fire at a property he owned in West Castle. But the arson investigators could never prove a thing. As usual, Mickey got off free and clear. When it comes to the law, he's as slippery as they come—nothing ever sticks."

"Thanks, Jack. Good work. I owe you one," said Gallagher.

"No problem, man. Keep in touch."

***

Gallagher parked his car in a Dunkin' Donuts lot about a half block away and across the street from Imperial Motors. He casually walked through the rows of low-priced used cars looking at the sticker prices and peering into the windows. Had he driven into the lot in his BMW, it would have been too obvious that he was here on some other business. Until he was sure that Mickey was working, he preferred to look like any other price-checking buyer trying to find a good deal on a car.

He stopped by a 1999 Honda Accord, and walked around the car repeatedly, carefully studying the body of the car as if checking for scratches and nicks. He crouched down to check the front tire on the driver's side. The sun was suddenly blocked by a large figure standing over him.

"Brand new tires on this baby," the man said, "You won't find an Accord in better shape than this one."

Gallagher looked up. A man as large as an offensive lineman

peered down at him: well over six feet tall with thick black curly hair and a stomach that looked like a storage container for a Sam Adams brewery. His shirt was not tucked in, giving him the appearance of wearing a tent. Gallagher guessed his age as late fifties. But despite his big belly and his age, he seemed to be a man of considerable strength. His large frame cast an intimidating shadow on Gallagher.

"Yeah, the car looks like new. Did it come off a lease?" asked Gallagher as he stood up from his crouching position.

"No, just a one-time owner. A lady traded it in to move up to an SUV. It's got low mileage. If you're interested, I can give you a good deal."

He extended his hand out to Gallagher, "I'm Mickey Ryan. You wanna take it for a test drive?"

"I might like to do that later, but first I'd like to ask you a few questions," he said as he handed Mickey one of his cards.

Mickey's facial expression flashed from a half-smile to a snarl as he looked at the card.

"Who the hell are you?" he bellowed.

"Like the card says, the name's Gallagher. I'm a private investigator checking a real-estate transaction that took place in West Castle about twenty years ago. I believe you sold a piece of land to a guy named Nickerson."

Mickey threw his hands up in the air.

"Maybe I did. What's it to you?"

"Well, I thought you might want to comment on the sale and the medical building that was eventually built on that property.

"Look, wise guy, anything you need to know, you can find out from the recorder of deeds. That's all I've got to say. So get the hell out of here!" he growled with a sweeping motion of his hand toward the street.

"The recorder of deeds office will be able to tell me the price of the land you sold, but not what it was really worth. I think only you can do that," said Gallagher with a knowing smile on his face.

Mickey walked up close to Gallagher. Mickey's stomach pushed into him so that he was forced to lean back on the side of the car.

"Those doctor bastards screwed me on that deal. They sent a straw buyer to make a bid on my lot, and then, after I sold it to him, the son of a bitch turned it over to his partners so they could put up that building. Without that piece of land on Central Street, they could have never built that fuckin' place. Screwed me out of two-hundred grand!"

Mickey's breath was hot. Droplets of saliva sprayed out of his mouth as he became more agitated. Beads of perspiration formed on his forehead. He looked like someone about to go into a rage.

Gallagher resisted the onslaught.

"Do you know anything about what happened to a few of those guys during the past month?" he asked, still probing and trying to push Mickey's buttons.

"Sure, I read the papers. All I have to say is: what goes around comes around. Those doctors probably got what they deserved. Who knows who else they screwed!"

Then, he reacted like a switch in his brain had suddenly been flipped. Mickey stepped back from his new adversary, no longer crowding his space.

"Hey," he said, almost apologetically, "hold on here. You don't think I had anything to do with those murders, do you? If I wanted to kill those bastards, I would have done it twenty years ago before they had a chance to enjoy all the money."

"Well, frankly, Mickey, the thought has crossed my mind. People hold grudges for a long time, and then one day, they decide to get even."

"Look, Gallagher, or whatever the hell your name is, I had nothun' to do with those murders, and I can back it up with an alibi. What happened twenty years ago has nothun' to do with today. I'm a respectable business man just tryin' to make a living here," he said in a conciliatory tone.

"Does that include your bookmaking operation?" asked Gallagher, finding it hard to hide the coy smile on his face.

Mickey shrugged, exhaled loudly, and then nodded his head.

"You've really been doin' your homework, Mr. Detective. You seem to know a lot of shit. But I've got a question for you—if I've got such a successful side job here, why would I risk that just to get even with some jerks over in West Castle? Is there any money to be made in revenge?"

*Mickey is actually making some sense.*

Gallagher didn't have a chance to acknowledge the good point Mickey had made.

"Besides," Mickey continued, "I've had too much goin' on myself. I've got my own problems. Maybe if you're such a good detective, you could tell me who's been breaking into my place during the past few months."

"Break-ins?"

"Yeah, I had two robberies. One here and one at my house."

"What was taken?"

"I'd rather not say. That's my business, but if I catch the sons of bitches, they're gonna be sorry."

"Well, solving break-ins isn't my specialty. Sounds like you should just call the police."

Mickey began to laugh sarcastically.

"Right, Mr. Detective—first you tell me I'm a bookie, and then you expect me to call the cops about a couple of break-ins. I guess the next thing I should do is let them search all around my house until they find some betting slips, some names and addresses, or a pile of cash. You're a real fuckin' genius!"

Gallagher laughed at himself, and once again, had to say that the blusterous Mickey had scored another point. They ended their discussion almost on amicable terms.

"Look, Mickey. I'm looking into all business dealings of the partnership—trying to see if there's a link to the murders."

"I told ya' everything I know."

"Ever been to a place called Quechee?"

Mickey looked perplexed.

"Where?"

Gallagher smiled. "Never mind, Mickey. It's alright."

Gallagher turned to walk away as he said, "See you around."

Mickey stood with his arms at his side and a blank expression on his face.

As Gallagher walked to his car, he glanced back over his shoulder a few times, watching Mickey as he slowly ambled his way to the office at the rear of the used car lot. He was glad to have finally met him. But there was much more to be learned about this cagey, street-smart character who seemed completely at ease living outside of the law.

Mickey Ryan may have just proven himself to be a clever poker player, bluffing his way through their meeting with a combination of bluster and intimidation. Now the burden rested on Gallagher—he had even more questions but few answers.

It seemed as if he had no clear-cut path to a solution.

*If I don't come up with some fresh ideas in a hurry, this investigation is going nowhere.*

# Chapter 23

It was a tedious process, and he seemed to be stuck in mud. Gallagher once again sat in his office sifting through the papers and appointment books of Dr. Jonathan Becker, hoping to find some new clues that might shed a little light on the problems within the real-estate partnership.

Nothing jumped out at him.

He grew more impatient by the minute.

Two days earlier, the police in Hartford, Vermont, had held a news conference and announced that Phil Lombardo's death had been officially ruled a homicide. The medical examiner's office had determined that the cause of death was blunt-force trauma to the head. It was suspected that the perpetrator then pushed the body down the slope to the rocks at the base of the Gorge. As with the two West Castle murders, there were no witnesses to the incident. The police had been unable to find foot prints or hair samples that might provide a starting point to launch their investigation.

As Gallagher read the newspaper account of the press conference, he couldn't help but think that the police had no chance to solve this crime. Like the West Castle murders, the person or persons who committed the murder had carefully studied the daily patterns of the victim and then selected a time and place where the murder could be carried out without witnesses or interference.

*This was not some amateur; it bears all the markings of a professional job—someone with experience, someone who operates with brutally cold efficiency.*

He looked through Dr. Becker's papers and minutes of the partnership meetings. Everything continued to look vanilla—nothing but run-of-the-mill real-estate business: rent formulas, lease arrangements, condominium expenses, and distribution of profits to the partners. No points of contention, disagreements, or conflicts were evident in any of the minutes. Even the buy-out of Dr. Phil Lombardo in 1999 was handled in a totally amicable manner. Both sides agreed to the amount of the buyout, and the transaction was completed within a short time of Phil's announcement that he was interested in selling his share of the real-estate partnership.

Both Dr. Becker's current and old appointment books also showed nothing of particular interest. Partner's meetings were listed simply as "Ptr's Meet–6 PM." There was no indication in the appointment book that the partners were meeting in executive session, but Randi's absence from the meetings and the lack of minutes made it obvious that the partners had met alone. There were ten meetings between May and October that had no corresponding minutes, and according to Randi, each meeting lasted at least an hour and a half, requiring that she arrange for a takeout dinner.

*What were these guys talking about? Why was it such a big secret?*

Dr. Becker's cell phone was lying on the right side of Gallagher's desk. He picked up the phone, turned it on, and pressed the "OK" button. The "Contacts List" appeared on the screen. He scrolled down the list, past the numbers for "Home," "Hospital," "Lab," "Office," "Randi," "Suzanne Cell," and the expected assortment of speed dial numbers for a doctor, until, near the end of the alphabetized list, he came to the initials "WJP." The initials didn't match any of the partners or anyone else Gallagher had ever heard of in connection with Dr. Becker, so he pressed the "Send" button. The message "Dialing (202) 555-8600" appeared on the screen as the phone rang, and a young woman's voice answered the call.

"Good afternoon, Congressman William Prendergast's office. This is Laura. How may I help you?"

Gallagher looked at the cell phone incredulously and slid his thumb over to the "End" button, pressing it down to terminate the call. Gallagher was not a political junkie, but he prided himself on at least knowing the names of the representatives in Congress from Massachusetts. The name "Prendergast" was not among them. He pondered what had just transpired. Why would a doctor in West Castle have the number of an out-of-state U.S. congressman on his speed dial list?

He pushed the intercom button on his desk. Diane's voice responded immediately.

"Yes, Dan, do you need me?"

"Diane, could you arrange a flight to Washington, D.C. for me tomorrow morning? Reagan National is closest to downtown; I think US Air or American may be your best bet. And I'll need a room at the Hotel Washington."

"Sure, I'll see what I can do."

Gallagher continued to stare at the cell phone and the Washington, D.C. telephone number on the "recent calls" screen.

*Congressman William Prendergast? Where does this guy fit in?*

# CHAPTER 24

Johnny Nicoletti took a long drag from his cigarette as he looked out from the deck of his penthouse suite at the Venetian Hotel in Las Vegas. Resting on a chaise lounge beside him, a beautiful, buxom young woman put down her copy of *People Magazine* and glanced up at him.

"Getting hungry, Johnny?"

"We've got dinner reservations at six. I can wait. It's only another hour and a half. Relax—grab somethin' from the fridge if you're hungry," he said.

"Maybe I will," she said.

She got up and walked into the small kitchen and opened the refrigerator. As she scanned the shelves, deciding what looked appetizing, she continued the conversation.

"I was just reading about the new shows on Broadway. I'd love to go there sometime. Don't you miss New York?"

Johnny exhaled forcefully through his nose and exclaimed, "Are you kiddin'! Those poor suckers in the East are rakin' an endless pile of leaves, puttin' on their snow plows, and gettin' ready for winter. None of that crap for me! Can't believe I waited so long to come out here."

"How long you been here, Johnny?"

"Five years. Shoulda' come out here a long time ago. Look at this weather—eighty degrees—beautiful. I love this place!"

In Las Vegas, Johnny had it made. It was the perfect venue for him. He was not one to take his money to the casinos and lose it; that was for the tourists who thought they could get lucky and beat the house. Instead, the casinos were the indirect source of his livelihood and a comfortable lifestyle that gave him lots of time to relax, play some golf, and indulge in the natural beauties of the town—also known as the women of Las Vegas. Today's playmate was an all-day treat—twenty-four hours of companionship and indulgence. Expensive fun, but Johnny had plenty of dough for this type of entertainment.

She returned to her chair with a peach and a napkin in her hand.

"You must have a good job to afford a place like this, Johnny."

"Hey! No personal questions! Remember?" he shot back.

Then he smiled facetiously, letting her know it was all a tease.

"Look, Sugar, let's just say I'm a consultant—a highly paid consultant."

Johnny didn't want to say that his job description and compensation were completely off the books. He didn't know the identity of his employers, but they were most likely owners of the casinos and the syndicates that operated them. He had one contact person, a man named Jerry Murray, who called him every few weeks and gave him an assignment. The nature of these jobs was usually pretty simple—take care of a situation that his anonymous employers deemed important but too messy, dangerous, or illegal for them to get involved with. The only downside to this undefined job was that Johnny had to be available at a moment's notice, seven days a week, twenty-four hours a day.

Since he didn't know the names of his employers, he could never identify them to the police. No matter how severe the interrogation techniques might become, Johnny had nothing to tell. His sole contact was Jerry Murray, a guy whose name was probably a fabrication. But that didn't matter to Johnny. He confined his thoughts to things that did matter: his lavish life that included living rent-free in this beautiful condo, dining privileges throughout the hotel, and a nice cash payment delivered by Jerry every two weeks.

His assignments were varied and unpredictable—convincing a gambler with incredibly good luck in one of the casinos that he should leave Las Vegas and never come back again or punching out someone who repeatedly made passes at one of the female dealers or, worse yet, tried to meet with her after a shift. Whatever the assignment, Johnny was up for the challenge and managed to skate along the fringes of the law without ever being detected.

He prided himself on being efficient and never going to extremes unless absolutely necessary, and above all, never leaving a trail for someone to follow. He never asked why a particular assignment was given to him, how the characters were interrelated, or what he should do if he were caught. The ground rules were simple—here is a job that needs immediate attention, and we trust that you will do it without delay.

When he completed an assignment, there was no one to whom the results were reported. He merely waited until his next visit from Jerry Murray, informed him that the mission had been accomplished, and collected his money. For extraordinary jobs, involving considerable risk and travel, Johnny was rewarded with a bonus—a little extra cash for his efforts—but he never had to ask for the bonus. His employers gladly paid for the services rendered.

Johnny nestled an arm around his smiling companion.

"Do you think I could get into the consulting business?" she asked.

"Maybe. What's your specialty?" he asked.

He tickled her and watched her collapse with a peal of giggles.

Johnny knew a lot of people in Las Vegas, but no one really knew him or what he did for a living. He was a mystery man to most people, and that perception, as a guy with a lot of dough and no real job, was just how he liked it.

# CHAPTER 25

Gallagher knew it wouldn't be easy, but he had no choice. He had to see a few people before his trip to Washington, so he would have no time for dinner with Kate. It was already near five o'clock, and they were scheduled to meet at seven. He had to reach her before she drove into Boston. He was trying to be logical about an entirely emotional situation—always a flawed reasoning process.

Their relationship had grown even closer during the past few weeks, and he could no longer deny his feelings for her. She was something very special, and he knew that he could easily spend the rest of his life with her. He felt the same emotions emanating from her, but sensed her frustration and hesitancy about the unpredictability of his life as a private investigator.

Although she was confident in herself and the person she had become, Kate needed an orderly pattern in her life—maintaining a certain schedule was important. Knowing what she would be doing on a particular day and who she would be seeing were critical to her comfort level. In Gallagher, she had discovered a whole new wave of emotions that drew her to him. With each day and night they spent together, she was more eager to make a full commitment to him. However, the unpredictability of his schedule—the emergency calls, last minute changes in plans, and irregular hours—made her cautious. She feared that sharing her life with such an unconventional man, who was usually consumed with chasing some bad guy, might be too much to bear.

The depth of their feelings for each other had brought about some subtle, but significant changes in their relationship. Kate now had her own key for Gallagher's one-bedroom condominium in BayView Towers, a luxurious complex in downtown Boston with fabulous views of the city and harbor. She was not ready to commit to full-time cohabitation, but it was certainly easier to meet at his place some evenings and not have to wait in the lobby for him to arrive. She kept some clothes, cosmetics, and personal items in his condo so she didn't have to drive back to her apartment before going to the office in Needham.

Gallagher's condo was located on the seventeenth floor. From the balcony off the living room, the sunrise over the ocean created a breathtaking scene. Kate often told him, however, that one of her favorite times was sitting on the balcony with a glass of wine in the early evening, enjoying the peaceful serenity of twilight settling in on the horizon.

Gallagher dialed Kate's number at her office.

"Hey, it's me."

"Hey, you. I was just getting ready to leave. Are we still on for seven?" she asked with anticipation.

"Kate—I'm sorry. Something urgent has come up in this West Castle case. I have to see some people tonight before I head to Washington tomorrow morning." His voice was low, measured and apologetic, "I won't be able to meet you for dinner."

There was a long silence on the other end of the telephone.

Finally, she replied, "Another cancelled dinner? How many more times will this happen? Why can't you see what I need? I spend most of my day looking forward to being with you, and then I'm let down by these disappointments. Maybe I'm just not right for a relationship with a private eye."

He knew this conversation would go badly. He tried to recover.

"Listen, Kate, you know how I feel about you."

"Then how come I always find myself in second place?"

"It's not that way. I just have to act on a lead in this case before it gets away. I only need one day in Washington. I promise I'll see you when I get back the day after tomorrow. And then we'll be able to spend the Thanksgiving weekend together."

"Why is it so important?"

"It's complicated."

"I guess you could say the same thing about us. Give me a call sometime next week; I need a few days to sort out some things," she said.

The phone clicked as she hung up.

Gallagher's mind was whirling. His head throbbed.

*How can you give up a woman like her?*

He put his head down and ran his fingers through his hair. Dozens of questions were spinning all around. He needed time to find the answers. He had some critical calls to make.

*What can Randi Stockdale or Suzanne Becker tell me about a congressman from Pennsylvania named William J. Prendergast?*

# CHAPTER 26

Gallagher turned on his computer and Googled William J. Prendergast, hoping to find some helpful information about the congressman. A fourteen-term Republican congressman from Erie, Pennsylvania, he had gradually advanced to a ranking position on several congressional committees including chairman of the Joint Committee on Economic Development and Emerging Technologies. Despite his rise to prominence in Congress and longevity in office, he was a little-known figure on the national scene. Gallagher had never heard his name before.

Gallagher called Randi Stockdale, hoping to see her and ask if she knew of any connection between Prendergast and the real-estate partners. He reached her at home but was careful not to mention the main reason for the call.

"Hi Randi. It's Gallagher. Could I stop by to see you for a minute tonight?"

"Is it about Phil? I heard that the police in Vermont have ruled his death a homicide."

"No. Actually, I've come up with something new and wanted to run it by you."

"Sure. I'll be home for the night. Come over whenever you want," she said.

*Not quite an enthusiastic invitation,* he thought. *What else could I expect?*

Their previous conversation had not exactly ended in a pleasant manner. He didn't know why, but he wanted to see her reaction to Prendergast's name. Even though she had been providing critical information that he needed to investigate this case, he could not escape the feeling that she was holding something back and was afraid to tell him the whole story.

Randi's house in West Castle was located in one of the nicer neighborhoods of the town. It was a large, white Colonial with New England red shutters and a distinctive six-panel front door with an antique black knocker. A pumpkin left over from Halloween and a display of Indian corn served as seasonal decorations on the front porch. Gallagher rang the doorbell, assuming that the knocker was ornamental rather than functional. The door opened. Randi invited him in. She looked perplexed by his visit as they stood in the hallway near the front door.

"What's this new information you've come up with? Something related to Jonathan and Dick?" she asked.

"Well, possibly. Have you ever heard of a congressman named William J. Prendergast?"

Randi took a slight step backward, paused for a second, and said, "Prendergast? No—I've never heard of him. How did that name come up?"

"He was listed in Jonathan Becker's cell phone. I thought it was odd that he would have the number of a U.S. congressman from Pennsylvania on his current speed dial list," said Gallagher, hoping to get a response.

"No, I don't know who he is and why he would have his number. I never heard Jonathan or any of the other partners mention that name."

"You told me in our first meeting that Dr. Becker and Dr. Evans went to Washington years ago to settle a problem with the FDIC. Do you know if they saw Congressman Prendergast on that visit?"

"No, they never told me who they saw or talked to in Washington.

It's been quite a few years now, but I believe I made their travel arrangements for an early morning flight with US Air. They came home the same night. It was a quick trip. They never talked to me about it."

He waited a few seconds for her to continue, but no further information was forthcoming.

"Well—I just hoped you might know the name. I'm planning to fly down to Washington tomorrow to nose around and see what I can come up with. If I'm lucky, maybe I can sneak in a word with the congressman and find out why Dr. Becker would be calling him. Give me a call if you think of anything," he said as he turned toward the door.

"Sure," she said with a slight hesitation. "Good luck tomorrow."

Gallagher walked out to his car feeling uneasy. Something had made Randi very uncomfortable. Once again, her responses were too cautious and measured. He doubted her honesty. He suspected that some issue lurked in the background. Eventually, her secret would help to unravel the twisted ball of yarn he faced.

*What can I do to make her reveal everything she knows?*

He called Suzanne Becker. Had her husband ever mentioned a congressman named William J. Prendergast? Once again, a negative answer. She had never heard the name. Her husband never called him in her presence. She could not come up with a reason why his phone number would be logged into her husband's cell phone. She vaguely remembered her husband's trip to Washington many years ago, but could not tell him any of the details. The frustration of every road leading to a dead end was beginning to set in.

"Mrs. Becker, I know you told me in our first meeting that the cost was no object," he said, "However, I have to tell you that this investigation is going to be very expensive. In fact, tomorrow, I'm flying down to Washington. Hopefully, to see this congressman."

"Don't worry," she encouraged. "Do whatever it takes. There

was evidently a lot that I didn't know all these years. It's about time I learned the whole story."

Gallagher hung up. One more stop before driving back to Boston. Almost nine o'clock—getting late. He drove past Barry Nickerson's home. Perhaps he would get lucky, and Barry would agree to speak to him, even if just for a few minutes. He pulled up in front of the house. The lights in the small sitting room were still on. He rang the doorbell and waited for a few minutes. No response. He rang the bell again and heard some shuffling inside the door. Evidently, Barry had fallen asleep on the couch and was awakened by the doorbell.

Gallagher stood on the porch as someone peered out between the curtains to the side of the front door. Barry recognized him and slowly opened the door. He stood in the doorway, not extending an invitation for his guest to come in. He seemed to prefer the distance and the security that the doorway afforded.

"What do you want, Gallagher? This has been a long day. I went to Phil's memorial service today—guess I just dozed off on the couch," he said groggily.

"Sorry, Barry. Hate to bother you so late, but something has come up. I think it may be important."

"What is it?" he asked. His eyes narrowed and he tilted his head backward, looking down the bridge of his nose at his late-night visitor.

"Did you ever hear of a congressman from Pennsylvania named William J. Prendergast? His phone number was in your partner's cell phone directory."

Gallagher stared at Nickerson, letting the full impact of the last sentence register. Nickerson's face seemed suddenly alert.

Barry Nickerson stammered at first and then blurted, "How can you—uh—what makes you think I would know this guy just because Jonathan had his phone number?"

"Well, that is precisely the question. Do you know Congressman William Prendergast?" he asked.

Gallagher's question was pointed. He spoke in a methodical manner, as if he were cross-examining a witness in a trial.

Nickerson put his head down for a few seconds without saying a word. Gallagher's question had obviously unnerved him. He grasped for a way to respond. He looked up at Gallagher with an icy stare, but his voice quivered as he spoke.

"I need you to leave my house and don't ever come back. I have nothing further to say. My advice to you is simple— stay out of this! People get hurt when they stick their noses where they don't belong."

With that, he closed the door, leaving Gallagher standing alone on the porch, realizing that, finally, he may have found the link that brought all the puzzle pieces together.

# Chapter 27

Kate was wearing a blue, silk Japanese kimono that shimmered slightly despite the dim light in the room. She rearranged the pillows on the couch to get comfortable. Racked by self-doubt and indecision, her mind was in turmoil.

*Why did I act so rashly? Should I be staying here, or packing my things to leave?*

She knew Gallagher could never resist the thrill of the chase—always putting her on a back burner while he tried to sort out the facts in another mystery case.

*Do I want that kind of life? Is this relationship going anywhere?*

But there was something about him, an undeniable attraction that could not be ignored. She was drawn to him in a way she had never felt before. No, she couldn't leave now. She needed to feel the closeness of his body and the safety of his embrace at least one more time.

***

During the drive back to Boston, Gallagher's heart was racing. Barry Nickerson's reaction to Gallagher's questions had made it clear—Congressman William J. Prendergast was a major figure in understanding what had happened in the partners' secret executive sessions.

*Could he also be the key to finding the killer of the three doctors?*

Nickerson's demeanor was not simply defensive.

*It was full of fear, like a man whose life had unexpectedly been turned upside down by the realization that a deep, dark secret had been revealed.*

Almost eleven o'clock. Gallagher could hardly contain his excitement to get on the plane to Washington the next morning. He knew the answers to his questions were most likely there, just waiting for him to find them. How could a United States congressman be involved in the murders of three physicians in New England? It seemed like such an unlikely scenario. If true, Gallagher had entered a new arena—playing with the big boys. The personal risks were greater than ever.

He parked his car in the garage next to BayView Towers and walked along the brick sidewalk to the lobby. He nodded to Joe, the nighttime security guard at the desk, stepped into the lobby elevator for Tower II and pressed "17" for his floor. After a quick, non-stop ride, he put his key into the lock of his unit, 17 C, and opened the door.

He had turned off the lights when he left that morning, but a single lamp near the couch in the living room was dimly lit. It cast a soft shadow across the room. As he closed the door, someone suddenly sat up from the couch. It startled him. His knees buckled. He began to reach for the gun in his shoulder holster.

False alarm! His adrenaline began to subside as he realized it was not an intruder, but Kate, who had been waiting for him to come home.

*She's here! I never expected her to be here.*

She walked toward him with a sexy, flirtatious swagger.

"Just for the record, I'm still mad at you," she said coyly.

When she reached him, she put her arms around his neck and pulled him closer.

"But I'm weak," she whispered as she kissed him deeply and pressed her body into his.

Her actions conveyed the intensity of her feelings—she loved him more than any man she had ever known.

He put his arms around her, fully aroused by the feel of her warm, soft skin through the silk robe and knowing she was wearing nothing underneath it.

He wanted to move slowly to savor the smell of her hair, the touch of her lips, and the excitement of her body coming alive. But the heat of her response would not tolerate patience. As he kissed and caressed her, the thoughts that had been swirling through his mind all night began to completely fade away. He was left with only one thought, one immediate purpose, and nothing else seemed to matter.

"*A chuisle mo chroi*" he said, reciting the Irish phrase: "pulse of my heart."

"*Mo chuisle*," she replied softly, as she moved her arms to let the blue, silk kimono slide quietly to the floor.

Gallagher had not yet checked the e-mail itinerary that Diane printed out for his flight the next day. He just hoped it wasn't too early in the morning.

# CHAPTER 28

The wind blew gently across the fairway of the first hole on the Legends course at the Ibis Golf and Country Club in West Palm Beach, Florida. Bill Prendergast stood on the tee box, looking out to the fairway where the group ahead of him prepared to hit their second shots.

"Great day to play some golf," he said to his friend, Jerry.

Prendergast waited patiently, swinging his driver slowly and methodically, one practice swing after another, trying to instill into his muscle memory the swing tempo he needed. One thing he truly hated was mishitting the first shot of the day and costing himself a penalty stroke at the beginning of the round. He had become a pretty decent golfer, logging in at a very respectable ten handicap. In fact, he was one of the better golfers in the halls of Congress. Nowhere did he enjoy playing golf more than right here in beautiful South Florida where he and Linda, his wife of thirty-five years, had bought a vacation home several years ago.

Bill Prendergast and his wife were playing golf with Jerry and B. J. Lanoux, a couple of their same age who had retired to Florida about the same time that Bill and Linda had bought their new home. Congress continued on its extended Thanksgiving holiday break, so he and his wife had flown down to West Palm Beach the previous night to play golf and spend the holiday with their family and friends in Florida. As a ranking congressman, his current status in life made him happy and comfortable.

He had risen from rather humble beginnings in Erie, Pennsylvania. His first job at only nine years of age had been as a newspaper boy. He had worked hard in school, always trying to excel in both academics and sports, though he was not a gifted athlete. He won a partial scholarship to the University of Pittsburgh and, through a combination of work and loans, eventually graduated with a bachelor of arts degree with a major in political science.

After college, he worked for the mayor's office in Pittsburgh for a few years before returning to Erie where he took a job with the county commissioner. He became active in the Young Republicans Club and, at age thirty, got his big break when the congressional seat for the Third District in Pennsylvania was vacated by the retirement of the incumbent. He decided to enter the race. He was young and inexperienced but had great communication and debating skills. He won over the voters.

After a bitter campaign battle in which his Democrat opponent cited his lack of experience by referring to him as "Silly Billy," he was elected by a margin of less than a thousand votes. Since that time, his popularity had skyrocketed; he never received less than 60 percent of the vote and had been unopposed for the past four congressional elections.

At age fifty-nine, he had achieved rank and stature in Washington and, not coincidentally, considerable wealth. He had homes in Pennsylvania and Washington, and his vacation home here in the Bay Pointe community of the Ibis Golf and Country Club was worth over $1.5 million.

"Say, Bill, how are they keeping you busy in Washington these days?" asked Jerry.

Bill continued to swing his driver, smoothly clipping the top of the grass with each stroke.

"I spend most of my time as chairman of the Joint Committee on Economic Development and Emerging Technologies."

Jerry laughed. "Sounds impressive. But, have to admit, I never heard of it."

Bill smiled. "Don't feel bad. A lot of voters never heard of it. We're a committee that's wrestling with a highly controversial subject: whether to turn former military bases into federally operated casinos. If our committee approves the current bill, legislation could be enacted by Congress to create dozens of new casino and resort areas. These new casinos would rival those already existing in Las Vegas, Atlantic City, and Biloxi, Mississippi."

"Ooh—could be a lot of money at stake with that legislation," said Jerry.

Bill smiled widely.

"There's always a lot of money at stake in Washington!" he said with a laugh.

"If it's alright to ask, where do you stand on the issue?"

"No problem. I'm on the record as being opposed. The last things we need are more casinos. I don't think the government should be involved in the gambling business. So far, our committee is pretty much divided on party lines. The Democrats are in favor of the bill; the Republicans are opposed. As committee chairman, I have a lot influence on how the Republican members cast their votes, and we've got the majority. We have a couple of weeks of hearings after the Thanksgiving break. Then, the committee will vote on whether the bill goes to the full House."

"But, won't these government casinos bring in a lot of tax revenue?" Jerry asked.

"You sound like a Democratic sympathizer! That's a two-stroke penalty!" Bill joked.

The wives heard his comeback and chimed in with laughter. He stretched back, took another practice swing, and then gave a serious reply.

"Take my word for it, Jerry. It's a complicated issue. With all the corruption and additional government employees, those casinos could well end up costing more money to the taxpayers than they generate revenues."

The group ahead of them finally cleared the first fairway. Bill and Jerry usually played a friendly game of golf with a five-dollar Nassau wager. At the end of the day, not a lot of money exchanged hands. Nevertheless, Prendergast loved money, and he loved to win.

Bill teed up his Callaway golf ball on an extra long tee and rested the head of his Taylor Made R-7 driver behind it. His swing was long and smooth. His head stayed down through impact. His ball soared high and far, out toward the fairway, faded over the sand traps on the right, and landed directly in the middle of the fairway.

"Holy Schmoley!" exclaimed Jerry, "You really hammered that one! Good thing I brought my wallet today."

It was another great shot from a man who always seemed to come out as the winner and he had plenty of money in the bank to prove it.

# Chapter 29

The wheels of Flight 2029 hit the runway smoothly at 11:15 AM at Reagan National Airport in Washington, D.C. Gallagher had slept lightly for most of the flight, still tired from a lack of sleep the previous night. But he had no complaints; the hours of lovemaking with Kate were so incredibly satisfying and meaningful for both of them that he could only see their relationship growing stronger. It seemed as though they had just begun to explore the joys of being together. He never wanted it to stop. When he finished resolving all of the issues in this case, he planned to ask her to marry him.

Gallagher had no illusions about this trip to Washington. He knew that most of Congress was off on an extended Thanksgiving holiday break.

*The rest of the country got a day off on Thanksgiving Day; the people we elect to represent us take a week and a half.*

Nevertheless, he hoped to nose around and come up with some information about Congressman Prendergast or even, with luck, manage to secure an appointment to talk to him. That, he knew, would be very tough; you just don't walk into a United States congressman's office, introduce yourself as a private investigator, and get invited to come in for coffee. His Irish charm had to be finely polished to accomplish that trick.

He took a cab to the Hotel Washington, one of the most convenient locations in the city. It was an older hotel—nothing fancy—but the rates were reasonable, and you could easily walk to the White House, the museums, or the Capitol Hill office buildings within a short time. One of the Hotel Washington's claims to fame was that a scene from the movie, "The Godfather," was staged there. The marquee of the Hotel actually appeared in the film. Another famous Washington landmark was located next door—the Willard Hotel, that housed one of Gallagher's favorite bars, the Willard Bar, which had been frequented by presidents and celebrities for more than a hundred-and-fifty years.

Gallagher checked in at the desk and rode up in the elevator with Stanley, the short-statured bellman who took his suitcase.

"Pretty quiet in D.C. this week, huh, Stanley?"

"Thanksgiving week. All the politicians gone home to eat turkey," Stanley said with his heavy Indonesian accent and laughing at his own remark.

Gallagher tipped Stanley and barely waited for him to leave before he started to make phone calls. He called the Library of Congress and the main office of the Federal Deposit Insurance Corporation to make sure he could access the information he needed. He obtained the location for Congressman Prendergast's office in the Rayburn House Office Building but decided not to call in advance. He planned it as his first stop, and just hoped, by some stroke of luck, that he might get to see him or one of his top aides.

He walked from the hotel to the Rayburn Building and entered through the entrance on South Capitol Street. The building was designed in a modified H plan with four stories above ground and two basements. One hundred sixty-five representatives had three-room suites in this building to serve as their Washington-based office. Gallagher did not travel to Washington with his handgun, and he had no problem passing through security. He listed his destination on the log as the office of Congressman William J. Prendergast, Room 2782.

On his walk through the corridors, he noted that Stanley, the bellman, had been correct—the place was nearly empty. Most of the employees had gotten an early jump on the Thanksgiving weekend. As he arrived in Room 2782, a very pretty young woman greeted him. She was in her early twenties and sat behind a plain desk that was bare except for a telephone and a computer monitor. She was idly surfing the Internet for something of interest.

The flag of Pennsylvania hung on one of the walls alongside the flag of the United States. A photograph was prominently featured just below the flags. It showed a man with glasses and graying hair, shaking hands and smiling with President George W. Bush. The man was about the same height as the president but had a much stockier frame. Gallagher assumed that this had to be Congressman William J. Prendergast.

The young woman looked up at Gallagher and flashed an instant smile, "Hi. Good afternoon, how can I help you?"

Gallagher returned her smile and added a wink, "Looks like Pennsylvania has the prettiest secretaries."

Her fair skin blushed, and she tried to hide an even wider smile, "Well, I'm actually not a secretary; I'm a congressional intern. I'm filling in on the phone because everyone else is away for the holiday. You can cut out all that sweet stuff any time now."

"Sorry. Didn't mean any offense—just having a little fun. You look like a person with a good sense of humor. What's your name?" he asked.

"My name is Laura," she smiled. "No offense taken. What can I do to help you?"

"Hi, Laura. My name is Gallagher. Any chance I can set up a meeting with Mr. Prendergast sometime?"

"Well, you probably know that the Congressman is very busy these days. What is the nature of your business? Are you from his district?"

"No, I'm actually from Massachusetts. I have a few questions about some banking issues and the FDIC," he said, trying to avoid telling her his real occupation. "I believe he can shed some light on an old problem involving a bank that went out of business during the Savings and Loan problems of the 1980s."

"Well, all of the Congressman's appointments are cleared with his chief of staff, Mr. Tane. I'll give your name and contact information to him, and someone will be in touch with you. Do you have a business card?"

Gallagher was afraid of that question, but decided not to try to fake it any longer. He reached into his jacket pocket and handed her one of his business cards. She looked at it for a few seconds. Her eyebrows rose as she absorbed everything on the card.

*A private investigator?*

"Okay, Mr. Gallagher, I'll make sure he gets this information."

"Thank you, Laura, have a great holiday."

He walked out of the office, feeling that the barriers to a meeting with Prendergast might be too difficult to overcome. People in such powerful positions have a staff to triage access. He couldn't think of a way to make Prendergast want to meet with him.

He spent the next few hours at the Library of Congress and the main FDIC office building on F Street. He searched through dozens of documents related to the S & L scandals of the 1980s in which a wave of over one thousand savings and loan institutions failed in the United States. Many economists believed that this banking crisis led to the great recession of the early 1990s. The crisis was also not without its share of scandals as a prominent figure, Charles Keating, was convicted in 1993 of fraud, racketeering, and conspiracy and eventually pled guilty to bankruptcy fraud. Keating's attempts to escape regulatory sanctions led to the Keating Five political scandal in which three U.S. senators found their political careers cut short as a result of their involvement.

*Looks like some members of Congress really got their hands dirty during all of this.*

As he skimmed through a list of FDIC Enforcement Decisions and Orders, he eventually came to Docket No. FDIC – 89 – 1029

B (9/21/89) in the matter of the West Castle Bank for Savings. In this decision, the bank was ordered to cease operations following hazardous lending and collection practices and for operating with excessive loan losses. A later document stated that the bank's loans went into receivership and were controlled by the FDIC until they were transferred to another loan-processing agency. However, since privacy laws prohibited revealing the list of loans transferred, Gallagher was unable to find specific reference to the loan made to the West Castle real-estate partnership in question.

"Come on—come on!" he mumbled. "There's got to be a way to find out what happened to that loan."

Gallagher stayed in the Library of Congress reading documents until a security guard informed him that it was closing time. He packed up his pile of photocopied papers and scribbled notes and walked down to Independence Avenue where he hailed a cab. He dropped all the newly acquired documents in his hotel room, except for a lengthy biography of Congressman William Prendergast.

*The best way to properly absorb and digest this is over a glass of scotch!*

He took the biographical information with him, walked over to the Willard Hotel and took a seat at the circular bar.

He ordered his usual drink—Johnny Walker Black on the rocks with a splash of club soda and a small glass of club soda on the side. He read through the details of Prendergast's biography.

*Interesting. After his fourth term in Congress, Prendergast became a member of the House Committee on Banking, which had considerable dealings with the board of directors of the FDIC. In fact, very interesting!*

Gallagher was also impressed by Prendergast's current status and recognized the power-broking potential of a position to which the casino industry was forced to pay homage.

*This guy has quietly set himself up for one of the biggest paydays in congressional history. His vote in either direction on this casino bill is worth millions to him.*

He sipped his drink and contemplated his trip back to Boston the next day. He wanted to interview Tony Cognetti and Dan Oblas, the other doctors who were partners in the real-estate group.

*Yes—pursue this Prendergast connection and then come up with a plan to force a meeting with the congressman.*

He knew that none of this would be easy, but he was convinced that the answer to the mystery of the murders was rooted in the partners' problems with the FDIC and their relationship with William J. Prendergast.

Of course, he couldn't wait to get home to see Kate again. He had been away from her for less than twenty-four hours, but he missed her already. His cell phone rang. He looked at the screen, "Call from Randi Stockdale."

"Hello, Randi. Got something good for me?"

She spoke quickly. Her voice sounded excited.

"Gallagher, I thought you would want to know. I got a call from a high-school friend who's a cop in West Castle. They're holding a press conference tomorrow morning to announce that Mickey Ryan has been arrested for the murders of Jonathan and Dick. Said they've got him cold. They came up with the murder weapon. It passed all the ballistics tests. The gun is registered in Mickey's name."

"What time is the press conference?"

"Ten o'clock. You might want to be there."

Gallagher put down his drink, stunned by the news of Randi's call.

*Mickey Ryan? Arrested for the murders?*

Had all his theories about this case just exploded into dust?

*Mickey Ryan?*

*How could it be?*

# Chapter 30

During the flight back to Boston, Gallagher stared out at the clouds from his window seat.

*How could Mickey Ryan have fooled me so easily?*

Sure, Mickey was a big, strong man with a bad temper—he had personally witnessed that side of Mickey in action. However, Mickey's rationale for not being involved in the murders actually made sense. Despite having had only one experience with him, Gallagher viewed Mickey as a clever survivor and a guy who knew just how far to go to skirt around the law and make an easy dollar.

*What could Mickey earn from killing the three partners? Nothing—unless someone had paid him a boatload of money to bump them off. Could I have missed this possibility? Is that how Mickey recovered the money he lost on that real-estate deal? Or, is someone setting him up?*

It seemed to Gallagher that the old adage, popularized in stories about the Watergate scandal of the 1970s, was clearly apropos in this case: follow the money. Everything about these murders pointed to money. When he figured out who had the most to gain financially from the death of the three partners, he would know who committed the crimes.

US Air Flight 2112 touched down at Boston's Logan International Airport at 9:20 AM, twelve minutes behind schedule. By the time the plane taxied to the terminal and the passengers began deplaning, it was 9:35 AM. He still thought he could get to the press conference on time, but it would be close.

Gallagher had no luggage, just a carry-on bag. He raced from the gate toward the parking garage in Terminal B. Within a few minutes, he was on his way toward Route 93 North. Luckily, he was traveling against the traffic and made good time in the short ride to West Castle. He counted on the fact that police press conferences never started on time. Always some last minute hang-up. He was right. When he walked into the West Castle Town Hall at 10:15, newsman and photographers were still milling around. He hadn't missed anything. He stepped to the back of the room and took a seat in the last row. He tried to be inconspicuous.

Detective Jack Hoskins stood at the front of the room. He leaned over a table and appeared to look over some papers with a uniformed police officer. His right hand was inserted into his right rear pocket, causing his brown suit coat to be pushed back, revealing his protruding gut—and, of course, his striped suspenders. After a few minutes, the uniformed officer nodded to Hoskins several times, turned, and stood at the podium in front of the microphone.

"Good Morning, ladies and gentlemen, my name is Tom Tackage, Chief of the West Castle Police Department. This morning, after six weeks of intensive investigation, we are pleased to announce an arrest in the murders that took place at the Parker Hill Medical Building last month. A .357 Magnum revolver was discovered in the glove compartment of a stolen car that was abandoned in Dorchester. The muzzle of this gun had been machined so it could accept a silencer. This gun also underwent extensive ballistics tests that confirmed that it was the same gun used in the murders in question. Last night, with the cooperation of the Everett Police Department, we took into custody Mr. Mickey Ryan, to whom the gun was registered, and charged him with the murders of Drs. Jonathan Becker and Richard Evans. Mr. Ryan is known to have had a major financial dispute with the doctors and their partners that dates back to a real-estate transaction in the 1980s. Mr. Ryan is being held without bail and will be arraigned in the Middlesex County Courthouse Monday at 11:00 AM."

During the police chief's prepared statement, Jack Hoskins stood impassively behind him, looking out to the sea of reporters and cameramen in the audience. After a short while, his eyes stopped moving as he caught a glimpse of Gallagher sitting in the back of the room.

Their eyes met in a hard stare.

Hoskins' bland facial expression slowly changed to a smug smile, looking like Felix the cat just after having swallowed the family parakeet. Gallagher eventually broke the stare-down and looked back at the chief. He hated losing at anything, but when the opponent rubbed it in your face, it was twice as bad.

The police chief finished his prepared remarks and opened the forum to the audience of news media.

The first reporter asked the obvious question, "How do the police think the murder weapon ended up in a stolen car?"

"The murder weapon was stolen from Mickey Ryan's office at his used car business," said Chief Tackage. "A car from his lot was stolen at the same time. The thieves placed the murder weapon in the glove compartment. Then, for reasons unknown, they abandoned the car in Dorchester. They may have been scared off by a police cruiser in the area, or maybe they were young kids—afraid to be caught with a gun."

The chief continued by saying, "Our sources also tell us that Mr. Ryan was inquiring on his own about a break-in to his office and was looking for the person or persons responsible. We believe that he never reported the theft because he knew that the murder weapon had been stolen."

A news reporter from a local television station asked if there was any connection with the murder of Phil Lombardo in Vermont.

"That is a continuing part of this investigation," the chief responded, "and we are working with the authorities in Vermont to determine if there is a link between that homicide and the two that occurred here in West Castle."

A few more questions were asked pertaining to the upcoming arraignment, but the press conference was essentially over. Everyone got up from their seats and made their way out of the room.

Gallagher walked to the door and was met by Jack Hoskins who smirked again and asked, "Still looking for your retirement home in West Castle?"

Gallagher tried to stay cool, but he was boiling inside.

"Could be. Seems like it's a safer place to live now that you've arrested the guy who's been shooting up the town."

Hoskins didn't appreciate his attempt at humor.

"Look, Gallagher, I told you once before that we didn't need your help solving this crime. Why don't you go back to Boston and try to find some runaway kid? Leave the police work to us."

Gallagher paused for a few seconds and then calmly looked at Hoskins.

"Let me ask you something, Detective. Do you really think you've got the right guy?"

Hoskins chortled.

"Have you been paying attention? This case is a slam dunk! We have the murder weapon, and it's registered in this guy's name. He had threatened the victims in the past and had a motive to get even with them. What else do you need, hotshot?"

"Something that doesn't look like a frame-up," Gallagher fired back.

The direct response took the smile off Hoskins' face and left him pondering the thought. Gallagher turned, walked through the doorway and down the stairs to the main doors of the Town Hall.

As Gallagher walked outside, a few television news trucks were still parked on the street. A large group of reporters remained in front of the building, busily preparing their stories for the evening news broadcasts and the morning newspapers. Gallagher stopped for a minute and surveyed the scene.

A reporter approached him and said,"Excuse me. I saw you talking to Detective Hoskins inside. Do you have any comments on the arrest of Mickey Ryan?"

"No. No comments," replied Gallagher as he brushed by the reporter and walked toward his car.

# Chapter 31

When it came to dealing with stress, depression, or a personal crisis, Daniel Cormac Gallagher Jr. subscribed to the "Hot-Fudge Sundae Theory" of life. This was really quite simple: when faced with a serious setback, a perplexing problem, or something that made you want to jump and scream, go out and order a hot-fudge sundae. Nothing else could serve better as a tranquilizer to help you relax and sort out your problems.

After the Red Sox playoff loss to the Yankees on October 16, 2003, Gallagher remembered walking the street in disbelief and shock. The Red Sox manager, Grady Little, had left Pedro Martinez in the game too long and effectively blew the pennant. Gallagher had trouble putting it all in perspective. He found a small coffee shop that was still open and ordered a hot fudge sundae. He felt instantly better.

In fact, Gallagher was convinced that hot-fudge sundaes should be served in the United Nations Security Council; certainly none of the delegates would ever consider voting in favor of a policy involving warfare while they were eating something so soothing and delicious.

Gallagher drove to a local ice cream shop, sat at a small table, and placed his order. The arrest of Mickey Ryan, the press conference in West Castle, and the condescending arrogance of Jack Hoskins had put him into a genuine funk. He thought he might need several doses of his favorite dessert to get himself through.

He felt certain that Mickey had been set up as the fall guy for the murders.

*Who could have done it? How were they able to get Mickey's gun before the murders and then make sure it ended up in the hands of the police? So far I haven't been able to prove anything in this case!*

The secret meetings, Randi Stockdale's evasiveness, and Barry Nickerson's fearful denial of Congressman William J. Prendergast—had all of these factors been rendered meaningless?

He had to force the issue to create a break. He needed another meeting with Mickey Ryan. He doubted that Mickey would welcome him as a jailhouse visitor—he probably felt that Gallagher was involved in framing him. Perhaps he could speak to Mickey's lawyer after the arraignment next week and try to impress upon him that he had some information that could potentially help Mickey's case.

He sifted through all the possibilities in his mind. The picture was bleak. His thoughts were interrupted by the ring of his cell phone— Suzanne Becker. She sounded ecstatic.

"Gallagher? I was so relieved to see the news today. It's a wonderful Thanksgiving present to know that the police have arrested that man."

Gallagher listened to see if she had anything further to add, then paused before speaking. He hated to put a damper on her obvious enthusiasm, but couldn't find an easier way to express his feelings.

"Mrs. Becker, I think the police have the wrong man."

He heard the gasp on the other end of the phone.

"Wrong man? How can that be? The chief of police said they have the gun. It matched the ballistics tests."

"I'm sure they have the correct murder weapon, but I don't think they have the man who pulled the trigger. I believe the man they arrested has been set up, probably to divert attention from what's really going on. This whole thing runs deep—more than anyone imagines."

Suzanne Becker's voice became emotional, almost frantic, as a result of this new interpretation of the day's events.

"But the police said he had a motive. He wanted to get even with Jonathan and his partners," she continued.

Gallagher stopped her in mid-sentence.

"Mrs. Becker, I know you would like to see this come to an end and be wrapped up into one neat little package, without any further problems for you or your family. But I have to be honest with you. This isn't over. The answer to your husband's murder is in Washington. I'd like to continue checking some sources until I am satisfied that we've gotten the whole story. Is that all right with you?"

"Oh, god—I don't know."

She hesitated while she organized her thoughts.

"I don't know if it does any good to keep digging up the past when it seems that everything is already settled."

There was pain in her voice. He knew she had reached the breaking point.

"I don't know what to say," she said. "I'm so confused now—give me a few days to think about this."

With those words, she clicked off the phone.

Gallagher sat at the small table in the restaurant, staring at the melted remains of his hot fudge sundae, somehow feeling a strange loss of appetite.

If he wanted to continue with the investigation of these murders, it looked like he was completely on his own.

# Chapter 32

"Kathryn Daisy McSurdy!" Aunt Heather exclaimed as she opened the door at Kate's parent's home in Brewster, Massachusetts.

Then she shrieked, "We just don't see you often enough!"

She reached out and hugged Kate.

"And who do we have here?" she asked, looking at Gallagher with a mischievous twinkle in her eye.

"This is Daniel Gallagher. Don't worry, Aunt Heather, just call him Gallagher, and he'll be happy," said Kate as she nudged Gallagher in the ribs.

Kate's parents' home was a beautiful contemporary cottage-style house overlooking Cape Cod Bay. In the distance, approximately seventeen miles across the Bay, the Provincetown monument could be seen clearly—creating a serene, but stunning view from the large window of the family room. Her parents, Bob and Barbara McSurdy, both in their late sixties, were retired and divided their time between winters and springs in Florida and summers and fall at Cape Cod. This was Gallagher's first invitation for a Thanksgiving dinner celebration at their home in Brewster. The topics of conversation were the delicious food prepared by Kate's mother and the upcoming drive south to their winter home at Valencia Shores in Lake Worth, Florida.

This was also the first time that Gallagher had heard Kate's full name—Kathryn Daisy McSurdy, a name so Irish that it should always be written in green ink.

*Daisy—I like that. I wonder why she never told me her middle name.*

Kate's parents were extremely fond of Gallagher. The feeling was mutual—both parties hoping that the relationship between Kate and Gallagher would become formalized in the very near future. Kate's father, in particular, appreciated Gallagher's gentle approach to his daughter, which was a far cry from her previous liaison that had been wrought with intimidation and emotional stress. With Gallagher, he felt that his daughter was safe and secure and that he was a man who could be trusted. He also loved to ask about Gallagher's latest cases but respected the fact that some matters were shielded by a code of privacy, self-imposed by the private investigator. Nevertheless, as they sat alone in the family room after dinner, Bob couldn't resist asking him what he'd been up to lately.

"How's your work going these days? Kate says you've had to do some traveling."

"Yes, I had to fly down to Washington, D.C."

"Another missing person?"

"No, it's actually a murder case. Unfortunately, I really can't say too much about it at this time."

Gallagher hated to be so vague with someone who was nearly a family member, so he tried to soften his response by adding, "I haven't even discussed it with Kate."

"No problem at all. I just find it fascinating to hear how you are able to solve some of these mysteries."

"Yeah, sometimes I even surprise myself," replied Gallagher, thinking that Kate's father had no idea about the turmoil that the West Castle case had been causing him.

He had found his mind drifting away in the middle of dinner and even during casual conversations to thoughts of Dr. Jonathan Becker, Randi Stockdale, Mickey Ryan, Jack Hoskins, and Congressman William J. Prendergast. He had come to know these names so well in just two weeks.

*Were they interrelated? Or was his cynical mind overworking and looking for connections that just didn't exist?*

He was biding his time, waiting until Mickey Ryan's arraignment on Monday when, hopefully, some new information would surface to help him determine where his next move should be.

*What about Suzanne Becker? Has she suddenly ended my employment? Is it worth pursuing this case by myself? To show Hoskins that I really know how to investigate a murder?*

These thoughts kept dancing through his mind as he sat by the fire in the family room making a futile attempt to seem interested in Bob's talk about the New England Patriots and their chances for another Super Bowl title.

After dinner, Gallagher and Kate drove from Brewster to Plymouth to have dessert with his parents at their home at Pine Hills.

During the ride, he looked over at her and playfully asked, "Daisy? Where did that come from?"

Kate blushed and laughed.

"It was my grandmother's name. My parents wanted to preserve her memory by naming me after her. I had so much fun visiting her in Mount Carmel, Pennsylvania, when I was a little girl. She was a great lady. You would have liked her."

Then, after a short pause she asked, "How come you brought it up? Don't you like my middle name, Mr. Daniel Cormac Gallagher Jr.?" emphasizing the "Cormac" in a teasing way.

Gallagher laughed and said, "Yes, in fact I do like it; it's one of those special names that you don't hear often enough these days. And, as far as your grandmother is concerned, I wish I could tell her what a wonderful granddaughter she has. I'm sure that would make the great lady very happy."

Kate smiled but said nothing. It was one of those moments, shared by two people who truly cared about each other, where no other words were necessary. Just before seven o'clock they arrived at Pine Hills—one of the newer developments a short distance from

Cape Cod with small, winding roads carved out of the pine hill bluffs near the Atlantic Ocean. The houses were nestled on the hillsides around two championship golf courses. The graying clapboards were weathering unevenly indicating the newness of the construction. Gallagher's parents had moved there two years ago after his father retired from his job as a history teacher at the Rivers School in Weston, Massachusetts. This was their dream retirement home. During the summer, his mother spent hours in the garden and along the blue stone walkway tending to her lush flowering plants.

Although the exterior of the house was traditional and somewhat conservative, the interior had a definite contemporary flair with light-colored, polished hardwood floors set against a beautiful blend of yellow-and-white painted walls. The living room and dining room were dominated by massive windows with sweeping views of the golf course and were decorated with a fascinating collection of Asian artifacts. An eighteenth-century Chinese religious altar served as the liquor cabinet that was opened by Gallagher's father almost as soon as they walked in the door.

"Sit down, son, and have a drink. And tell me what you've been doing for the past few weeks."

Kate and Gallagher's mother hugged and walked into the kitchen where two pies—a chocolate cream and an apple crumb—sat on the counter waiting to be sliced. Gallagher and his father sat down at the dining room table, fulfilling the time-honored Thanksgiving tradition of men being served by women on this holiday of abundant food.

"Thanks, Dad, but I'll just have one. We still have to drive back to Boston tonight."

"You're absolutely right; no sense getting a DUI in holiday traffic."

His father scooped some ice out of the ice bucket and poured a modest amount of Jameson Irish whiskey over the ice cubes into a glass.

He handed it to Gallagher and then continued, "How's everything going? We haven't heard much from you lately; you must really be wrapped up in your work."

His father's words sparked an immediate flash of embarrassment. The West Castle case had consumed his thoughts so completely that he had been neglecting many of his basic family obligations. The sad truth was that he hadn't even noticed.

"Yes, I'm sorry I haven't called for a while; I guess there's just been a lot on my mind. I've been investigating the business dealings of three doctors who were murdered last month. The police have arrested the guy who owned the murder weapon, but somehow the pieces don't fit together. There is something about the whole case that doesn't make sense. I haven't figured it out yet. I wonder if I ever will."

His father gave him a knowing look.

"Sounds like this case has you a bit frustrated."

"Frustrated is putting it mildly."

As his father slowly stirred his teaspoon around his cup of coffee, he looked across the table at Gallagher, smiled, and said, "You know—if there is one thing I learned in all the years I studied and taught world history, it's that most of the wars were less about ideology and more about money. So, if you're stymied in this case, try to find the person who had the most to gain financially, and then maybe you'll find the murderer."

The words were spoken so calmly and simply, but they resonated in Gallagher's head like the sound of a ten-piece band, echoing the conclusion that he, himself, had reached days ago—this case had to be all about money.

When this weekend was over, it would be time to follow the money trail to see where it led.

# Chapter 33

For the rest of the Thanksgiving weekend Gallagher was edgy. He felt like he was jumping out of his skin. He desperately wanted to move on with this investigation, but none of the principals in the case were available. Washington, D.C., was virtually closed—like a store that had gone out of business. Mickey Ryan was locked up in the Middlesex County jail, and except for his lawyer, no visitors allowed until his arraignment on Monday morning.

Gallagher was powerless to do anything but sit and wait. Kate sensed his uneasiness and tried to come up with suggestions to keep him busy.

"I've got to pick up an outfit I ordered from a dress shop in Revere. Would you like to come along?"

Gallagher hesitated.

*Clothes shopping? I don't think so.*

Then, considering that his alternative was sitting around, ruminating about the frustrations of the West Castle murder case, he acquiesced and said, "Sure, I'll go with you. How long will it take?"

"Just about an hour. Then I'll take you for lunch to a great little Italian spot nearby. It'll be my treat, Mr. Private Eye, and maybe it will get you out of your state of depression."

Gallagher smiled. He couldn't hide his inner feelings from her. He knew she was right. There was nothing he could do until Monday. Why not accept it and take the opportunity to spend more time with Kate?

They drove toward Revere Beach from Boston. Their destination was Selma's Dress Shoppe, located on Revere Beach Boulevard in the remodeled basement of a red-brick house. The entrance to the shop was found at the bottom of a steep driveway. Lauralee, the shop's owner, immediately greeted them. She hugged Kate as if she were a relative, not just a customer.

"It's great to see you again. You look wonderful. Is this the man you've been telling me about?"

"Yes, this is Gallagher. He's my special guy. Thought I'd drag him along today; he's never been to a woman's dress shop before."

Kate locked her arm with Gallagher's and playfully pulled him into the waiting area, which was lined by a row of chairs on the left and a rack of clothes with sale items on the right. The showroom itself was located one step up and through a door in the right-hand corner of the waiting room. It was filled with racks of perfectly coordinated dresses and pants suits, shelves with sweaters, and a display case of costume jewelry. A floor-to-ceiling mirror took up one entire wall. Lauralee motioned to a chair across from the mirror. Gallagher took that as his cue to sit down and enjoy the upcoming show.

For Gallagher, this shop was unique in that it only catered to one customer at a time. Outside of the showroom, there were no fitting rooms. He quickly figured out why no other customers were allowed in the showroom while someone was trying on clothing, as Kate stood in the center of the room and immediately began undressing. Soon she was wearing nothing but her panties and bra, displaying her beautiful figure. He couldn't help but stare.

*How did I get so lucky to have a woman who looks like this?*

Lauralee and her assistant brought out one outfit after another, helped Kate try them on and then looked to Gallagher for his approval. This whole process took most of an hour, until Kate had finally made three new selections to add to the outfit she had already ordered.

They drove from the dress shop in Revere toward Winthrop.

They parked on a side street just around the corner from Rossetti's Restaurant, a small Italian bistro operated by two brothers whose menu consisted of recipes they had learned from their mother. Twelve thirty— but the restaurant was almost empty. Evidently, most people had stayed home to finish their leftovers from Thanksgiving dinner. Kate and Gallagher sat quietly at a table near the window where they could look out and see the waves crashing against a stone retaining wall in the distance. Despite the sound of the gusty wind and the sight of the white-capped surf, there was a certain peacefulness and solitude to the scene.

After they placed their order, Kate lifted her glass of Pinot Grigio and tenderly took Gallagher's hand in hers.

"I'd like to make a toast to you, my private investigator—the man I love. I know how much you are bothered by anything that doesn't fit into its proper place in life. Something that's not right causes you pain. And right now, I know this case in West Castle is causing you a lot of pain. But I believe in you and know you'll eventually put all the pieces in order. No one else may be able to figure it out, but I know you will."

Then, in a halting, emotional voice, she added, "I just have this fear that there is more danger in this case than you realize. Someone may try to hurt you to keep you silent. Promise me that you'll be careful. I couldn't bear to lose you."

He squeezed her hand gently and then lifted it to his lips and kissed it.

"Don't worry, I'm always careful. Besides, I couldn't bear to be without you, knowing that some other guy was holding your hand."

They both smiled and made a toast to being together forever.

But in his heart, Gallagher knew that Kate was right—the person he was trying to find had already killed three people and wouldn't hesitate to kill again.

# Chapter 34

The Middlesex County Courthouse, located on Thorndike Street in Cambridge, had a unique distinction—the Middlesex County Jail occupied the uppermost floor of the ten-story building. Once the criminals were convicted, they didn't have to travel very far to begin serving their time.

Gallagher arrived several minutes before the scheduled eleven o'clock arraignment and casually sat in an aisle seat in the middle row of the courtroom. He wanted to be sure to hear all the details of the indictment against Mickey Ryan, as well as any response from either Mickey or his defense attorney.

The room filled up with reporters and news people. Only one camera crew was allowed. They positioned themselves in the left corner at the front of the room in order to have a good angle to film the proceedings. Several members of the Middlesex District Attorney's office sat at a table at the front of the room facing the judge's bench. They conversed with Tom Tackage, the West Castle chief of police. Right next to the Chief sat Detective Jack Hoskins.

*Guess he's here to gloat some more. Maybe I'll be lucky and he won't notice me.*

Gallagher had no time to dwell on his dislike for Hoskins. In an emotional twist, an attractive woman in a flattering, charcoal-gray business suit was seated with the prosecution team. She was his ex-wife, Lesley, now an assistant district attorney for Middlesex County. The sight of her made Gallagher feel uneasily warm. He could feel beads of sweat beginning to form and run down the inside of his shirt.

Promptly at eleven o'clock a door opened on the right side of the courtroom. Mickey Ryan walked in. He wore an orange, county-issued scrub suit, handcuffs, and leg irons and was escorted by two uniformed court officers. They led him to a table where an elderly, distinguished-looking, white-haired gentleman sat waiting. He had a neatly trimmed mustache, gold-framed glasses and wore a dark blue, three-piece suit—undoubtedly Mickey's lawyer. The man stood up, greeted Mickey, and patted him gently on the back in a reassuring manner. Almost a comical scene since Mickey, with his massive frame, towered over his lawyer, whose head barely reached the top of his client's shoulder. They spoke to each other in quiet tones; Gallagher could not hear any of their comments.

After a few minutes, Mickey turned awkwardly, clearly bothered by the handcuffs around his wrists, and looked around the courtroom, curious to see who had come to witness his appearance before the judge. His eyes scanned the room, glanced at Gallagher, and looked away. Then his eyes darted back, as if his memory had suddenly been jogged by a shocking revelation. He eyes narrowed as he stared at Gallagher, obviously remembering their recent encounter in his used-car lot.

He nodded his head with a scowl as if to say, "You bastard. I should have known you were part of this."

Gallagher looked back at Mickey with a blank expression on his face, understanding how his role in the whole scenario could have easily been mistaken and knowing he had no way to convey that message at this time. He just hoped he would have the opportunity to speak with him sometime after the legal proceedings.

The booming voice of a court officer interrupted Mickey's stare.

"All rise for the Honorable James Walsh," he bellowed.

The judge walked to his chair, sat down, and motioned to everyone in the court to do the same.

He looked over to the prosecutor's table and asked, "Does the district attorney's office have a motion?"

The Middlesex County district attorney stood up and responded, "Yes, Your Honor. The people would like to seek charges for murder in the first degree against Mr. Mickey Ryan of Everett, Massachusetts, for the deaths of Dr. Jonathan Becker and Dr. Richard Evans, both of Middlesex County."

"Please recite the evidence for the charges," advised the judge.

"The police have recovered a Smith and Wesson .357 Magnum revolver that was tested and proven to be the weapon used in both murders. This gun is registered to Mr. Ryan. In addition, Mr. Ryan was known to both victims and their business associates and had threatened them with bodily harm in regard to an old dispute over a real-estate transaction. The people also have a witness who saw a person fitting Mr. Ryan's description leaving the scene of the crime on the morning of Dr. Evans' murder."

*A witness?* thought Gallagher.

There had never been a suggestion of a witness following either of the murders. Certainly, the case against Mickey looked more compelling than ever.

*Has the man who slipped through the clutches of the law for so many years finally run out of luck? Looks like he's facing a growing collection of hard evidence. How's he going to escape this time?*

The judge listened to the rest of the district attorney's charges and the request for holding the defendant without bail.

He then turned to Mickey's table and asked, "Will the defendant please rise?"

Mickey and his lawyer stood up and faced the judge.

"Mr. Ryan, how do you plead to the charges of first degree murder against you?"

Mickey stood rigidly at attention.

He hardly waited for the judge to finish his question before firmly exclaiming, "Not guilty."

The judge then asked, "Will counsel for the defendant respond to the request for holding without bail?"

"Yes, your honor, I am David Gorkin, attorney for Mr. Ryan. We request that the defendant be released on bail. We look forward to our day in court where we can prove that he is innocent of these charges. He will testify to the fact that the murder weapon was stolen from his home prior to the murders and was not in his possession when the murders were committed. Furthermore, he has a witness who will testify that he was not in the area on the days the victims were murdered. Mr. Ryan is an upstanding member of the local business community, has no previous arrests for crimes of this nature, and is not a risk for flight. Therefore, we feel that the district attorney's request for no bail is not warranted."

The judge looked over to the district attorney's table for their response.

Lesley, one of the younger members of the prosecution team stood up and replied, "Your Honor, we disagree completely. Mr. Ryan's story about the stolen weapon is a concocted fabrication designed to obscure the facts in this case. We also have witnesses who claim that Mr. Ryan has connections with the underworld and has been conducting a gambling operation from his business location for years. We consider him to be a substantial flight risk and strongly recommend that bail be denied."

The judge glanced over some papers in front of him for a few seconds and then spoke in a terse, direct manner, "The request from the district attorney is approved. The defendant is to be held without bail and is remanded to the Middlesex County Jail until trial. Will counsel please approach the bench?"

Mickey's lawyer and the staff from the district attorney's office gathered in front of the judge for a few minutes, trying to agree on a schedule for a trial date in the spring. As soon as the meeting concluded, the lawyers returned to their seats. The judge stood up and left the courtroom.

Mickey, still in handcuffs and shuffling his feet due to his leg irons, was escorted out of the room through the side door by two court officers, while his attorney sat at his table putting a small pile of papers into his briefcase. Since press conferences were not allowed inside the courtroom, the herd of reporters hurried out through the rear door, hoping to get a good spot on the outside stairs where they could question Mr. Gorkin about his client's defense. Gallagher walked slowly behind them—in no hurry and willing to wait until everyone had left so that he could speak to Gorkin alone.

As he walked along the corridor, he suddenly heard a familiar voice calling his name.

"Gallagher?" the voice called a second time as he turned to look back toward the source.

Lesley had just spotted him in the crowd. She moved quickly down the hallway, in what could only be described as a near sprint, and caught up to him.

They stared at each other for a few seconds, smiled, then gradually embraced—two people still drawn to each other by an undeniable, sexual chemistry, but both knowing that the bond had too many flaws to endure. Their hug continued, oblivious to the crowd walking past them. She eventually leaned back and looked up at him, slowly lifting her hand to gently place it on his cheek.

"You know—you're still as handsome as ever," she said softly.

The closeness of her body reminded him of the passion they once shared. His reply was instinctive.

"And you feel as good as ever."

There had never been any real animosity between them. Seven years ago, they knew their relationship was over. They ended it before any further hurt was realized. Then, they moved on with their lives.

"You looked pretty good up there today, Counselor. I liked the way you handled that judge to keep the defendant in the big house," teased Gallagher.

Lesley smiled, "Just trying to protect the public, you sexy sleuth.

But tell me, what brings you to this type of arraignment? Besides shooting two doctors, was this guy running around on his wife, too?"

She smiled wider.

"No, actually, I'm doing a little business investigation. Just came here out of curiosity," he said, not wanting to give her any specifics.

"I'm not buying that and you know it! I won't hit you with a cross examination this time. One of these days you'll confess, and I'll get the real story."

"If you're as tough on me as you were in that court, I'll have no chance."

She laughed. Then her face took on a more serious look.

"Are you okay?" she asked.

"Yes."

"Is there someone in your life?"

"Yes."

"Is she special?"

"Very."

"I'm glad. You deserve someone special."

"And you?"

She smiled and shook her head side to side.

"Everything is fine—just crazy busy. I've got to cut back on my schedule. We're thinking it's time to start a family."

She blushed and looked away for a second.

"That would be great, Lesley. I'm happy for you."

They spoke for a few more minutes. Their brief encounter ended when a call from the lobby informed her that her ride back to the DA's office was about to leave. She scampered down the stairs, waving as she went, and disappeared from sight.

Gallagher barely had time to rearrange his emotions when he pushed into the midst of a huge crowd standing on the staircase of the courthouse. Newspaper reporters and TV news people shoved and pushed themselves toward Mickey's lawyer trying to get the first quote or sound bite for their story. Mr. Gorkin, however, remained completely composed and spoke calmly, in a matter-of-fact tone despite all the microphones that were pressed into his face, leaving him little room to move. Although a man in his mid-seventies, he seemed to be at the top of his game. He was a veteran of the courtroom, obviously comfortable with the media, and knew how to handle the pressures of being a criminal defense attorney. He explained that he was confident that his client would be cleared of all charges.

A newspaper reporter asked, "Were you surprised to hear that the DA's office has a witness who places someone fitting the description of your client at the scene of the second murder?"

"Yes. Today was the first time we heard any mention of a witness. But," he said without any reservations, "I expect that it is a simple case of mistaken identity, and that a well-meaning person has gotten confused."

Another reporter asked, "What about your witnesses?"

"We have a witness who will testify that Mr. Ryan was at Foxwoods Casino on the morning of Dr. Becker's murder and was nowhere near the scene of the crime."

The questions continued in rapid fire succession, but Mr. Gorkin handled every one of them with such a confident aplomb that a casual onlooker could think that Mickey might find a way out of this mess after all. In a few minutes, the crowd of media began to disperse, all heading to make their final reports for the next edition or telecast. Mr. Gorkin, walking with a slight bounce in his gait, proceeded down the steps toward the street.

Gallagher walked alongside of him and said, "You handled those guys like a pro. Looks like you've been down this road more than once in your career."

"Yes, a few times, I suppose. But it's not the media I have to win over. There'll be a jury to convince, and that's where the real test comes."

Gallagher laughed in agreement.

"You're right about that. My name's Gallagher; I'm a private investigator hired by the wife of one of the victims. I think I have some information that can be helpful to you and your client. Can we get together to talk?"

Gorkin paused for a few seconds and then turned to face Gallagher.

"Doesn't that seem to be a bit of a conflict of interest? My client is accused of murdering the husband of your client. Isn't that so?" Gorkin asked pointedly.

"Yes, I guess that is technically correct. Mrs. Becker actually retained me to look into the business dealings of her husband's partnership before his murder. But along the way, I've come up with a few things that may help your case. I think Mickey is being framed, and I don't think Mrs. Becker will be happy if the wrong person is convicted for her husband's murder."

"I suppose you are right, Mr. Gallagher," Gorkin answered in his low, raspy voice. "When would you like to meet with me?"

"Well, I would like to meet with you and Mickey at the same time—if that's alright with you?"

"I can certainly arrange that. Let me have one of your cards. After I speak to Mickey, I'll give you a call."

Gallagher took a business card out of his wallet and handed it to Mr. Gorkin.

"If I'm not in the office, you can reach me on my cell any time," he added.

"No problem, Mr. Gallagher, I expect that you'll be hearing from me very soon."

Gorkin tucked the card into his suit pocket, turned, and jauntily walked down the street. He seemed to have a bounce to his step, walking more toward his toes than on the heels of his feet.

Gallagher watched him as he strode away, admiring his unfazed approach to the entire situation and feeling that, in this wise old man, Mickey Ryan may have found a trump card that would give him another winning hand.

# Chapter 35

The sound from the nineteen-inch television set blared loudly across the small living room of the third-floor, one-bedroom apartment in West Somerville. Old newspapers were scattered around the floor and on both ends of the faded brown couch. An open bag of Cape Cod potato chips had been spilled on the wooden coffee table next to several empty bottles of Sam Adams beer. An irregular stack of dirty dishes filled the kitchen sink. The stench from the garbage can in the corner of the kitchen was a sign that too many days had passed since someone felt the need to empty it.

None of these petty distractions concerned Jimmy Nolan. His attention was completely focused on the television screen as the local evening news on Channel 7 shifted to an on-the-scene reporter who recounted the story of Mickey Ryan's arraignment.

As the video of Mickey Ryan rolled on, showing him in handcuffs, standing in his orange jumpsuit before the judge, the reporter's voice in the background summarized the proceedings and the charges levied against him.

The screen then switched to a young woman reporter, standing on the street in front of the courthouse: "Mickey Ryan is being held without bail at the Middlesex County Jail until his trial next spring. This apparently brings to an end the nightmarish fear of the residents of West Castle who had been afraid that a serial killer was living in their midst, about to strike at any time."

The raunchy, unshaven Jimmy stared at the screen, hoping the reporter would provide more details about the story. He impatiently grabbed the remote control from the table near his chair and tried to find the same story on another local channel. He was disappointed that none of the reports had anything else to add; everyone seemed to have the same spin on the West Castle murders—evidence found, killer arrested, case closed.

Jimmy Nolan walked to his refrigerator and took out another bottle of Sam Adams. He popped off the cap, took a long drink, and then walked over to the couch where he threw himself back into the cushions and stretched his legs up onto the coffee table, knocking over one of the empties in the process.

"So the case is closed?" he said as if someone was sitting there listening to his commentary on the news.

He leaned further back on the couch and looked up at the ceiling aimlessly. This beaten man, living in squalor, with nowhere to go and nothing in life that gave him pleasure, began slowly muttering to himself, "Three down, three to go—three down, three to go," as he purposefully sipped on his bottle of beer. "Everyone thinks this case is closed, but they're in for a real surprise."

# Chapter 36

Tuesday morning—still half-asleep—Gallagher walked in to his office at his usual late arrival time of eleven o'clock. Diane had left a few items for him to review, including a schedule for the hours of the Library of Congress and information about the documents available through its online website. Hours of research would be required to learn about Congressman Prendergast and his role on the banking committee in the 1980s, and Gallagher had to get on with it.

There had been no calls from Suzanne Becker. Gallagher couldn't help but wonder if his brief term of employment had ended. He decided to have Diane call her regarding the invoices that would soon be mailed and to determine where she stood on continuing the investigation.

He had hardly finished that thought when Diane's voice over the intercom interrupted with a message, "Dan, there is a phone call from Mr. Gorkin."

Gallagher immediately recognized the old man's raspy tones.

"Mr. Gallagher? This is David Gorkin. I spoke to my client, Mickey, this morning and, yes, he certainly does remember you. I assured him that you were not an informant for the district attorney's office," he said chuckling, enjoying his own attempt at humor. "He has agreed to meet with you. Are you available this afternoon around one-thirty?"

"Sure. Where should I meet you?"

"Right in front of the courthouse will be fine. You won't be able to get into the visiting area of the jail without me. See you there."

"Okay. I'll be there at one thirty."

Gallagher hung up. He reconsidered his plan to have Diane call Mrs. Becker. Better to meet with Mickey first to see for himself if there was any need to continue. Gallagher had information that could be meaningful to Mickey's defense. More importantly, he had a theory that, if proven correct, could bring about his release from jail and the elimination of all charges against him.

Maybe now, in the dire situation in which he found himself, Mickey would recognize that Gallagher was not the enemy.

# Chapter 37

Gallagher arrived at the courthouse a few minutes early. Not to Gallagher's surprise, David Gorkin stood outside the main door waiting for him. He looked quite dapper in his black three-piece, pin-striped suit with a white shirt, a colorful blue and red tie, and a matching handkerchief in his lapel pocket.

*Is he about to step into a television studio for an interview?* Gallagher wondered.

They checked through the security area and got clearance to meet Mickey Ryan in the prisoners' visiting area on the tenth floor.

They sat in a small room, starkly furnished with only a table and several wooden chairs, and waited for Mickey to be brought down from his holding cell.

Gorkin turned to Gallagher and said, "You know, I'm anxious to hear what you and Mickey have to say to each other. Something tells me that you may hold the key to his ultimate release."

"I'm not sure about that. At this point I'm a long way from figuring this whole thing out, but I have a few..."

A metal door clanged open and interrupted his sentence. Two security guards escorted Mickey Ryan into the room. Jail life was definitely not agreeing with Mickey. Unshaven and disheveled, it looked like he had not slept all night. The guards seated him at the table, briefly checked the barren room, and then stood outside the closed door.

Gorkin wasted no time getting on with the business at hand,

"Mickey, you remember Mr. Gallagher, he's a private investigator from Boston who's been looking into the West Castle matter."

Mickey glared at Gallagher, "Sure. I remember him. He was snoopin' around my car lot, askin' me questions. The next thing I know, I'm in the fuckin' slammer."

Gallagher leaned across the table to get a little closer, "Look, Mickey, I had nothing to do with your arrest. In fact, I believe you were set up as the fall guy for these murders."

Mickey looked at Gallagher as if trying to measure the sincerity of his words. "Okay, so we agree that I'm being framed. How's that goin' to get me outta here?"

"I'm not sure. But I have an idea that the murders of the two doctors in West Castle and the one in Vermont are all related to a business transaction twenty years ago, and I'm not talking about the one where you sold that piece of land to Barry Nickerson. The guys in that real-estate partnership got into a legal dispute with the FDIC and ended up owing a lot of money to the government. Then, two of them flew to Washington for a one day meeting with someone. After that meeting they owed a lot less money to the government—more than a million dollars less."

Mickey's eyes blinked rapidly, but he sat quietly, listening as Gallagher provided the details of this new information.

Gallagher continued, "Coincidentally, those are the same two doctors who got murdered in West Castle. The doctor who was murdered in Vermont was a very active member of the partnership until he sold his interests a few years ago. He knew the inner workings of the group and helped orchestrate most of the early transactions of the partnership. It figures that he knew all about that trip to Washington."

"So maybe that's why he got hit, too," said Mickey.

"Right," agreed Gallagher. "It's logical to assume that he was a target. And there's more: Dr. Becker's cell phone had the number of a congressman from Pennsylvania. At one time this congressman was an active member of a committee that had dealings with the FDIC. I'm looking into that connection to see if the congressman is somehow tied to the murders."

After a few seconds, Gorkin sat up in his chair and remarked, "Well, Mr. Gallagher, it is an interesting theory, but I don't think the Middlesex District Attorney will care much about it unless you come up with ironclad proof. It's pretty tough to implicate a United States congressman in a plot to commit murder."

Gallagher shook his head in agreement, "I know that, but I'm going back to Washington to see if I can find a connection. I have a good friend from college who works for the Democratic Party. He may be able to open a few doors for me. But first, I have a few questions for Mickey."

"Go ahead. I've got all day; I'm not goin' anywhere," said Mickey.

"Tell me about those break-ins. I think they're part of the frame-up."

Mickey rolled around on his chair, trying to get comfortable.

"A lot of strange shit was happening. First of all, I got a call from a guy who ran quite a bit of action through Vegas. Jimmy Galdieri from Malden. Whenever I had too much money comin' in on one team, I would lay some of it off with Jimmy, just so I wouldn't get hurt if that team covered. Jimmy's a good guy. Always played it straight with me. Anyway, one day he calls me and says, 'Mickey, you havin' trouble with the boys in Vegas?' I said, 'Whaddya mean? I've got nothun' to do with Vegas.' He told me that some guys from Vegas were making inquiries—wanted to know all about me, where I lived, where I hung out—asking all kinds of questions. I didn't know what to make of it, but then, a couple of weeks later, somebody breaks into my house and takes a whole bunch of stuff including my gun. I had that piece for years. Kept it in my bedroom drawer, just in case I ever needed it."

"What about the break-in at the used car lot?" asked Gallagher.

"Happened about a week later. I didn't think too much about

that because it happened before. Usually some kids wanting to take a car for a joy ride."

"Did you ever call your friend, Jimmy, to ask if he had heard anything about the break-ins?"

"Yeah, in fact, I did. But Jimmy said the street was quiet. Nobody was talkin'."

"When the Vegas guys were trying to find out about you, did they ask if you carried a gun?"

"Yeah. When I got back to Jimmy Gal, I told him my gun was taken. He told me that they were askin' if I packed a piece. Made him think that I was gonna be hit for not payin' off some money or somethun'. If I had known they were gonna steal my gun, I wudda hid it in a better place."

Gallagher's mind was racing with possibilities. He looked at Gorkin and asked, "Do you think you could get this guy Jimmy to testify that Mickey's gun was stolen before the murders?"

Gorkin smiled and shrugged, "In view of Mr. Galdieri's profession, I don't think he'd be willing to step into a court of law."

Gallagher grimaced.

"You're right about that," he said. "And I guess that conversation would be considered hearsay and wouldn't carry much weight in a murder trial. We'll need to do better than that."

Gallagher, aware that he needed to pursue other options, turned back to Mickey, "Would Jimmy Galdieri talk to me?"

"Probably not. Guys in the business don't like to discuss their business with people they don't know. It increases their risk; we don't like the odds of increasin' our risk."

"Well, did he ever mention the names of the Vegas people who were making inquiries about you?"

"Nah, Jimmy Gal wouldn't do that either. Don't forget, these guys from Vegas help him make money." Then pausing for a second, Mickey looked up, rolled his eyes and then nodded, "But he did say somethun' about someone named 'LT.' Sort of like 'LT was asking me if you carried a piece all the time.' Somethun' like that, but I don't know anybody named LT."

Gallagher jotted the initials down on a small lined notepad he always carried in his pocket, adding them to a small list of items that now included "Vegas and Jimmy Galdieri."

The meeting lasted for another half hour, but nothing of significance was forthcoming. Mickey became much more relaxed and now seemed to view Gallagher as an ally, not an antagonist.

"You know, I've got an alibi that puts me nowhere near that medical building when the first doctor was killed," said Mickey.

"Yes. I heard Mr. Gorkin mention something about an alibi at your hearing," said Gallagher.

"Yeah, my girlfriend and I went down to Foxwoods in the morning and got there for lunch."

Gorkin smiled and then interrupted.

"I've told you, Mickey, we have some work to do in that area. We need someone else besides your girlfriend to corroborate your story and verify your whereabouts for the entire morning before you left for the casino."

Gallagher didn't want to disappoint his new friend by telling him that he agreed with his attorney. Even if Mickey showed up on security tapes from the casino at noontime, the murder had occurred early enough in the morning to allow him plenty of time to complete the drive from Massachusetts to Connecticut.

The security guards signaled that it was time for Mickey to return to his holding cell. Before he left the room, Gallagher shook his hand and said, "Mickey, I believe you had nothing to do with these murders. Hopefully, I can find the evidence to get you out of here. If you think of anything else, let David know. He'll contact me."

Mickey now looked more like a gentle giant than an intimidator. He muttered, "Thanks, man, I appreciate it."

He left the room without saying another word, allowing the two guards to replace his handcuffs and leg irons and then following their lead down the hallway.

As Gallagher walked down the stairs from the courthouse, Gorkin asked, "So, Gallagher, you certainly have some work cut out for yourself. What's your next step?"

"Well, I guess the first thing is to find out if I'm still being paid for this job."

Gorkin looked puzzled.

"Why not?" he asked.

"I'm not sure if the woman who hired me wants to pursue this. If she decides to continue, I've got a lot to do in Washington. I didn't mention it to Mickey, but the congressman whose name appeared on Dr. Becker's cell phone is currently the chairman of a congressional committee that's deciding whether casinos can be built and operated by the federal government on former military bases. I'd be willing to bet that he's had some interesting discussions with a few guys in Las Vegas."

Gorkin listened and waited for a few seconds before responding, as if needing time for the latest of Gallagher's theories to settle in.

"If you're right about all of this, it's a sinister, convoluted plot. But you may be on to something. In the end, you could be my client's only hope. Keep me posted on your progress, and, above all, keep an eye on your back."

Gorkin waved his finger toward Gallagher as if to emphasize the warning in his next point.

"You're embarking on dangerous territory, Gallagher. You're taking on two major institutions: the United States Congress and the syndicates of Las Vegas. They both have some very heavy hitters; people can get seriously hurt in many different ways when they mess with them."

With that admonition, the little old man tapped his hand on his forehead to make a salute and then winked at his younger friend. He turned and walked away, his characteristic gait more evident than ever.

Gallagher stood alone on the street trying to digest all the new information and expanded cast of characters in this case. His mind was tiring—he needed a hot cup of coffee and a jolt of caffeine before he called Suzanne Becker.

*Will she keep the investigation open? Where do I go from here if she cuts me off?*

Gallagher, however, knew himself all too well. The thought of Hoskins gloating at him in the courtroom had been enough to make his blood boil. This was his chance to prove Hoskins wrong.

*Even if she bails out on me now, I can't let this go until I have all the answers.*

# Chapter 38

The city of Las Vegas—the entertainment capital of the United States. Other resort casino operations have tried to imitate Las Vegas. Casinos in Atlantic City, Biloxi, Mississippi, and at Foxwoods in Connecticut have had moderate success. Las Vegas, however, has remained comfortably at the top of the gambling and entertainment industry with no rivals in sight.

And that's just how its owners prefer to keep it.

The federal initiative to convert abandoned military installations into federally operated resort casinos had been considered a pipe dream to cynical critics of previously botched government forays into legalized gambling. The casinos of Atlantic City were supposed to create a tax-relief boon to the state of New Jersey and revitalize the economy of a depressed city. Neither of these benefits had ever been realized.

Therefore, the current proposal sitting before the Joint Committee on Economic Development and Emerging Technologies in the United States Congress had not received much attention from national media or congressional observers. In Las Vegas betting terminology, this proposal was considered a long shot, at best, and would probably never make its way out of the committee hearings. To the owners of the Las Vegas resort casinos, however, this bill represented a genuine threat, not to be taken lightly. If approved in committee and proposed as a bill in Congress, its enactment could create dozens of casino complexes throughout the country, particularly in the warm climate areas of California, Arizona, and Florida—siphoning off millions of tourists annually and billions of dollars of revenue from Las Vegas.

The Las Vegas casino operators competed with each other daily to attract gamblers and visitors to their establishments. They were united, however, in recognizing that such losses to casinos outside of Las Vegas could not be tolerated. They were willing to expend every effort to quietly kill the proposal in committee. These owners shared a common bond when it came to resisting any discussion of a federally operated gaming initiative. They desperately wanted to protect the status quo that gave them license to continue reaping profits of staggering proportions.

This collective paranoia of the Las Vegas casino syndicate trickled down in a variety of ways to establish a philosophy of "whatever it takes to get the job done." Among the beneficiaries of this philosophy was Johnny Nicoletti, living in Las Vegas in virtual obscurity, but relishing all the pleasures the city had to offer. As Johnny lay poolside at the Venetian Hotel, his light brown, wavy hair glistened in the sun and his five-foot ten-inch frame showed a dark bronze tan. He looked down from his lounge chair at the red-haired, buxom young woman, who was resting on a towel by his side. She was clad in a bikini that left nothing to the imagination.

Johnny had hired her as a companion for the day. After several hours with her in his room, he decided to take a break and enjoy the fresh air at the pool. Later in the day, they would get dressed for dinner and a show at the Bellagio Hotel. Johnny never had it so good, and he would be the first to acknowledge it.

His life for the past few weeks had been relatively quiet; no trips or out of town assignments, giving him plenty of time to relax and recharge his batteries. When the next call came from Jerry Murray, with another problem to be solved or delicate issue to be handled, Johnny was ready to take action.

Like the powerful but nameless people who employed him, Johnny liked things just as they were.

He was willing to do whatever it took to get the job done.

# Chapter 39

For Suzanne Becker, Thanksgiving was over, but her pain was not. She had surrounded herself with family and friends during the four days of the holiday weekend. All the cooking, serving, and chatter had provided a mere temporary distraction—the hurt of losing her husband was deeper than ever. A person content to deal with reality, she worked to make life better and never expected a fairy-tale ending to a story. But her life had been a fairy tale story of its own.

She married her husband, Jonathan, just after they graduated from college together. She worked as a computer programmer for six years while he completed medical school and entered his residency in pediatrics at the New England Medical Center in Boston. Her husband's career in medicine was extremely successful, allowing them to send their two children to private schools, to live in a beautiful home, and enjoy some of the finer things in life. They traveled extensively, went to the theater and cultural events, and played golf at the West Castle Country Club. They had two wonderful children who were now grown and busy developing their own careers.

Everything seemed to be in place for a perfect beginning to a life of retirement and exciting new horizons. In a whisper, it all vanished—as if someone had blown out a candle. Without warning, Jonathan was gone.

Suzanne and her husband had shared a charitable commitment to society and worked together on fund raising efforts for West Castle Hospital where Jonathan admitted his patients. Ironically, his bullet-riddled body had been taken there after he was shot last month outside his office building.

Suzanne Becker didn't engage in trite phrases or sayings, but had to admit that the old cliché, "the first holiday is always the hardest" was painfully true.

At first, the shock and bitterness over Jonathan's murder had been mollified by a desire to find out why it happened. Who did this and what was the motivation? Why had her husband been acting so depressed and preoccupied by his partnership's real-estate holdings? What threats did he face and why couldn't he talk to her about them? But now, with the arrest of this monster of a man, Mickey Ryan, whose name she had never heard mentioned before, those feelings had dissipated.

She was left with the stark fear of loneliness and the need to come up with a new direction and purpose in her life. This would not be easy, but she was a woman of great reserve, high intellect, and the mental toughness to look forward and not be deterred by events of the past. She just needed some time to formulate her plans and begin the healing process; she was confident that she could, once again, find happiness in her life.

However, her phone conversation last week with Gallagher, the private investigator she hired, had created further turmoil in her mind. In just the few short weeks that she had known him, and in their brief personal encounters, she had grown to respect and admire him. She felt that he had the cunning ability to systematically comb through all the confusion and come up with plausible answers to her questions. She liked everything about him—his strength of character, his handsome looks and laid back style, and the confidence and self-assurance he expressed with his every mannerism. Nothing phony or pretentious. She knew he would never settle for anything but the truth.

Nevertheless, she wondered if he had wandered off course when he told her that the police had arrested and charged the wrong man with her husband's murder. The evidence against this man seemed compelling. The police had the murder weapon that happened to be his gun; he had a motive; and the police now claimed to have a witness who saw him leaving the scene of Dick Evan's murder. What could possibly make Gallagher think that this man was being framed? This very question brought out feelings of anger and frustration and made her wonder if Gallagher was stubbornly pursuing wild theories at her expense.

However, Suzanne Becker—a woman who lived in the real world and could not, herself, accept anything but the truth—knew there were no other options. What if he was right and someone else was responsible for her husband's murder? How could she go on, forever wondering if the killer was still at large?

A business card was taped to the bookshelf above her small desk at the side of the kitchen. She looked at the card, agonizing to herself for a moment, fighting back the tears that had suddenly welled up in her eyes, and knowing that any further investigation might uncover dark, hidden secrets that could bring embarrassment or shame to her family.

But in the end, she was guided by her need to know the whole story.

She dialed the telephone number below the name, "Gallagher: Private Investigator."

# Chapter 40

By the time Gallagher arrived back at his office, Diane had already taken the message and told him that Mrs. Becker wanted him to call as soon as possible. She had sounded very emotional on the phone, and at first, Diane thought that something terrible had happened.

"I felt so bad for her, Dan; she seemed very upset. You might want to call her now," suggested Diane.

Diane's advice in such matters was generally right on target. Gallagher stepped into his private office, picked up his telephone, and dialed the number. "Mrs. Becker, it's Gallagher. Are you alright?" he asked.

They spoke on the phone for nearly an hour. Mrs. Becker sobbed at times and, occasionally, even displayed anger. She explained her fears about the potential outcome of the investigation but also acknowledged her need to know what really had happened. In return, Gallagher offered her consolation for the ethical dilemma she faced and the roller coaster of emotions she had to endure since her husband's murder. He reviewed the facts he had gathered during the past three weeks and went over his theories on the FDIC issue, Congressman Prendergast, the federal gaming proposal, and the possible link to the Las Vegas syndicates. He discussed his thoughts on Mickey Ryan's arrest, pointing out that Mickey's story was believable and that Gallagher thought he was the apparent victim of a plot to frame him. Incredible as it might seem, this plot appeared to have a Las Vegas connection.

She listened intently, so engrossed in the details that her tones of emotional despair were now replaced with one of firm resolve, reflecting a need to know more and get to the bottom of the matter. By the end of their discussion, it was clear how she wanted to proceed.

"We can't stop now. If this was all a terrible plan to murder my husband and his partners, and then put the blame on an innocent man—just so someone could make a lot of money—we can't let them get away with that."

"I agree with you completely, "Gallagher said. "There may be much more to this story than we imagine. I think we are only at the beginning; there's a lot that we don't know yet."

She began to retreat somewhat in her tone.

"The people you are talking about are dangerous. If they could so cleverly arrange to kill Jonathan and two of his partners and then pin it all on this guy, Mickey, what else are they capable of doing? Do you think you should take this information to the police?"

His response was immediate, "No, I don't think we should get the police involved at this time."

"But you could be in serious danger if you threaten to expose these people."

"Don't worry. If we go to the police, it would be all over the media in a heartbeat. That would give the killers more time to cover their tracks and make themselves scarce. Worse yet, they might go back on the offensive. Right now, they're relaxed and confident that no one is looking for them. Mickey's locked up and everyone is saying the case is closed. I can function a lot more effectively if I work on my own and take advantage of secrecy and the element of surprise."

"I'm willing to go on with this, but how long do you think it will take to resolve these questions?" she asked.

"Give me two more weeks. If I don't have the answers by then, we'll get together and decide how to proceed from there."

"That sounds fair. I think you should transfer me to Diane, so I can take care of some business with her," she said, realizing that she had just made a significant monetary commitment as well as an emotional one.

Gallagher transferred the call and sat at his desk for a few minutes thinking about all the elements of their recent conversation. He eventually got up from his chair and walked over to the wall where the picture of Jason Varitek and Alex Rodriquez was hanging. He carefully removed the picture from its hook, disclosing a hidden door to a wall safe. He unlocked the safe, opened the drawer, and removed the single item stored within: a .38 caliber Smith & Wesson snubbed-nose revolver.

For the past few days, it seemed that almost everyone—Kate, Mr. Gorkin, and Suzanne Becker—had been warning him that he was dealing with a very dangerous situation. Gallagher understood their concern and tried to put them at ease with a confident air of bravado. Still, he was well aware of the treacherous territory he had entered. The person or persons he was seeking would do anything to keep him from revealing their identities. They would not hesitate to kill him.

He stared at the gun in his hand. When the ultimate confrontation occurred, Gallagher knew he'd better be ready.

# CHAPTER 41

A private investigator and his gun have a vacillating relationship at best. The gun offers security—the first line of defense in a life threatening crisis—and is the ultimate means of protection when facing an enemy at a distance and an equalizer to ward off multiple attackers using their fists or knives as quiet, but deadly weapons.

However, the private investigator's gun can also be a downright nuisance. In the post-9/11 world of increased security at airports, government buildings, office buildings, and virtually every place of importance, any person who walks though a security checkpoint carrying a gun in a shoulder holster might just as well announce a declaration of war.

Even the bored museum guard who spent his whole day looking through the pocketbooks of little old ladies would have no tolerance for the story that this .38 caliber revolver was merely for personal protection, to remain holstered the whole time that paintings by Renoir were being admired. There would be no use trying to convince an airport security screener that a handgun would only be used to defend the other passengers in the event a hijacker tried to overtake the cockpit. Alarms would sound, buzzers would go off, and the private investigator would be on the ground in handcuffs, with several other guns pointed at his head before he got a chance to flash his business card.

Gallagher had learned to adjust to this dilemma. When flying to other cities, he packed his gun according to FAA regulations: in a locked steel container that was placed in his suitcase and then loaded into the luggage hold. For local traveling, he stored his gun in a lock box that was secured to the frame of the car inside the trunk. Then he'd place it in his shoulder holster after arriving at a destination that posed some threat. This was a cumbersome system, at best, but at least it provided him some access to his .38 if he felt it was needed. Most of the time, he was forced to just go "bare," without his weapon, relying solely on his ability to recognize a dangerous situation and keep himself out of trouble.

Gallagher was good with a gun. While in the police academy, he had been cited for proficiency in marksmanship and always took great pride in knowing that his hands remained steady, even in times of stress or pressure. He had the ability to slow things down, to sort out the important targets from the maelstrom all around him and to focus his mind and body on executing a gunshot with precision and accuracy. Although he had not needed to use his gun in self-defense for many years, Gallagher practiced frequently at a gun range in Hudson, New Hampshire, in order to maintain his edge, knowing that it could be a fatal mistake to allow his skills to diminish.

He had been forced to use his gun in a lethal manner on only one occasion in his career—while he was a Boston cop, in only his second year on the force. He could remember the details of that incident, second by second, as if it had happened yesterday. He and his partner, Ray, had been called by dispatch to respond to a report of a burglary in process at a convenience store on Tremont Street, near the entrance to the Mass Pike West. When their police cruiser pulled into the parking lot in front of the store, everything seemed to be in order. The clerk could be seen through the glass door standing calmly at the register. Customers casually walked into the store. Ray entered the store while Gallagher stood at the door guarding the parking lot in case a perpetrator tried to escape through a rear exit.

Ray asked the clerk if there were any problems.

The man responded, "No—everything's okay."

Through the doorway, Gallagher could see the clerk's eyes nervously shifting to the farthest aisle on the left side of the store. A tall man stood there with his back leaning against the stock aisle, unaware that he could be seen in the angled mirror in the corner of the wall above his head.

As Gallagher yelled, "Ray! Watch out on your right!" the man quickly stepped into the main aisle with a gun pointed directly at Ray.

Gallagher, now inside the store with his service revolver drawn, extended his arm perfectly straight at his target, and fired one shot, striking the ill-fated robber precisely in the middle of his chest. The man was dead by the time his body crashed to the linoleum floor in a heap.

After that incident, Ray swore that Gallagher's quick reflexes and accurate shooting had saved his life and frequently reminded him by stating, "I owe you one, Gallagher."

On social occasions, whenever he saw Ray and his wife, Janice, she always gave Gallagher a long hug that he felt was her way of acknowledging what he had done to save her husband.

Although he was thankful that he had saved his partner, the thought of taking another person's life was not appealing under any circumstances. This was one of the major reasons he felt uncomfortable in police work and had opted for the less violent life of a private investigator. Now, he faced another highly volatile, potentially violent situation and was no longer looking for a simple answer to a real-estate deal gone bad. He knew, in the coming weeks, he could be confronted by a person who would not be intimidated or yield easily—someone who had fired a gun with deadly results on two occasions and bludgeoned another man to death. This person had coolly left all three scenes without leaving a single trace of evidence for the police and had successfully conspired to implicate another man in the murders. This person would not surrender without a fight.

Gallagher knew that this confrontation would require him to draw upon all of his cunning and reserve. In the end, under the worst circumstances, he would have to use his gun against the killer.

It had been nine years since he shot that robber in the convenience store. Self-doubt was now creeping into his psyche.

If he were faced with another life-or-death situation with a gun pointed at him, Gallagher wondered if his hands would be as steady.

# Chapter 42

Later in the day, Gallagher drove out to Belmont, Massachusetts, a wealthy suburb located about twenty minutes west of Boston. In his first meeting with Randi Stockdale, she had given him the addresses and telephone numbers of the principals in Jonathan Becker's real-estate partnership. He had not yet met or spoken to two of them, Tony Cognetti, who lived in Belmont, and Dan Oblas, who was retired in Bonita Springs, Florida. He did not have high expectations that either man would be willing to speak to him, especially since Barry Nickerson had practically closed the door in his face when he mentioned the name of Congressman William Prendergast a couple of weeks ago. Nevertheless, he felt he had nothing to lose as he parked his car in front of 1018 Statler Road, an impressive center-entrance colonial home in an upscale neighborhood not far from Route 2 and the Cambridge-Arlington town lines.

He rang the doorbell. After several rings, the door opened, and a man, about five feet six inches tall, in his early seventies with balding, gray hair, looked up at Gallagher.

"Hope I'm not catching you at a bad time. Are you Dr. Cognetti?" asked Gallagher.

"Yes, I am. What can I do for you?" replied the man with a suspicious, quizzical look on his face.

"My name is Gallagher. I've been retained by Suzanne Becker. Could I have a few minutes to ask you some questions about your real-estate partnership?"

Tony stepped back from the door in a manner reminiscent of the reaction Gallagher had seen in his partner, Barry Nickerson.

He simply uttered, "Sorry, no questions," as he slowly pushed the door shut.

Barry had obviously spread the word that it would be wise to avoid talking to the private investigator that Suzanne had hired to snoop around.

Gallagher returned to his car and used his cell phone to dial the home of Dr. Dan Oblas in Florida. A woman answered the phone; Gallagher identified himself to her and asked to speak to Dan.

"Are you Mrs. Oblas?" he asked cordially.

"Yes, I'm his wife, Phyllis. Could you hold for a moment?"

She returned to the phone after only a few seconds and spoke in a terse, edgy manner, "My husband is not available and asked that you not call again. Please abide by his wishes."

Before Gallagher could respond, he was on the end of a dead phone line.

The partners were definitely closing ranks and were united in their refusal to speak to Gallagher. Thus far, in his brief encounters with them, he had detected a strong underlying element of fear in their behavior.

*Why should they be so afraid, especially now that the police had arrested a man and charged him with the killings of two of the partners? Shouldn't they be relieved knowing that this vindictive nemesis from their past is behind bars and can't come after them to settle an old score? Or, is it possible that the three remaining partners know full well that Mickey Ryan is not involved and that the real killer is still at large, ready to strike again?*

# Chapter 43

In a booth at the back of the Old Ebbitt Grill on 15th Street NW in Washington, D.C., Tony Macmillan poured his second cup of coffee. He had arrived at eleven o'clock, knowing that this place became packed at noon. He wanted to be sure he had secured a table when his friend, Gallagher, walked in for their lunchtime meeting. He hadn't seen Gallagher for a few years, but their friendship went all the way back to their days at Boston College when they lived in the same dorm and drank beer together at BC football games.

Tony always loved politics and, after working as a volunteer on several election campaigns in Massachusetts, landed a job at Democrat Party national headquarters in Washington. His official title was "Democrat Party Operative," which, in simple terms, meant that he had a lot to do with grass-roots efforts to build support for Democrat candidates in state and local elections all over the country. A well-connected guy in Washington political circles, Tony always had his ear to the ground for the latest rumors or gossip.

The Old Ebbitt Grill was the quintessential restaurant for a lunch in which politics would be the main topic of discussion. Located just minutes from the White House and decorated in handsome, dark wood, highly polished brass, and antique gas chandeliers, it was a place steeped in tradition, as well as being known for its great food. Many political lunches took place here. The participants never had to worry about their conversations being overheard by eavesdroppers—the noisy restaurant made it hard enough to hear the voice of the person sitting across from you, let alone someone from another table.

Tony Macmillan had barely changed since his days at BC. His blonde hair and trademark handlebar mustache now had a few hints of gray scattered throughout. He still wore the same rimless, glass frames that always seemed to slip down past the bridge of his nose while he was speaking. The only significant change in his appearance was that he had swapped his abundant collection of sweaters from his college wardrobe for dozens of colorful bow ties that accompanied his pin-striped business suits. He was a likeable, if not lovable, personality.

"Hey—there he is!" exclaimed Tony, glancing up from his newspaper, his mustache dripping slightly from the coffee cup he had just placed down on the saucer. "Still looking trim and fit! How come the rest of us have a little paunch and you look like a fitness trainer?"

"This is what happens when you chase after missing people all day—you burn up a lot of calories," Gallagher said with a laugh.

"Guess I better start doing some of that," Tony replied, patting his stomach as he spoke. "Did you fly in this morning?"

"Yes," said Gallagher, looking a bit harried from the trip and sliding himself awkwardly into the booth. "You know what a pain it is to deal with the airlines. I miss the old days when you could just walk onto the Washington Shuttle five minutes before take-off, buy your ticket on board, and be here an hour later."

Tony laughed.

"I'm afraid those days are long gone, my friend, and you'll never see them again," he said. "Have a drink and relax, and then tell me all about this latest mystery you're investigating. Seems like there's never a dull moment in your life. When we were at BC, did you ever think you'd be having this much fun?"

"I don't know if I would always categorize this as fun, but it does make life interesting. And then sometimes you come up against a brick wall, and you feel like you've got nowhere to go."

"Ah—I see," said Tony, "You expect your old friend to drill a hole through some brick wall for you, maybe even open a few doors here in Washington? How's that for quickly solving a mystery? I should have been a private eye, myself."

"Yeah, I guess you're right, Tony; I could use some help."

They were briefly interrupted by the waiter who took their order for lunch, both choosing the seafood special—crab cakes and a cup of clam chowder.

While they waited for lunch, Gallagher proceeded to fill Tony in on all the details of the West Castle murder case, including the real-estate transactions, the FDIC loan, Congressman Prendergast, Mickey Ryan, and his theory about a Las Vegas connection. Tony listened intently, absorbing this information like someone getting a scoop from a gossip columnist.

When Gallagher finished his story, Tony leaned back in the booth, looked at his friend with a roguish smile, and said, "So, you want me to believe that Bill Prendergast, fourteen-term United States congressman, hopped on a plane, flew up to Boston, and shot a doctor and then a couple of weeks later, he shot another one? Then, if that wasn't enough excitement, he drove up to Vermont at the crack of dawn and threw another doctor down an embankment near some Keeshee Gorge.

"Natives pronounce it Kwee-chee Gorge," interrupted Gallagher. "It's spelled with a Q."

"All right, Quechee Gorge," said Tony, raising his arms in a frustrated, apologetic manner. Then he continued, "You want me to help you get an appointment to see Congressman Prendergast? What should I say? 'Excuse me, Mr. Congressman, I've got a friend who wants to ask you about those doctors you killed up in New England. How about tomorrow at two o'clock?'"

Gallagher laughed right along with Tony, admitting that the scenario described by his friend was absurdly comical.

Then he got serious again, "No, Tony, I don't think Prendergast pulled the trigger; but I do think he was somehow involved and may have direct knowledge about the person who actually did the killings. How can I find out more about this guy?"

"Well, the Democrats have suspected that he's been on the take for years. How else can you explain that a guy comes to Washington without a penny in his pocket and then twenty-eight years later, on a congressman's salary, he's a multimillionaire? The money had to come from somewhere. No one's ever been able to pin anything on him. He's really pretty slick. Word around town is that he took some big payoffs back in his days on the Banking Committee. We had our own private investigation consultants look into it, but they could never get anyone to admit they paid him off."

"Why were your private investigators so interested in Prendergast?" Gallagher asked as he leaned toward his friend.

"Well, he's got control of the Economic and Emerging Technologies Committee; we'd love to get something on him, force him out, and then maybe get that legislation rolling to turn those abandoned federal military bases into government operated casinos. You know, it's typical Washington hypocrisy. Prendergast is waving the flag, claiming that gambling is a vice that the federal government should suppress, not encourage, and that the government must stay out of the gambling business in order to avoid the potential of corruption. Meanwhile, he's probably on the take from the Las Vegas syndicates who will figure out a way to funnel millions of dollars toward him if he can kill the legislation in committee."

"I figured you'd be up to speed on all of that,' said Gallagher. "That's the same take I have on the whole situation. What did your investigators find?"

"I had heard they had a few possibilities; in fact, there were rumors circulating around that they had someone willing to testify that Prendergast had accepted a bribe. But nothing ever panned out. You might want to speak to Jack McKissock; he headed up the inquiries and could give you a lot more information than I ever could. I'll make a call to Jack and let him know you're a friend."

"And," said Gallagher, "What if I do want to speak to the inimitable Congressman Prendergast?"

"Remember, you're sitting across the table from a Democrat Party operative. The Republicans usually hang up when I call," joked Tony. "Prendergast's chief of staff is the person who screens all his appointments. He happens to be a pretty good guy. His name is Stu Tane—one of the nicest, most ethical guys in Washington. We all wonder how he ever got himself hooked up with a sleaze-bag like Prendergast. If you go to Prendergast's office, you might get lucky and be able to grab a few minutes with Stu. He's your only chance to ever get a meeting with Prendergast."

Gallagher wrote both names on his notepad and went back to eating his lunch. "I'll bet these crab cakes were delicious when they were hot."

"You see, the way it works in Washington, when I talk, you're supposed to be eating. Then, when you talk, I eat. If you follow that protocol, these lengthy conversations won't ruin your lunch," offered Tony.

"Okay. Next time I'll know what to do. Thanks for establishing the guidelines."

Tony had finished eating and now peered across the table with an impish look.

"Let's put the mystery aside and get to the important business of your visit. Are the women still knocking down your door to get into your bed? Please say 'yes' and give me all the scintillating, erotic details."

"No, Tony—I'm afraid those days are also long gone. There's just one woman now; her name is Kate McSurdy. She's pretty special."

"Oh, no!" mocked Tony, raising his glass to make a toast, "The

King of the Lady Killers has retired from playing the field; long live the King!"

Gallagher laughed along with his friend's familiar theatrics and raised his glass.

*Long live the King? I'll drink to that. When Congressman William Prendergast finds out who I am and why I'm in Washington, I doubt that he'll join in the toast.*

# Chapter 44

The next morning, Gallagher walked up the steps to the main entrance of the Rayburn House Office Building on South Capitol Street. His friend, Tony, had actually been quite modest in estimating his ability to arrange a meeting with a staffer of a Republican congressman. A phone call requesting a small favor, such as a brief meeting for a friend? No problem. Thanks to Tony, Gallagher had a ten o'clock meeting with Stu Tane, chief of staff for Congressman William J. Prendergast.

Gallagher walked into Room 2782 and announced his arrival to the receptionist. He had barely gotten comfortable on a chair in the reception office when a man, wearing an ecru-colored shirt with the sleeves rolled up and a tie hanging loosely from an open collar, briskly walked out of an office on the left and called over to him.

"Mr. Gallagher? Come on in. Thanks for being on time."

Stu Tane's office and desk told the story of a man with a very busy job and too many responsibilities. Papers and files were scattered everywhere. A large stack of bound manuals titled *Committee Briefings* almost obscured the seventeen-inch flat screen monitor on his desk. Although he was a man in his early sixties, Tane had a much younger-looking face, a broad smile, and an energetic personality that made him likable from the time you shook his hand.

"Tony Mac says you're an old friend of his. He's a great guy, isn't he? We'd love to convert him over to our side, but so far he's resisting," said Stu with a laugh. "Those liberals are tough nuts to crack!"

"Yes, I guess you're right; Tony will never change," agreed Gallagher as he smiled and tried to humor his host.

"What can I do to help you in Washington?" asked Stu.

Gallagher leaned over the desk and handed him a business card. He wasted no time cutting right to the chase.

"I'm a private investigator, checking into the transactions of a real-estate partnership in West Castle, Massachusetts. It was a group of doctors who put up a medical building in the mid-1980s, then ran into some problems during the S&L banking crisis a few years later. Their loan was taken over by the FDIC and eventually paid off. But there are questions related to the way the payoff was handled. Since Congressman Prendergast was a member of the Banking Committee at that time, I was hoping that he might be able to help answer some of these questions."

Tane looked perplexed by Gallagher's story.

"Why don't you just ask the partners about their settlement with the FDIC? It was their loan. Wouldn't they be the best source of information?" he asked.

Gallagher hesitated for a second, and then dropped what he knew would be a bombshell.

"Three of the doctors were murdered within the past two months, and the three remaining partners refuse to talk to me."

"Murdered? Holy Shit! You're not serious!" exclaimed Tane, clearly taken aback by the unexpected twist in the story. However, he quickly recovered and asked, "But isn't that a matter for the police, not a private eye or a member of Congress?"

"The police have already arrested a man and charged him with the murders. I'm here because Congressman Prendergast's office number was on the speed-dial list on the cell phone of one of the doctors. His widow has hired me to look at the business dealings of the partnership. The doctor was apparently acquainted with the congressman and had phone conversations with him or somebody in his office during the weeks before his murder. I thought Congressman Prendergast might be willing to help us," said Gallagher innocently, but laying the groundwork for his trap.

"Well, I can assure you that Congressman Prendergast has been very busy in Washington and has had no involvement in these murders," said Tane.

He stared straight into Gallagher's eyes.

Gallagher did not respond, but chose to wait silently, hoping that Tane would continue.

After a few seconds, he looked down at Gallagher's card and said, "But I will talk to Congressman Prendergast to make him aware of this situation. I'll call you if he's able to meet with you sometime."

"That would be great; thanks for your time," said Gallagher. He got up from his seat, shook hands with Stu and promptly left the office.

Their meeting had taken less than five minutes, but Gallagher had accomplished his goal. Congressman William J. Prendergast, a man who kept a close eye on the direction from which the political winds were blowing and a man who had made a career out of avoiding scandals, was now on notice. Someone had linked his name to one of the victims of the West Castle murders.

# Chapter 45

For Congressman William J. Prendergast, life was all about power and money. He had successfully wielded his power in Washington to create an affluent lifestyle for himself and his family. He looked forward to a comfortable retirement after a few more terms in Congress. He had enjoyed a great ride, but there was still much to accomplish in the next several years; he was in prime position to capitalize on his chairmanship of the Joint Committee for Economic Development and Emerging Technologies. Maintaining control of the vote in this committee and bringing about a result that was favorable to his supporters in Las Vegas could pay dividends to him for many years to come. After all, a retired United States congressman with business acumen and contacts all over the world would be the perfect choice for a lucrative seat on a board of directors, or as a highly paid consultant to the gaming industry.

Prendergast had arrived at his office at two o'clock in the afternoon, having completed a lunch-time briefing with more than a dozen congressional leaders at the White House. Although Congress was officially still on its Thanksgiving recess and would not resume legislative sessions until Monday, December 5, Prendergast and his wife had returned to Washington a few days early from their Florida vacation so he could take part in the briefing. More importantly, they came back to attend the Kennedy Center Honors Gala that was honoring several icons in the arts and entertainment industry including Tony Bennett, Robert Redford, and Tina Turner. Despite his status in Congress, Prendergast loved to rub elbows with celebrities and relished every opportunity to do so. Such events tended to fuel his ever-expanding ego as well as add to the dozens of photographs that graced the walls of his office, showing him with various movie stars and Hollywood celebrities.

He reviewed some letters left by his staff but was interrupted by a light tapping sound on his door.

"Have a minute, Bill?" asked Stu Tane.

"Sure—come on in," replied Prendergast.

"Just wanted to go over a few things with you. I've got the briefing reports all ready for the committee members. The first session is Wednesday morning at nine o'clock. We've had lots of calls from voters in our district; the staff has compiled the usual list of names, addresses, and whether they are pro or con. So far it's been about a fifty-fifty split. Actually a little surprising. All of us thought the majority would be against creating more resort casinos."

Prendergast didn't respond, but merely sat at his desk listening impassively.

Stu continued, "I also had an unusual meeting this morning with a private investigator from Boston. He's looking into some old FDIC business involving a real-estate partnership from a place called West Castle, Massachusetts. Three of the partners—all doctors—were murdered recently. One of them had our office telephone number on the speed-dial list of his cell phone. This private eye was wondering if you could spare a few minutes to talk to him. Maybe you might remember something about their loan from your days on the Banking Committee." As he finished speaking, he flipped Gallagher's card onto the desk.

A nerve had been struck.

Prendergast's curt reply was immediate.

"What the hell is wrong with you, Stu? I've got no time to talk to any private investigators—down here to dig up some old dirt," he protested. He waved his arm toward the door. "Tell this guy to get lost. He's probably working for the Democrats. They won't give up trying to get something on me."

Stu felt the rage spewing from his boss, but, as always, tried to be the voice of rational thinking in these matters.

"But Bill, what about the telephone number? How do we explain that?"

Prendergast—a little more flustered now—continued fuming, "Just tell him—just tell him that Dr. Becker was on our list of honored Republican supporters who received calls from the office requesting a campaign contribution. Make up something if you have to! But—uh—make it clear that I have more important matters pending and have no time to see him."

Stu Tane paused for a few seconds, waiting for the rampage to subside. But now he was the one with a surprised look on his face.

"Becker? Did you say Dr. Becker?" he asked. "This guy, Gallagher, never gave me the names of the victims. So, you did know him?"

His voice had an accusatory bite. But his words got out before he could retract them. He was caught in the awkward position of interrogating the man who employed him. Not a safe place to be. So he followed up with a softer tone, "I wasn't aware that you knew one of the doctors who was killed."

Prendergast fidgeted in his seat and licked his lip a few times. His eyes blinked nervously.

Then, he stood up, paced around the room, and said, "For Chrissakes, Stu, that story has been all around Washington for weeks. I've heard about it from a dozen different sources. I didn't know the guy had ever called here, but how am I supposed to know about the hundreds of people who call here every week? Just because they call here and put my number in their cell phone doesn't mean I know who the hell they are! I'm not paying you to meet with every Detective Columbo who comes through the door trying to get a story he can turn around and sell to the newspapers. What kind of crap is this anyway?"

Stu retreated uneasily toward the doorway, trying to escape his employer's wrath.

"Sorry. You're right, Bill. Don't worry; I'll take care of it."

***

Stu returned to his office and sat down at his desk. He clasped his hands behind his neck and stared up at the ceiling with a queasy feeling in his stomach. In his eight years in Washington, he had come to know the behavior of politicians; he watched them campaigning and giving political speeches to partisan crowds, granting interviews to the media, and speaking at hearings that they knew would appear on C-SPAN. He admired how quickly they could think on their feet and react with feigned outrage when challenged by a member of the opposition or the media. They were seasoned actors on a large political stage, conning their audience into believing they were honest and forthright, fighting for an honorable cause, always telling the truth.

Stu Tane was suddenly torn between two major forces in his life—his ethics, high moral standards, and honesty were now in conflict with his commitment to public service and sense of loyalty to his boss, a ranking leader in the halls of Congress. He was afraid that he had just witnessed a major acting job, a cover-up, a bit of feigned outrage.

And, most of all, Stu was afraid that his boss, Congressman William J. Prendergast, knew more about the West Castle murders than he was willing to admit.

# Chapter 46

William Prendergast rocked back and forth in his chair, staring at the business card that Stu Tane had left on his desk. He rubbed his thumb slowly over the name, "Gallagher, Private Investigator," all the while asking himself how this hotshot detective from Boston had gotten involved in this matter. His mind was teeming with paranoid, convoluted scenarios. He wondered who else had been questioned and how many people knew that his telephone number was on Dr. Becker's cell phone. Did this guy have phone records, access to old files, or depositions from anyone who might implicate Prendergast in a scandal? Was he hired by the Democrats? Was this their last desperate attempt to bring him down and pressure him to resign his committee chairmanship?

He knew he had made the right decision by refusing to meet with Gallagher. Why put himself in the potentially compromising situation of being forced to answer questions on the record and give credence to the notion that he had any direct knowledge of the details of this dreadful situation? Better to maintain a healthy distance from the topic and shrug off any suggestion that he knew the subjects personally or had any involvement in their financial affairs.

The timing of this Gallagher character's arrival on the scene could not have been worse. Pendergast was in the midst of critical negotiations with members of his committee, promising future concessions on other legislation in exchange for casting their votes with him. Although he had control of a majority of the members, he knew he could ill afford questions about his integrity and past record, let alone whispers that he may be implicated in a murder investigation. No, this was not a good time for any distractions from the business at hand; he knew he needed some help to decide how to handle this delicate problem—how to rid himself of this new pest before he could cause any real trouble.

Prendergast got up from his desk, walked over to his office door, quietly closed it and pressed the privacy button. He reached into his wallet and took out a small piece of paper tucked under his driver's license. The paper had nothing written on it, except a ten digit telephone number followed by the number "3." He dialed the number, waited a few seconds, and pressed "3." He lowered his voice and spoke slowly into the telephone, "Something's come up; we need to talk. It's important. Let me know when you can be here."

Congressman William J. Prendergast sat back in his chair and renewed rhythmically rocking back and forth, something he always did while he was deep in thought. Once again, he looked at the business card resting on his desk.

*This "one-name" son of a bitch is going to be sorry he ever started asking questions about me.*

# CHAPTER 47

The call from Stu Tane came early on Friday morning. Gallagher rolled over in his bed at the Hotel Washington and picked up his cell phone on the fourth ring, just before the call was sent to his voice mail. He fumbled the phone as he opened it, dropped it on the floor, and then recovered it quickly before the call was lost.

"Gallagher?" asked Stu. "Are you there?"

'Yes—uh—sorry, I was just stepping out of the shower," said Gallagher, not wanting to admit that, at 9:25 in the morning, he was still in bed.

"Listen," offered Stu with some trepidation in his voice, "The congressman is really tied up with a lot of pressing matters on his schedule. He's got committee hearings this week and some major votes coming up before the Christmas recess. So he doesn't have any time to meet with you. Besides, he couldn't recall anything about the matter up in Massachusetts. He didn't know any of the principals involved. I'm afraid there's nothing we can do to help you. You may want to check over at the FDIC building; if the documents are not protected by the privacy act, you might learn something there."

Gallagher had shaken the grogginess out of his mind and listened intently to Stu Tane's words. They were not spoken with conviction or commitment; rather, they sounded more like a prepared statement than conversational language. He wished he could see Tane in person to get a better read on his reactions but decided not to tell him that he intended to revisit the congressman's office very soon.

"OK, Stu, thanks for the call; I'll let you know if I come up with anything else and if it involves any of the committees the congressman served on. That may refresh his memory, and he might be able to help," said Gallagher, trying to be appeasing but knowing he had just gotten the brush-off.

Gallagher showered, got dressed, and decided to go back to Prendergast's office in the hope that he could have a face-to-face discussion with Stu Tane. He believed he was dealing with a person of good character and that, eventually, he could provide the information Gallagher needed to determine the congressman's role in the West Castle murders.

When he arrived at Room 2782, the reception area was once again nearly deserted. Only the receptionist sat at her desk. Gallagher always expected that this place would be a beehive of activity but attributed the quiet to the fact that even the constituents and lobbyists were taking an extended Thanksgiving break. He asked the receptionist if she could let Mr. Tane know that he had stopped by to see him. She got up from her desk and walked to the office on the left.

After a few minutes, Stu emerged from the doorway. With an annoyed wave of his hand, he said, "Look, Gallagher, we don't have any more time to spend on this matter. You'll have to stop coming to this office, or else we'll contact the security guards."

Gallagher did not respond with a look of anger, disappointment, or apology. Instead, he fixed his gaze on his new antagonist and calmly stated, "Stu, when we met yesterday, I didn't mention something important about this case, but I believe you should know it."

He stood impassively, completely composed and showing the confidence that comes with the belief that what you have said is true and factual. He said nothing else and waited for Stu to make the next statement.

Stu stared back at him; his initial aggressive posture with his hands on his hips slowly began to relax; his hands eventually slipped down to his sides. His face became expressionless—a blank stare.

Finally, he relented and said, "All right. Come in."

When they were alone in his office, Stu closed the door, turned to Gallagher and asked, "What's so important that I should know?"

Gallagher got right to his point, "You said this morning that the congressman didn't know any of the principals involved in the West Castle murders. I spoke to one of the surviving partners on two occasions. It wasn't like he wanted to open up his whole life to me, but he was willing to invite me into his house and have a conversation. Then, one night, after I found Prendergast's phone number on Dr. Jonathan Becker's cell phone, I went back to the partner's house and asked if he knew Prendergast. The look on that guy's face spoke volumes. He knew Prendergast and tried to deny it. He practically closed his door in my face and told me to never come back. Said I might get hurt if I went any further. It's pretty obvious to me that those doctors had some important dealings with your boss. Three of them may have been killed because of it."

Stu nodded his head but didn't say anything. The hurt in his voice was apparent when he looked up at Gallagher. "You just said the name Jonathan Becker. Yesterday, you never gave me the name of the doctor who was murdered. But the congressman blurted out that name during a tirade when I told him about your visit. Then he did a masterful acting job trying to pretend he heard it somewhere else."

He walked over to his desk, shoulders slumped, obviously disturbed by the gravity of the situation that was evolving.

"This is going to get pretty messy. I can see it coming and don't know if I want to be involved. I have a lot to think about here," he said, seemingly resigned to the desperate dilemma he faced.

Gallagher tried to console him, but also recognized the need to secure his assistance in possibly getting evidence against Prendergast.

"Look, Stu, I know this is a tough spot for you. I can't expect you to make any decisions right now. But keep your eyes open. Call me if you see or hear anything that may help to find the truth. You know it's the right thing to do. I think the congressman is going to react to my visit here and make a move during the next few days to keep a lid on all of this. My guess is that I've just become a target, so I could use your help."

Stu sat motionless at his desk.

"I'll do my best," he said.

Gallagher handed Stu a business card. Stu carefully placed it in his wallet.

Gallagher left the office without any further comments. As he walked down the corridor of the Rayburn House Office Building, Gallagher's own words echoed in his mind. He was no longer hiding in the background—a stranger asking questions about a real-estate and banking transaction that occurred twenty years ago. He had just become a recognized, defined entity—a person investigating the potentially criminal activities of a powerful United States congressman.

There was a target on Gallagher's back, and he knew it.

# Chapter 48

Six o'clock on Saturday morning, December 3.

Jimmy Nolan's hands were shaking. Was it the booze he had consumed the night before? Or, were his nerves just getting the best of him? He poured some cold water into the back of his coffee maker, dumped a few scoops of coffee in the filter, and flipped on the switch to start the brewing. Maybe he'd feel better after he got a couple of shots of caffeine into his system.

Still dark outside, and only one dim light was glowing in his apartment. His eyes were barely half open. No way he could handle a brighter room at the moment. Resting on the small table in front of the couch was a Smith & Wesson .357 Magnum revolver, Model 340, one of the smallest revolvers made by S & W. Its 1-7/8-inch barrel made it easy to conceal in a pants or coat pocket. Jimmy liked the way the gun was advertised: "maximum, dependable power in a small, lightweight package." He also liked the comfortable rubber grip and the black, matte finish. In fact, he had considered many other choices at the sporting goods store in Cambridge before deciding on this model that perfectly suited his needs.

Going back to his days in Vietnam, he had always been fascinated with guns. In fact, he had proven himself repeatedly as an excellent marksman. He was at his best with a rifle and personally preferred much larger handguns than this little dynamo, but the small size of the 340 offered many advantages for the purposes intended—especially when you relied on the element of surprise. The gun only held five rounds, but that would be all that he needed to complete this job. Actually, if he could just get control of his shaking hands, he would need only one or two rounds at the most.

Jimmy had carefully laid out his plan of attack. He had driven to West Castle on each of the past three days, parked his car in the area of Barry Nickerson's home, and watched for any activity around his house. He didn't have to wait very long to see a pattern. Every morning, between seven-thirty and eight o'clock, the garage door opened, and Barry slowly walked out to the driveway to pick up the morning newspaper.

Same routine every day.

An innocuous start, without a hint of danger or need to be on guard.

Jimmy surmised that Barry's three partners must have shared a similar sense of well-being on the days they were killed—never suspecting that someone was lurking nearby with evil intentions to bring about an end to their lives.

As he methodically loaded the shells into the revolver, Jimmy thought back to the pain and torment that he had felt for all those years since he was fired from the job as construction manager at the Parker Hill Medical Building. Everything bad that ever happened to him had started that day.

He lost his job, his family, and his dignity. Then, he found his only escape in alcohol. He had married the bottle, and it had been a love-hate relationship.

Three of the partners had already gotten what they deserved. He relished seeing the look on Barry Nickerson's face when he realized who was holding the gun that was pointing squarely at him.

Barry would suddenly know what this was all about—not just revenge; it was justice of the type you could only mete out personally.

# Chapter 49

The temperature was only in the low thirties. The dreary, gray cloud cover gave the distinct feeling that the first snowfall of the season could begin at anytime. At 7:15 AM, Jimmy Nolan parked his car across the street from Barry Nickerson's home on Evergreen Drive. The garrison colonial house was set back from the street by more than fifty feet and occupied a rounded corner lot that was protected from the busier main road by a row of tall, thick hedges. The large lawn in front of the house sloped slightly upward to the main entrance. A wide driveway to the left led to an attached two-car garage located a few steps below the level of the house. The morning edition of the *Boston Globe*, wrapped in a blue plastic bag, rested at the bottom of the driveway.

Jimmy nervously massaged the weapon in the right waist pocket of his jacket. He stomped his foot on the floor of the car when he realized that, in his haste to get to West Castle on time, he had forgotten to stop and fill his gas tank. The gauge registered near empty. He wondered if he'd have enough gas to get out of town and onto the highway heading north where he hoped to lay low for a few hours before driving home to his apartment in Somerville. Just in time, he thought, to catch the evening news and enjoy the shocking reports that another of the Parker Hill partners had been murdered.

*That poor bastard they have in jail will be celebrating tonight when the red-faced cops begin wondering if they're holding the wrong man. This will be sweet. Jimmy Nolan upsetting the old apple cart and throwing the whole town into chaos.*

Seven forty-five—still very quiet, with hardly any street traffic. No activity at Barry Nickerson's home. Jimmy's feet were cold. He squeezed his toes back and forth to try to keep them warm. A jogger, clad in a light blue, hooded sweat suit with a Tufts logo on the front, ran past the Nickerson home and out to the main street. Jimmy took his eyes off Barry's house to watch the jogger turn up the street and disappear behind the hedges. When his gaze returned to the house, the automatic garage door had already opened. Barry Nickerson, wearing a pair of brown work pants and a navy blue winter parka, had emerged from the garage. He walked down the driveway to retrieve the newspaper.

Jimmy's heart pounded as he got out of his car. He left the door ajar. He walked purposefully across the street toward Nickerson. As he moved closer, his right hand slowly came out of his jacket pocket and lifted the .357 Magnum so that it aimed directly at his unsuspecting target.

Barry, oblivious to the approaching danger, bent down to pick up the newspaper. When he straightened up, his first glance caught the barrel of the gun pointed straight at him.

His initial, defensive instinct was to hold the thick newspaper, full of ads and sale brochures, in front of his face to shield himself from the bullets. But his eyes looked past the gun to the face of the man holding it—a face he not seen in many years, but one he instantly recognized.

"Jimmy, you old fool, what the hell are you doing?" Nickerson blurted out.

"Just gettin' even, Barry. Just gettin' even for what you did to me. I worked my ass off for you guys, and you screwed me. You never gave me a chance."

Jimmy's voice cracked with emotion.

His body trembled.

His finger alternately started to squeeze and release the pressure on the trigger, trying to decide what to do, but apparently unable to force himself to discharge the gun.

Barry stood frozen, now helpless to think of any action that could deter his crazed attacker.

Suddenly, a blow of enormous power to his blind side sent Jimmy Nolan's body crashing to the driveway.

His right arm flailed wildly upward.

He fired a bullet harmlessly into the air.

The jogger had circled back on Evergreen Drive, and, coming upon the scene of a murder in progress, had hit Jimmy with a cross-body block that would make Bill Belichick smile.

The gun fell to the ground.

The jogger wrestled Jimmy onto his stomach, pinned his arms behind his back and leaned on him with all his strength and weight. Jimmy struggled mightily, but he was no match for the athletic young man who had overpowered him.

The jogger yelled to Barry, "Grab that gun and call the police. I'll hold him right here."

Barry, at first immobilized by the shock of what had happened, sprang into action, picked up the gun and ran into the house to dial 911.

Jimmy Nolan writhed on the ground gasping for air. His forehead bled profusely from the impact against the driveway. His arms felt like they were being broken as they were twisted and forced up towards his neck.

For Jimmy Nolan, there was neither revenge nor justice today. The real torment in his life had just begun.

# CHAPTER 50

At ten o'clock on Saturday morning, Gallagher looked out from the large bay window of his seventeenth-floor condominium at BayView Towers. No sign of the sun. The dense, gray clouds sent a message that fall was over in New England. A depressing thought to Gallagher, a person with seasonal affective disorder.

He had taken a late plane from Washington the previous night and didn't get home until close to midnight. He expected to fly back on Monday morning to meet with Jack McKissock, the private investigator who worked for the Democrat Party.

He had just finished his second cup of coffee when his cell phone rang. He flipped open the phone and the message "Incoming: Randi Stockdale" appeared on the screen.

"Hey, Randi, every time you call, it seems you have some earth-shattering news. What is it this time?"

There was no amusement in her voice when she responded, "Gallagher, have you seen the morning news reports on television?"

"No," he said. His back straightened as he sensed the seriousness of her call.

"There was an attempt on Barry Nickerson's life this morning at his house. A guy named Jimmy Nolan, who used to be a foreman for the construction company that built Parker Hill, tried to shoot him in his driveway."

"You've got to be kidding me!"

"Wish I was. Luckily, Barry is alright—just a bit shaken up.

Jimmy's in custody at the West Castle police station. Can you believe what's happening here?"

"Jimmy Nolan? Never heard his name mentioned before. What can you tell me about him?" asked Gallagher.

"He was the construction foreman for Forgione Brothers—the company that built the Parker Hill Building. They caught him drinking on the job and then the partners found out he had been submitting fraudulent invoices. He pleaded his case to the owner, but the partners insisted that the company fire him. Far as I know, that's the last time anyone ever heard from him."

"Have you spoken to that friend of yours in the police department?"

"No, but if I find out anything, I'll let you know. Bye."

The phone clicked. She hung up before he could ask any other questions. His interactions with Randi always left him wondering.

Gallagher turned on the television and flipped the channel to NECN news. After a few minutes, the news anchor turned the camera over to an on-the-scene reporter for the continuation of a breaking-news story.

The reporter stood in front of the West Castle Police Station and dramatically relayed the story: "In a bizarre twist in the West Castle murder case, early this morning police arrested a man who attempted to assassinate one of the surviving partners of the real-estate group that built the Parker Hill Medical Building. This brings into question the case of Mickey Ryan who has already been indicted for the murders of two of the partners. Ryan is currently being held without bail in the Middlesex County jail. We are awaiting a statement from the West Castle police chief and will bring it to you live as soon as further information is available."

Gallagher went into his kitchen and poured more coffee into his mug.

*Jimmy Nolan? How does he fit into this? Could he possibly know Congressman Prendergast? Does he have any connections to Las Vegas? What about Randi?*

He still wasn't sure he knew everything about her part in this whole scenario, but had to admit that her willingness to keep him updated on the developments in the case was earning her some points on his scorecard. He was certain it would all come out eventually; but would it be too late? Now that another one of the partners was almost killed, would the partners be willing to open up and tell him what they were hiding?

Gallagher stared out at the peacefulness of the Boston harbor below. He sipped on his coffee, hoping some ideas would spring into his head. He wondered out loud to himself, "Okay, Mr. Private Eye—where do you go from here?"

# Chapter 51

It didn't take long for Tom Tackage to sort out the confusion of Jimmy Nolan's attempt to murder one of the Parker Hill business partners. The West Castle police chief held a press briefing on Sunday morning and reported the results of several hours of intense interrogation. The chief stated that a despondent Jimmy Nolan acknowledged that he had been enthusiastically following the news reports about the murders of the first three partners—hoping that the killer would eventually kill all six. When Mickey Ryan was arrested and put in jail, Jimmy felt it was his responsibility to pick up where he had left off and finish the job.

Jimmy also confessed that he had been contemplating taking action against the partners for years, trying to seek revenge for their unfair treatment when he was fired as construction foreman at the Parker Hill Medical Building. The gun he intended to use on Barry Nickerson had undergone ballistics tests that confirmed it was not the weapon used to kill Drs. Becker and Evans. Furthermore, the police had no reason to suspect that Jimmy Nolan and Mickey Ryan knew each other or were involved in a plot to murder the six partners. Their actions were being viewed by the police as completely independent criminal acts and would be prosecuted in that manner.

Thus, the case against Mickey Ryan would proceed to trial as scheduled, and the arrest of Jimmy Nolan would have no effect whatsoever. Mickey Ryan's status remained the same: held without bail at the Middlesex County jail.

Gallagher attended the news briefing, having been tipped off about the time by Randi Stockdale. Her contact within the West Castle police department was proving to be valuable. When the chief had finished his comments, the crowd of reporters began to disperse. There were only a few questions. The situation seemed pretty cut and dry—a downtrodden, unemployed alcoholic, who had an ax to grind with his former employer, attempted a copycat murder and was foiled in the act by a courageous passerby. It was a good story for the Sunday newspaper and a chance for the jogger, who prevented the murder, to enjoy his moment in the limelight.

As Gallagher made his way to the exit at the back of the room, he came face to face with Jack Hoskins who was standing by the doorway.

"You know, Gallagher, your presence at every event related to this murder case has got to be considered more than a coincidence. What's your angle?" asked Hoskins.

"Nothing, Detective," deadpanned Gallagher, "Just an interested citizen watching the police do their job."

"Are you still harboring the foolish notion that we've arrested the wrong guy for those murders?"

Gallagher looked at him with a wry smile and asked, "Tell me, Jack. Are you a betting man?"

"What's that supposed to mean?"

"I'll bet you dinner for two at the Four Seasons Hotel in Boston that Mickey Ryan walks out of jail a free man within six months."

Hoskins grunted and then became quite animated, "Oh, I'll take that bet, Mr. Hotshot. How 'bout we also include the drinks? After all, I'll want to make a toast that I was right about your incompetence."

"You're on, Detective. I'll send you my address when Mickey gets out." Then, he leaned toward Hoskins—his face just inches away from his tormentor. He lowered his voice almost to a whisper, "I usually order the chef's tasting menu. It's outrageous!"

With that final comment, Gallagher turned and walked out of the building, leaving Hoskins with his mouth ajar.

Gallagher drove out of West Castle to meet Kate for lunch and then spend the rest of the day and night with her before leaving in the morning for another trip to Washington. Tomorrow's meeting with Jack McKissock had better open up a few more doors and give him some leads.

Gallagher's time was running out.

He was afraid that the killer might slip away.

# CHAPTER 52

The sign on the door read "Capitol Private Investigative Services." Gallagher studied it for a few seconds, thinking that Washington, D.C., known for its corruption and scandals, was certainly a place with plenty of things to investigate. He opened the door, walked in, and introduced himself to the receptionist.

"Oh, yes," she said, "You're here to see Mr. McKissock. Follow me." She led him back to the last office in the hallway, then stepped aside as her arm pointing into the room, "You can go in; he's expecting you."

Gallagher entered the room to see a man, about sixty years of age, sitting behind his desk. His tortoise-shell reading glasses rested precariously near the tip of his nose as he appeared engrossed in reading some papers in front of him. He wore a French-blue shirt with the collar open, and his matching yellow-and-blue tie was pulled off to one side.

He hardly looked up at Gallagher as he uttered the words, "Have a seat. I'll be right with you."

Gallagher sat down in the chair in front of the desk and studied the man for a few seconds: black and silver hair, thinning and slicked back on the sides; long sideburns accentuating the jowls of his cheeks.

*Something tells me this guy is a real character!*

Finally, his host looked up from the papers and extended his hand across the desk to his much younger visitor.

In a deep voice, he said, "Gallagher? Jack McKissock."

Gallagher leaned over, shook his hand and was about to speak, but the older man took the initiative.

"Tony Mac says you can be trusted; that's good enough for me. Also said you've been investigating a real-estate partnership in Massachusetts. After Tony's call, I decided to go back and review some of my notes on that group. We were looking at them, too. They've had their share of excitement in the past few months, haven't they?"

"Yes, they have. Three of them are no longer with us, and someone tried to kill a fourth partner two days ago."

McKissock looked surprised, "I knew about the first three, but haven't heard about the other one. What was that all about?"

"Nothing that really pertains to the case; just a former construction foreman who had too much to drink and decided he was a self-appointed vigilante on a mission to finish the job started by someone else. All he's going to get for his trouble is six to ten years for attempted murder. The poor bastard should have had some counseling before he went after somebody with a gun."

Gallagher glanced at the papers on McKissock's desk and shifted gears, "But I'd be interested in knowing why you were looking at that group. Were they in some kind of trouble with the Feds?"

"Not sure, but they could have been. We were hired by the Democrat Party to look into deals involving the Banking Committee going back to the time when the FDIC took over the loans from the failed S&Ls. There were thousands of loans to be settled; some of them slipped through the cracks; others got sweetheart deals. At the center of the chaos was one man who seemed to capitalize on the opportunities before him—Bill Prendergast."

"I'm not surprised."

"I hear ya'. His interest in helping businessmen find a way to satisfy their obligations to the government seemed to go well beyond the usual civic duty we see in Washington."

"What an American!"

"Right! We need more people in Congress like him," he laughed. "Anyway, the word from old staffers, who worked for the FDIC, was that he was relentless in pursuing some of these overdue loans. Then he would miraculously work out a compromise plan to satisfy the principle. Sometimes it would involve writing off some of the interest and penalties, but he would argue that it was more important for the government to get back the principal and not take a loss on the loan. Considering how many millions were being lost because of bad loans to companies that went belly up, you really couldn't disagree with that logic."

"Any proof that he ever took a payoff?"

"No. No one even suggested it."

"Weren't the administrators at FDIC keeping an eye on deals like that?" asked Gallagher.

McKissock waved his hand in a scoffing manner.

"They were so swamped with paperwork and phone calls that no one noticed what the hell was going on. They were just happy to have some cases settled."

"So what made you focus on the group from West Castle? What made them stand out?"

"Well, we couldn't access all the old files. But, of the cases we were able to review, we actually found about five deals that looked suspicious; one of them was the group in West Castle. They all had the same pattern: no payments or activity on their loan for a year or two, and then all of a sudden...," McKissock paused and his deep-set brown eyes widened. Then he slowly said, "The loan was paid off in full with all interest and penalties forgiven."

Gallagher seemed perplexed by the whole story.

"Wasn't any rationale provided for writing off the interest and penalties?"

"No, and that's the problem in trying to prove any wrongdoing. None of the documents we came up with contained any narrative or explanation of the methodology used in arriving at the settlement terms. It looked very fishy, but without someone coming forward, it was impossible to prove that any laws were broken."

"So what did you do?" asked Gallagher, anxious to get to the conclusion.

"Well, we played a little poker, figuring that we had nothing to lose. I sent one of my guys up to Boston to visit the partners in that West Castle real-estate group. Did the same with those other four deals that caught our attention. He informed them that we were hired by the Democrat Party to examine the possibility of corruption and bribery related to some old FDIC loans. He also informed them that the statute of limitations did not apply to cases involving bribery of a government official. So if evidence was found against them, they could be convicted and serve serious jail time. However, if they were willing to come forward and provide proof that an elected official accepted money to reduce the amount of their financial obligation to the government, we would intercede to help them gain immunity from prosecution."

Gallagher slumped back into his chair and rolled his eyes upward, feeling like a percussionist had just banged a pair of cymbals in his head.

*The meetings—the meetings,* he thought to himself. *That's what those secret meetings were all about. The partners were wrestling with the choice between gaining immunity from prosecution by coming forward and testifying against Prendergast or stonewalling the investigation by claiming they did nothing wrong.*

McKissock stopped talking and looked across at Gallagher who appeared dazed in his seat.

"Are you all right?" he asked.

"Oh yes, excuse me," said Gallagher, straightening himself up in his chair. "I've been trying to figure something out for the past three weeks, and you just spelled it out for me in about thirty seconds. But, go on. What happened after your guy spoke to the partnership?" asked Gallagher, having composed himself again.

"Frankly, nothing. Nothing at all. We could never get them to admit to anything."

"Did they talk much to your guy? Give him any clues as to what they were thinking?"

"No, they were coy about everything. He told them that we were looking, willing to dig deep, and that eventually we might find something. Our position was simple: wouldn't it be easier for you to cooperate and not take a risk of going to jail? But they denied doing anything illegal and just politely listened to what he had to say. I'd have to say, from what I heard, they were pretty cool about the whole thing."

"Weren't you at all suspicious when Dr. Becker and then Dr. Evans were killed?"

"At first, when we got the news, we thought that somebody took drastic action to keep them quiet. We got on it right away. But then we spoke to the detective from the West Castle PD who was running the investigation, a guy named Hoskins. He assured us that they had arrested the killer and that he had absolutely no connections to anything in Washington. Seemed to be someone who was settling an old score against the partners. Hoskins effectively told us to bug off."

"Sounds like Hoskins," said Gallagher. He let out a groan.

"Yeah, he sounded like a real pain in the ass, but he had a point. We were hired by a political party, not the federal government. He didn't have to tell us a thing. Since then, nothing else has happened; there has been no word about that investment group or any of the other deals we studied. I'd have to say that the trail is dead. If the Democrats were relying on this to embarrass Prendergast and force him to resign, they're going to be disappointed. There is no hard evidence that he did anything illegal."

McKissock shook his head as a sign of surrender.

"Do you think Prendergast got wind of your investigation?"

McKissock laughed.

"This is Washington, my friend! The president has a hard time keeping private meetings with the secretary of state out of the newspapers. What makes you think we could keep something like this quiet?"

He paused to laugh even louder at his own comment, his ample belly bouncing up and down. Then he acknowledged, "Yes, I suppose it didn't take Prendergast very long to know all about our investigation, and I'll bet he wasn't happy."

Gallagher continued his discussion with Jack McKissock for another half hour, sharing his belief that Mickey Ryan was innocent and that there was still much more to be determined about the role of Congressman Prendergast in the murder of the West Castle partners.

"So where do you go from here?" asked McKissock.

Gallagher shrugged and shook his head, "I guess from a technical point of view, you could say my assignment is over. I was hired to find out why the partners were holding secret meetings and what was causing Dr. Becker to act so depressed and worried in the weeks before he was killed. You just answered those questions this morning. So when I get back to Boston, I'll have a meeting with Mrs. Becker to give her the full report. Then I'll see what she wants to do with it. The key now would be to get one of the partners to talk. If that happens, we could turn the information over to the FBI, put pressure on Prendergast, and then maybe find out who really pulled the trigger."

"That's a long shot, for sure," warned McKissock. "Those guys have shown no tendency to start talking. Each one of them must be afraid that he'll be the next victim."

"You're probably right."

Within a few minutes, Gallagher was on his way back to the Hotel Washington. Until he met again with Suzanne Becker, there seemed to be little else to do in Washington. Gradually, the pieces of this puzzle were falling into place; he finally knew why the partners needed those secret meetings without Randi Stockdale in attendance to record the minutes. They were debating a problem about which they wanted no paper trail, no witnesses. For them, it was a choice between an admission of guilt, public humiliation, and professional embarrassment or a claim of innocence with the risks of indictments and possible jail sentences.

In the end, however, Gallagher wondered what made them targets for murder? Why were they chosen over some of the other suspicious deals that Jack McKissock's team had uncovered? Suzanne Becker may be satisfied just to know what had been troubling her husband; she may come to the conclusion that this information is too inflammatory to allow it to become public through any further investigation.

For Gallagher, it was an entirely different story. He knew he couldn't stop here and leave so many unanswered questions. An undeniable force kept pulling him into this case: *Three men have already been killed. I'll bet Congressman William J. Prendergast knows where I could find the murderer.*

# Chapter 53

Back at his hotel, Gallagher packed up his travel bag for his return flight to Boston. He was eager to see Suzanne Becker in person. He didn't feel comfortable giving her the information he had learned from Jack McKissock over the telephone.

The case was clearly circumstantial—no proof actually existed. Yet all signs pointed to the likelihood that her husband's real-estate partnership had bribed Congressman Prendergast to gain his assistance in reducing their loan to the FDIC. Suzanne Becker's reaction would undoubtedly be one of shock and disappointment. Gallagher wanted to be with her to offer any emotional support she needed. But how she would react to his intention to continue searching for the real murderer?

Gallagher's thoughts were interrupted by a call on his cell phone from a Washington number he didn't recognize. When he opened the phone and answered, the voice on the other end was quiet, almost hushed.

"Gallagher—Stu Tane here. Something's come up that I think you should know."

"Sure, Stu. What is it?"

"We had a meeting scheduled tonight with several other congressmen and their aides. We were supposed to go over some important issues related to the upcoming committee hearings on the casino proposal. Bill would never put off a meeting like that; he's too much of a control freak. But, an hour ago, he got a call and then abruptly came in to my office. Told me to cancel it and said something urgent came up at home that he had to take care of—some kind of family issue. Then, after he left the office, I noticed something on his desk that didn't fit with his story. He has an unconscious habit of doodling notes on a pad while he's on the phone. On a small notepad on his desk were the initials "LT" and right below it, "Gerard's 7."

"Gerard's 7?"

"Yes, Gerard's Place. It's a restaurant on 15th Street, Northwest; do you know where it is?"

Gallagher listened intently, focusing on all the details of Stu's call. He was so distracted by something Stu said, he almost forgot to respond—then caught himself and said, "No, but I'll find it. Thanks Stu; I really appreciate your calling me. I know this wasn't easy for you. Thanks again."

With those final words of gratitude, Gallagher clicked off the phone. He sat down on the edge of the bed, leaning forward with his head resting in his hands, his elbows tucked into his knees.

*LT—LT? Where have I heard someone use those initials before?*

Then, it came to him. He stood up and excitedly paced around the room. His mind churned with random thoughts, all coming together to a startling conclusion.

*Jimmy Galdieri, the bookie from Malden, told Mickey Ryan that LT had asked if he carried a gun. LT must be a major-league figure in Las Vegas who had been asking about Mickey Ryan's gun just weeks before it was stolen. The same gun used to kill Dr. Becker and then Dr. Evans! Now LT is having dinner in Washington with Congressman Prendergast, just a few days after his chief of staff tells him that I've been making inquiries about him.*

Gallagher flipped his travel bag over the closet door and unzipped it. He began to unpack his clothes and hang them carefully in the closet. He checked his digital camera and made sure it was charged.

Another night in Washington? Not such a bad idea after all. Taking some pictures of the patrons dining at a restaurant known as Gerard's Place?

*This could be a very revealing evening.*

# Chapter 54

The ambiance of the small restaurant was hardly elegant or ostentatious. In fact, it was rather understated in its décor. The simple, straight-backed chairs had a rectangular lattice pattern near the top. Except for a few paintings and several floor lamps, the white walls of the main dining room gave almost a stark appearance. Gerard's Place was not about appearances; it was all about the food. The extraordinary French cuisine served in this restaurant was among the best in Washington, D.C. Certain dishes, such as the poached Maine lobster and the sautéed sea scallops, were considered classics among fine-dining cognoscenti.

Gerard's Place was not a restaurant for noisy gatherings or the raucous drinking crowd but rather a place for quiet conversation and formal service while enjoying delicious food. For the man sitting alone at the corner table for two in the rear of the restaurant, those were the prerequisites for tonight's meeting. He loved dining in restaurants where you could enjoy a bottle of wine with a friend and the specialty of the house was a meal you could savor for weeks. The man with a tanned, ruddy complexion, that revealed his penchant for living in a warm climate and sitting in the sun, carefully studied the menu. He interrupted himself only occasionally for a sip from his glass of 2004 Gruner Veltliner Terrassen Federspiel, a lighter-styled white wine that was suitable for almost any choice of food. A man in his mid-sixties, he was a formidable figure—his broad shoulders and heavy arms still retained their muscular appearance, but his bulging waistline betrayed his love of food and the need for more exercise.

He was dressed impeccably. His polished black Armani shoes, black shirt, silver cuff links, and perfectly tailored, gray sport jacket highlighted his thick, white hair. As he held the menu in his left hand, his right hand, bearing a large, beautiful, blue sapphire ring, lightly tapped on the table as if he were gently keeping time with the background music. On the chair next to him rested a black leather briefcase engraved with the simple monogram, "LT."

The arrival of his dinner companion interrupted his perusal of the menu. He quickly moved the briefcase to allow his guest to sit down next to him. Both chairs were placed so the men could sit in the corner with their backs to the wall, looking out to the dining room. They preferred to sit this way, never having to worry that someone behind them could lean over to listen in on their conversation.

Congressman William J. Prendergast pulled his chair in close to the table and looked at his dinner mate with a serious expression on his face.

"Glad you could make it so soon," he said.

His companion put down his menu, studied him attentively for a few seconds as if analyzing his frame of mind, and then smiled broadly, "Hey—relax, Congressman. You look like you've seen a ghost. What's the problem?"

"A private eye has been snooping around and asking a lot of questions. He came by my office and spoke to my chief of staff, trying to get a meeting with me. Says he's checking into the West Castle real-estate deal and the settlement with the FDIC," explained Prendergast nervously.

"So what's new about this? Didn't those investigators hired by the Democrats do much of the same thing? And they got nowhere, right?"

"Yes, but this guy had access to Dr. Becker's cell phone and found my number on his call list. He's probably got phone records that show I talked to Becker. Something tells me he's not going to go away easily. You know, some of these guys keep digging until they find what they're looking for."

The man sitting next to Prendergast calmly folded his hands on the table, undisturbed by the worries of his dinner companion. He spoke in the manner of a teacher lecturing to a pupil who had forgotten to do his homework.

"When we first laid out our plans, didn't I ask you if there were any old skeletons to deal with? Anything that might cause you some political embarrassment? Didn't we take care of them for you?"

He didn't wait for an answer but continued along with his point.

"We're on the brink of some very important business. No amateur private eye is going to get in our way. So don't worry; we'll take care of this character. He won't cause you any problems."

The man took another sip from his glass of wine, letting his taste buds slowly enjoy the flavor. Then, it was his turn to take on a serious look.

"Tell me, have you gotten complete control of that committee? Anyone threatening to break ranks and vote against you?"

Prendergast shook his head emphatically side to side.

"No, I still have enough votes to beat it down. There have been some last-minute promises that I've had to make to hold a few of them in line. But I don't think there'll be any defectors before the vote is taken."

The man leaned closer to Prendergast.

"Now, listen carefully. We can't have any doubts about this. I'm a betting man, but I only believe in sure bets. There can be no risks here, only zero tolerance for losing that vote, do you hear? If there is anything you need to do in order to absolutely guarantee that vote, you have to do it. If it takes money, you let me know. Got it?"

The last two words were spoken with a bluntness that could only be interpreted as a threat. Prendergast clearly understood the message and nodded his head in acknowledgment.

The rest of the hour was spent in idle chatter, with more attention being devoted to the food being served than the heavy business matters at hand. Congressman Prendergast became more at ease as the calming influence of several glasses of wine took effect and relaxed his entire demeanor. At the end of the dinner, the gray-haired man picked up his cloth napkin, wiped his mouth, laid the napkin on the right side of the table, and then rested both hands calmly on the table again. He opened his hands toward Prendergast with a gesture asking for help.

"So where do we find this private detective you're so concerned about?"

Prendergast reached into his suit pocket, took out a business card, and placed it on the table in front of his host.

The man stared at it for a few seconds and then said, "Gallagher? Another Irish guy? Have you noticed how many of these private eyes are Irish; it must be something in their blood. Well, don't worry; this guy won't be causing you any more problems."

The man reached down to the floor, picked up the narrow briefcase he had placed there earlier, and slid the business card into a small pocket on the front. A few minutes later, the waitress brought the dinner check. While the man waited to settle the bill, Congressman Prendergast shook his hand, got up from the table, and left the restaurant alone.

The well-dressed, dignified, older gentleman sat at his table, idly looking around at the few patrons who remained on this quiet Monday night in this little restaurant with exquisite food. He could easily have been mistaken for a corporate executive, a prosperous attorney, or perhaps a highly-paid Washington lobbyist. His fingers slowly guided the business card out of the small pocket of his briefcase. As he studied the inscription on the card, no one could have guessed that he was a calculating, ruthless businessman whose agenda would not be denied.

No one could have guessed that he was about to issue an order for murder.

# Chapter 55

Gallagher had positioned his rental car in a parking space about three cars down from the front of Gerard's Place. From this vantage point he could see everyone who entered and left the restaurant. He saw Congressman Prendergast arrive alone just before seven o'clock and then hail a cab at approximately 8:20 PM when he had finished dinner. The patrons who left Gerard's Place were all in groups of two, three, or four diners, except for one man with white hair, wearing a black topcoat, who emerged from the front door at eight thirty. He casually looked around the street, stepped to the curb, and signaled to a cab waiting at the traffic light at the corner. Within a few seconds, he had gotten into the back of the taxi and was driven away.

Sitting on the passenger side of the front seat of the leased Chevy Malibu, Gallagher had a great view to get photos of both the congressman and the white-haired man as they waited on the sidewalk in front of the restaurant. Since no other patrons had departed the restaurant alone, he had to assume that this distinguished looking man was the mysterious LT who, to this point, was only known by his initials.

Gallagher waited for a few more minutes, then walked into the restaurant and looked all around as if trying to find someone. The hostess saw him from the entrance to the kitchen and immediately came over to him.

"*Bon soir.* May I help you, sir?" she asked with a French accent.

"Capitol Limo," deadpanned Gallagher, "Was called to pick up a fare at 8:20; I've been waiting for fifteen minutes, but no one's outside. The guy only gave dispatch his initials, 'LT.' Anybody here with those initials?"

The hostess walked behind her podium and looked over the reservation book, using her index finger to help scan down the list. She stopped by one of the names, and then looked back to the corner of the dining room where the small table for two was vacant.

"That would be Mr. Lan Tauber, but he and his guest have already finished dinner and left the restaurant. I believe you may have just missed him," she said, almost apologetically.

"Yeah—guess he got a ride from someone or decided to walk. These things happen to us all the time; thanks anyway," he said as he turned quickly and walked out the door, not wanting to engage in any further conversation or have another customer offer to be his next fare.

Once in his rental Gallagher carefully jotted the name on his notepad. He stared at it for a few seconds.

*Okay, LT. Looks like I need to find out all about you.*

# Chapter 56

Back in Boston the next day, Gallagher drove out to Suzanne Becker's home for a meeting at noon. When she had hired him, she had asked for the whole truth. Today was not the time to sugar-coat the facts.

As with his first visit to this house, she was at the door when he arrived and invited him into the cozy sitting area in the living room. Between the two love seats in the room, the rectangular ottoman was covered with a large black serving tray that held a pitcher of iced tea, two glasses, an assortment of cookies, about six neatly arranged fresh strawberries, and a small stack of black napkins.

Suzanne Becker looked elegant as always. Sitting on the edge of the love seat across from him, she wasted no time getting to the point.

"I've been nervous for two hours waiting for you to arrive; I feel like you have some important news for me," she said.

"Yes, I met with several people in Washington and think I know why your husband and his partners were having those secret meetings in the weeks before his murder," said Gallagher.

He waited for a response.

Nothing.

She simply stared at him, her mouth half-open, suddenly appearing like a person dreading the results of a medical test.

Then she inhaled deeply and replied, "Go on."

"As I told you the last week, your husband's cell phone contained a number on the speed dial list. The number of a Congressman from Pennsylvania—Congressman William Prendergast. The congressman refused to see me, but I was able to meet with his chief of staff, a guy named Stu Tane. To make a long story short, Prendergast denied ever knowing your husband and put on an emotional tirade when Stu brought up the subject of the Parker Hill Medical Building and the loans with the FDIC. But Prendergast blurted out your husband's name before Stu ever mentioned it. So, Stu knew he was lying."

Suzanne listened intently, her eyes fixed on Gallagher as she tried to absorb all of the details.

Gallagher continued.

"I also met with a private investigator who was hired by the Democratic Party to look into the activities of Congressman Prendergast and his relationship to the FDIC loans."

"I'm sorry," she said, "but I don't know much about these loans."

Gallagher paused for a few seconds as he tried to convey this next part as gently as possible.

"It seems that your husband and his partners may have paid money to Congressman Prendergast in exchange for his help in reducing the loan commitment on their building. Once the investigators from Washington told them they were looking at that transaction, the partners had to decide whether they wanted to turn state's evidence against the congressman or risk the possibility of an indictment for bribery."

Suzanne Becker had held her emotions intact, but tears welled up in her eyes when she heard the word, "bribery." She looked down at the floor for a moment, her right hand dabbed at the corner of her eye. Then she looked across at Gallagher.

"Jonathan would never have done anything illegal. There must be some misunderstanding."

"I wish I could say there was, but everything I've learned seems to lead to that conclusion. And I suspect that when they finally made their decision to tell the truth, someone made sure they didn't talk."

No matter how hard he tried to soften it, he knew that the impact of this disclosure would be hard to handle.

She looked away, shaking her head, her voice trembling as she spoke, "This is all so bizarre—a nightmare; who would have thought that these things would happen? Even that crazy man who tried to kill Barry the other day. Could this all be the result of a bribe to one congressman? It seems there has to be much more to the story."

Gallagher leaned over closer to her.

"You're right; there is much more. It all ties into a dramatic change in the multibillion-dollar gaming industry. This same congressman is in charge of a committee that is deciding whether places like Las Vegas, Atlantic City, and Biloxi will have major competition from federally sponsored casinos on former government military bases. There are huge dollars at stake. The established gaming sites will do anything to keep their friend, Congressman Prendergast, in charge of that committee. If he had to face questions about taking bribes and his credibility was in jeopardy, he'd be forced to resign. That could change everything."

Mrs. Becker wiped away her tears and seemed to regain her composure as she listened to Gallagher's explanation. He went on to tell her about his covert surveillance at Gerard's Place where Congressman Prendergast had dinner with the mysterious gentleman from Las Vegas who went by the initials, LT. By coincidence, this same man was reported to have expressed a curious interest about whether Mickey Ryan carried a gun.

Gallagher didn't have to complete the picture; the look of resignation on Suzanne Becker's face told him that she grasped the interconnection of all the characters and now fully understood the undeniable danger that these people posed.

"Shouldn't you immediately take this information to the police?" she asked, but her words were more of an admonition than a question. "The people who killed my husband didn't know who you were before, but now they do! They'll be coming after you. You have to protect yourself."

"I'm still not ready to go to the police. Frankly, at this point, I don't trust the police to handle this the right way. I have to give them a solid case, one that is flawless, so they have no choice but to arrest and prosecute the real killers and anyone who may have ordered the murders."

Gallagher's words were emphatic.

"Besides," he pointed out, "Congressman Prendergast may know that I've been checking on him, but Mr. LT has no idea I'm aware of his identity. I'd rather keep it that way until I find out a little more about him."

"So, if you don't contact the police, where do you go from here?"

"I want to meet with Mickey Ryan and his lawyer again. Maybe Mickey has some information about LT that his friends in the underworld can provide. And Randi Stockdale—she's on my list for another visit."

"Randi? Do you think she could be involved in all of this?"

"Well, she seems reluctant to tell me everything she knows. There's something about my conversations with her that always leaves me wanting more."

"I don't know what to say," she said. "This is all too much to fathom."

As she walked him to the door in the atrium to say goodnight, she reached her hand out to his. Then spontaneously, she moved closer, put her arms around his shoulders, hugged him and kissed him on the cheek.

"Please be careful. I'm worried about you. You're much more than just someone I hired."

At first Gallagher was somewhat taken aback by her affectionate gesture, but he understood that they now shared a common interest and a bond that would never be broken.

"Don't worry. I won't take any wild chances. I'll report everything

I find to the FBI as soon as I have enough information for an airtight case."

Gallagher got into his car and headed back toward his office. As he drove down Route 2, across Alewife Brook Parkway and then on to Storrow Drive toward Boston, his mood had become decidedly upbeat.

*I'm finally getting close to putting this all together.*

# Chapter 57

It was a clear and sunny December day in Las Vegas, but the temperature was only in the low 60s and certainly not a day for sitting by the pool. For Johnny Nicoletti, it was a great day for a late lunch, a chance to relax, read a good book, and be thankful that he no longer had to put up with the icy, cold winters of the Northeast. His hired date from the previous evening had already left his suite.

He had just finished his morning cup of coffee. His phone rang. He picked it up—nothing. The familiar pause let him know who was calling.

After a few seconds, a voice said, "Johnny, I need to see you this morning. I'll be over at eleven."

"Okay, I'll be here," he replied.

Johnny had come to recognize the relative importance of upcoming assignments simply by their method of delivery. For most of the small jobs, those with little risk and involving some simple scare tactics, Jerry Murray would give Johnny his instructions over the telephone. For anything major, situations in which the offending party needed a brutal, physical lesson to get a message across, Jerry would come to Johnny's suite and deliver his orders in person. The tone in Jerry's voice and the urgency to see him this morning told Johnny that this assignment was something big. He took a shower, got dressed, and then waited for his guest to arrive.

Jerry Murray rang the doorbell just before eleven o'clock. He was dressed sharply as always, wearing a black, crew-neck cotton sweater, black pants, and an ice-blue sport coat. He came into the suite and immediately sat in the swivel arm chair to the right of the couch. He folded his legs and let his hands hang off the edges of the arms of the chair. His signature blue sapphire ring on his right hand sparkled from the halogen spot lights in the ceiling and the sunlight that came through the large windows overlooking the Las Vegas Strip.

"Can I get a drink for ya', Jerry?" asked Johnny.

"No, Johnny."

He waved him off with a flip of his right hand. Johnny took a seat across from him, knowing that no further time needed to be wasted on pleasantries.

The well-dressed older man seemed to be the picture of elegance, composure, and class with his perfectly combed, white hair and highly polished, black Armani shoes. He started speaking, slowly and deliberately, to make sure there was no misinterpretation of his words.

"Johnny, I've got a job for you back East. You're going to have to do some traveling again. There's a private detective who's been nosing around into our business. He's trying to make trouble for us. We need to get him out of the picture—permanently."

He paused after the last word to guarantee that his message had fully registered.

Then he added, "And I mean permanently."

Johnny simply nodded a few times to acknowledge that he understood the intent of the order.

The white-haired man continued, "You need to arrange a terrible accident; something that doesn't draw too much attention outside the area. If you can't do that, you have to at least make this character disappear for a while. Maybe they find him a few months from now—whatever—I don't care. We need him out of the picture soon, before he causes any problems."

Johnny continued listening, dutifully nodding his head in agreement with the objectives being outlined.

The older gentleman then reached into his jacket pocket, took out a business card, and flipped it across the glass topped coffee table as he said, "That's all I've got on this guy for now, but I'm sure you'll be able to find him."

Johnny picked up the card, stared at it for a few seconds, pushed out his lower lip, shrugged his shoulders and said, "No problem, Jerry. You know me. When it comes to these jobs, I've got no match. I'll start making my plans right now."

The older man stood up and adjusted his sport coat to smooth out the lapels.

With no expression on his face he said, "Good, Johnny. I always know I can count on you. I'll be in touch. You'll let me know when it's done." Then he reached into his pocket, took out a thick, white envelope and handed it to his host. "You'll be hearing from me soon, Johnny."

The man that Johnny knew as Jerry Murray walked to the door and left the suite.

Johnny Nicoletti opened the envelope and fanned the thick stack of hundred-dollar bills that were neatly aligned inside. He smiled.

*More than five grand as a down payment! This guy must be really causing trouble. I'm gonna put an end to that.*

# CHAPTER 58

Gallagher and attorney David Gorkin cleared through security at the Middlesex County Jail.

"You know, you're awfully close to proving that your theory is correct," said Gorkin. "But that last link is going to be the hardest. How will you prove that Prendergast or an accomplice from Las Vegas actually gave the order to murder the partners?"

Gallagher shrugged.

"I don't know yet. If I can find some information about Tauber—who he is and what he does in Las Vegas—I could take it to the FBI. They've got much greater resources for checking travel records, bank accounts, and phone calls. They may be able to put the final pieces together and get someone to talk."

Soon, the door to the meeting room opened. Mickey Ryan, looking haggard and in worse physical condition than at their first jailhouse meeting two weeks ago, walked into the room. As the security guards took off his leg irons, Gallagher noticed that Mickey's eyes were puffy and bloodshot. He looked like he hadn't slept in days.

The guards left the room.

"Hey, Mick. Looks like things are pretty tough for you here," said Gallagher.

"Well, the food sucks and I can't sleep at night because of all the noise. Other than that, this place is great. What've you been doin' to get me the hell out of here?"

Gallagher moved closer.

"Actually, Mickey, I found out a lot of things that can help you, but I need to learn more about that guy, LT, who was asking Jimmy Galdieri about you. I think he's the one who set you up for the murders."

"I told you before; I don't know nothun' about that guy. I just heard Jimmy Gal mention his name," said Mickey. He waved his hand in the air to indicate his annoyance at having to rehash the story.

Gallagher pressed on, "I know that, but could you get some word out to your friend and let him know that this guy, Lan Tauber, holds the key to your release from jail? Maybe he'll be willing to help you."

"Not likely."

"Look, Mickey, if I can locate Tauber, I may be able to tie together the plot to frame you and identify the real killer of the partners in West Castle."

David Gorkin had been sitting quietly listening to the dialog between his client and Gallagher. Then he interjected, "Maybe I could go to see Mr. Galdieri and speak to him on Mickey's behalf and try to impress upon him how critical his help will be. He might listen to me."

Gallagher leaned back in his seat and motioned to Mickey, indicating that he approved of his lawyer's suggestion.

"All right," said Mickey, "but I doubt that Jimmy Gal will talk. Besides, he may not even know where to find the guy, himself."

Mickey looked over at Gorkin.

"Check around Tiel Square. He hangs out around there. Just ask any of the locals—they all know Jimmy Gal."

"Tiel Square? I know it well. I'll find him," said Gorkin. Then, Gorkin turned to Gallagher and said, "I'll need a few days. A guy running a bookmaking operation might take awhile to place his trust in me—especially when I'm asking him to finger a high-ranking member of the Las Vegas syndicate."

Two security guards arrived to escort Mickey back to his cell. Mickey ambled out of the room. The door closed with a loud shudder.

As Gallagher and Gorkin walked out to Thorndike Street, Gorkin looked up to his younger friend and asked, "If I find out how to reach LT, are you sure you want to go to Las Vegas and handle this on your own? Maybe this is the time to back off and turn it over to the FBI. You'll be up against a tough bunch of characters. They'll view you as a threat. They wouldn't think twice about eliminating you."

Gallagher stopped and put his right arm around the older man's shoulders. "Thanks, David, but I'm afraid that money rules in this case. I don't want too many parties getting involved and having the chance to bury the truth in exchange for a payoff. No, I'm going to have to do things on my own for a little while longer. Don't worry, my friend—I'll be all right."

# Chapter 59

At seven o'clock on Thursday morning there were only a handful of people waiting in the arrival area in Terminal B at Logan International Airport. America West Flight 66, the red-eye from Las Vegas, had landed on time at 6:53 AM. The passengers were beginning to make their way up the long walkway to the left of the security check-in area.

A tall, husky man wearing a black ski jacket and a navy-blue New England Patriots cap stood near the end of the walkway. Nick Roberto had done this same pickup several times already, so he knew the routine: The passenger would only have one carry-on suitcase; there would be no need to wait at the baggage claim area; as soon as they left the airport, they would drive to Three Yolks Breakfast and Lunch in Revere where the scope of the assignment would be discussed and the plans to carry it out would be formulated. Then, the passenger would crash at Nick's apartment for a few hours to get over his jet lag and adjust to Eastern Time.

Nick Roberto, a hired thug with a rap sheet as long as a yardstick, had moved to Boston from New York five years ago. He had numerous arrests for assault and carrying an unlicensed weapon and had served three years in prison for his part in the robbery of a delivery truck. His specialty was money laundering and the sale of hijacked merchandise, but he was also good at collecting debts for bookies and loan sharks. He was a tough guy who loved the action—it was the "juice" that kept him going. When he got the call from his old friend from New York, who was now based in Las Vegas, he jumped at the chance to pick up another big payday.

As the passengers filed by, looking half asleep from the overnight flight, Nick looked on without interest until a brown-haired man with a deeply tanned face slowly approached, carrying a black suitcase in his left hand and a black leather jacket over his right shoulder. The two men acknowledged each other with no words, only a quick nod. Nick reached out and took the passenger's suitcase from his hand, led him through the terminal and out to the parking garage.

Johnny Nicoletti had arrived in Boston with a single purpose in mind—to make sure that Daniel Cormac Gallagher Jr. had investigated his last case.

# Chapter 60

Two days had gone by. Still no word from David Gorkin.

Gallagher had tried to get the inside story on Lan Tauber from several of his contacts in Las Vegas, but no one had ever heard of him. He was not listed in the telephone directory; not a member of any board of directors; not a part owner or developer of a casino; not listed as an owner of real estate in Las Vegas County. He was officially a nonentity. Gallagher's hunch told him otherwise.

*As soon as I saw Tauber walk out of that Washington restaurant after his meeting with Congressman Prendergast, I knew he was a major player in the West Castle murders. Now I've just got to prove it.*

The investigation was at a standstill. Gallagher could do nothing until he got the information he needed. He felt paralyzed by the dormancy that had been forced upon him. He had been so absorbed with the implications of the case that he had hardly spoken to Kate in the past several days.

She had left a message on his cell phone: "Hey, Mr. Private Eye, if I'm supposed to be the woman you love, how come you never call me?"

The thought occurred to Gallagher that if Mr. Gorkin came through with some leads, it was likely that he would be in Las Vegas for much of the next few weeks. This would mean more time away from Kate just when they should be together for as much time as possible. The feelings of guilt were beginning to affect him. He contacted Kate at her office.

"Sorry I've been out of touch. This West Castle case has gotten control of my mind. I feel like I'm running in mud and going nowhere fast."

"I figured there had to be a reason why you haven't called me. You need to get away from it for a while. Is there any chance we could be alone for a few days? Maybe then you can escape some of the pressure and return with a fresh look at it," she said, sizing up the situation in an instant.

"Well, I'm actually in sort of a limbo status—waiting for some leads to develop," he replied, considering her proposal as he spoke.

She wasted no time jumping on his availability.

"Then this is good timing. How about if I arrange a little getaway for us? I'll find a romantic setting."

"You're getting me wildly interested."

"How about that area you visited a few weeks ago? I hear that the Woodstock Inn in Vermont is a great spot. What do you think of that, big guy?" she asked teasingly.

"I'm always up for an idyllic setting with a sensuous woman. I could be convinced to go."

"Well, let me check with my travel agent to see what I can arrange. I'll call you back in a few minutes."

"Okay, I'll be here," he said as he hung up the phone.

Gallagher was unaware that two men had positioned themselves outside his office on Commercial Street. They knew his car and the address of his condominium at Bay View Towers. They had plans to monitor his every move until the time was right for them to strike.

# Chapter 61

In Washington, Congressman William Prendergast seemed distracted as the briefings continued in the small House conference room. A group of twenty people, representing members of the Joint Committee on Economic Development and Emerging Technologies, listened to economic reports on the tax implications of the proposed conversion of closed federal military installations into resort casinos. Since Congress was not officially in session, many of the senators and representatives had sent their senior staffers to gather the data prior to the beginning of the public hearings and eventual vote in February.

Prendergast had felt uneasy for the entire week, fearing that some TV newsman would shove a microphone in front of his face and ask him how much he knew about the West Castle murder case. However, the week had passed rather uneventfully—his sources in the Washington grapevine had no new rumblings to report.

He was beginning to think that he may have cleverly survived the encounter with his chief of staff and the inquiries of the private investigator from Boston. The rest was up to his friends in Las Vegas. They had their ways of solving these delicate problems in a masterfully efficient manner.

As he presided over the briefing, his mind wandered between the facts being presented and visions of the future. The actual committee convened and voted in just eight weeks. He had secretly made all the arrangements for favors and payoffs and was sure he had the votes to win no matter how the hearings proceeded. It didn't matter how much tax revenue would be generated or how vociferous the arguments became for the benefits of added competition and expansion of the free-enterprise system. Prendergast was supremely confident that he would overcome all of these obstacles.

In the end, he could convince his constituents in Pennsylvania that he was acting in the best interests of the country by fighting against the corruption that would accompany an expansion of the gambling industry. He was on the verge of ultimate victory—about to deliver the most decisive vote of his congressional career, catapulting him to the brink of a personal financial triumph and setting himself up for life.

Prendergast was a man who was used to winning and willing to rig the odds in his favor to guarantee success. He would not allow anyone to get in his way or stop him from achieving his goal.

In his twisted, Machiavellian approach to self-preservation, eradicating a pesky private detective from Boston was just business as usual.

# Chapter 62

Gallagher arrived at Kate's house by ten o'clock in the morning. He tossed her small travel bag into the trunk of his car. After so many weeks of distractions, airports, and dead ends with the West Castle case, he was excited about the chance to spend the weekend with the woman who had become the most important person in his life.

They drove out of Boston on Route 93 North for almost an hour, passing into New Hampshire and through the toll booth in Concord. Except for the pines, the trees on the side of the highway were bare, having lost their beautiful color weeks ago when the leaves came down in the fall winds. The weather had been cold, but so far, no heavy snowfall.

A few miles north of the toll booth, they exited onto Route 89 North toward Vermont. The road was almost desolate; the lack of snow had kept the skiers at home, biding their time until the slopes had a thicker base of man-made snow and the conditions were less icy. As they drove up Route 89, they passed Stickney Hill Road near Exit Three. Gallagher looked into his rear view mirror at the empty road. Only one car could be seen, off in the distance, nearly a quarter of a mile behind them. Although he was driving at seventy miles an hour, the gap between the two cars closed rapidly as the car to the rear accelerated to a high speed.

He looked over to Kate and said, "Look at this cowboy coming up behind us. He must be going ninety!"

Kate turned around to her left, looked back through the rear window and said, "Oh, let him go by. It's just another idiot in a hurry."

The approaching car moved into the passing lane and came up next to Gallagher's BMW. Gallagher curiously looked over to see who was driving past. But the car suddenly slowed down to keep pace with him. Two men sat in the front of the car. The man in the passenger seat wore a black leather jacket. He glanced at Gallagher. The passenger window of the car was open.

The man extended his arm out of the window. His hand held a Glock 9mm pistol. Gallagher stepped on his brakes and turned his steering wheel to the right, trying to avoid the shooter.

His maneuver didn't help.

The man aimed directly at his left front tire and fired two shots.

The tire was destroyed in an instant blowout.

The combination of the blown tire and the sudden turning of the wheel sent Gallagher's car into an uncontrolled tailspin. He used all his strength to try to stabilize the vehicle, but the momentum generated by the centrifugal force was too great to overcome.

Kate screamed as the car slid wildly across the breakdown lane, spinning its way toward a violent ending.

The car careened over a wide ditch on the side of the highway and crashed into a tree on an embankment.

Gallagher felt his skin burn as the airbags exploded into his face, forcing his head violently backward against the neck rest. There was smoke, shattered glass, blood, and the smell of burning fuel everywhere.

Gallagher struggled to see what had happened. But he was pinned to his seat, unable to move his arms.

His head throbbed with pain.

He called out, "Kate—are you all right?"

An eerie silence now replaced the noise of the crash.

Smoke billowed through the inside of the car.

His eyes watered.

The force of the impact had seriously damaged the passenger side of the car. He could see nothing but an outline of Kate's body. He felt himself drifting into unconsciousness. He fought to stay awake, all the while shouting, "Kate—Kate—are you okay?"

No response; no other words were spoken in the burning car.

His brain was stunned by the powerful force of the crash. Gallagher could not resist the anesthetic-like fogginess that was overtaking him.

He slipped further and further out of reality, slowly and continually mumbling, "Kate—are you all right?"

Kate never answered his question.

# Chapter 63

The blue Mercedes sedan continued on the highway at a moderate speed, slowing down only briefly as the driver looked into his rear view mirror at the burning crash in the distance. The passenger had turned around completely in his seat, watching with great interest the scene of havoc he had created on the side of the road. His first instinct was to have the driver stop the car in the breakdown lane and reverse direction, allowing him to inspect the scene more closely. However, another car approached on the horizon behind them and posed an immediate threat of identification. So, he let his driver continue putting added distance between them and the crash.

The driver looked over at his passenger, "Nice shot, Johnny."

The passenger, now turned to the front of the car and, looking straight ahead, replied with a half-smile, "You know me, Nick. I never miss. I've had lots of practice."

Johnny Nicoletti continued staring straight ahead, his mouth partially open and his jaw locked in a rigid position. He seemed distracted and deep in thought.

Nick darted a few looks at him and finally asked, "You okay, Johnny?"

"Wanted to check that car to make sure they were dead."

"Have to be dead, Johnny. You saw the way their car blew off the highway into that tree. Look at all that smoke back there. They're fryin', man!" Nick exclaimed gleefully.

"Yeah, but I always like to be sure."

"That other car was comin' up fast behind us. He wudda I.D.'d us and gotten our plates and called the cops. No way we cudda gone back there."

Johnny shrugged his shoulders in terse agreement with his partner's rationale and stared blankly at the roadway ahead.

The two men had little to say to each other for the rest of their trip. They could have taken the next exit, reversed their direction and driven back to Boston the same way they had come. But they had no interest in passing the crash scene and possibly being stopped by the police. They continued on Route 89 North, passing over the Contoocook River, past Georges Mills, heading further north through New Hampshire. They pulled over to the side of the road just after Exit 12-A where Johnny faked making a stop to relieve himself. Instead he used his shoes to scrape a shallow hole beneath a pile of leaves in the woods. There he buried the gun. It was an unregistered piece that Nick had procured, but nevertheless, he was taking no chances in case they were stopped and searched.

They drove for almost another hour, sticking to the sixty-five mile-per-hour speed limit to avoid calling any attention to their car. Just past Lebanon, New Hampshire, they crossed the Vietnam Veterans Memorial Bridge above the Connecticut River and entered Vermont. Then they turned right on Route 91 and proceeded on a southern course toward Massachusetts—a long way to get back to Boston, but they didn't care.

This excursion took them far away from the gruesome scene that was miles behind them.

No hurry to return home.

For Johnny Nicoletti, it was another successfully completed assignment. As Nick drove the car, Johnny stared quietly out the window planning his next move.

*Think I'll go to New York tomorrow and hang loose for a few days.*

*I'll fly back to Vegas from there, just in case someone inspects the flight logs from Boston. That'll throw them off. Then I'm just gonna relax and enjoy the good life until Jerry calls me again. I'm the perfect guy for these jobs. Like I always say, there's no match for me.*

# Chapter 64

As Paul Slobozien, a seventy-five year old retired teacher and ex-football coach, turned onto Route 89 North on his way to his weekend winter home in Vermont, he had no idea of the physical and emotional challenge that awaited him, nor did he expect that the unlikely role of a hero would be thrust upon him.

As Paul passed Exit 2, he could see cloud of dark smoke about a mile ahead on the right side of the road. At first, he thought the smoke was the result of a forest fire, but as he drove closer, he could see that the smoke was coming from a car that had run off the road into an embankment on the edge of the tree line.

He sped up to get closer, expecting to see the driver standing somewhere away from the smoking car, possibly waving for help from a passing vehicle. But he saw no one near the scene of the accident.

He pulled his Lexus RX 330 SUV onto the shoulder of the road about twenty yards behind the disabled car, opened his door, and ran up the road. He stood directly across the ditch so he could see if there was anyone trapped within the smoking vehicle. He felt his heart beginning to pump forcefully as he saw the outline of two people in the front seats; neither person moved as the smoke and the powdered dust from the detonated air bags engulfed their bodies. He thought to himself that this accident had happened only minutes before he arrived.

He staggered down the ditch, half-tripping as he rushed. In the process, he twisted his ankle on the uneven terrain; then he struggled up the embankment to reach the front door of the smoking car. He could see that the driver was still breathing, moving his head from side to side as if trying to clear his head from the trauma he had just sustained. The passenger, a woman, did not move. The door on the passenger side of the car had caved in from a collision with a tree. Paul was sure he would be unable to open it. The only way to get her out of the car would be to first remove the driver and then drag her out, over the console, and across the driver's seat.

His first instincts reminded him that accident victims could have spinal cord injuries that could be worsened with the added trauma of forcibly removing them from a vehicle. But he was alone—no one else to offer help—and this car could catch fire and explode at any moment.

No time to waste.

He pulled open the front door, unfastened the driver's seat belt, and shoved his arms under the man's shoulders. He pulled him back and out of the car and dragged him on the embankment until a safe distance away from the car.

Then, he rushed back toward the smoking car, breathing heavily from inhaling the fumes and smoke and nearly exhausted from the sudden demands on his system. He climbed into the driver's seat and struggled to unsnap the seat belt of the woman whose face was covered with blood from a gash in her forehead.

He prayed for the jammed seat belt to open.

Finally, after several tries, the latch released. He first moved her legs to free them from the dented door panel that extended into the car. Then, with his back arched toward the roof of the car, and his knees resting on the driver's seat, he reached under her arms and gradually, but carefully, pulled her out of her seat, across the console between the bucket seats, and out of the car.

His energy was totally spent—his heart pounded and he could scarcely catch his breath.

Sweat covered his face despite the cold outdoor temperature.

He kept reminding himself that the gasoline tank could catch fire and explode, so he forced himself to continue. Mustering strength he had only known as a young man, he picked up the injured woman and carried her back to a flat area on the grass and laid her down on the ground.

Her pulse was weak. Although he was not a doctor, he could tell she was going into shock. He took off his coat and covered her, trying to maintain as much warmth as possible. He lifted her chin to maintain her airway.

"Hold on, lady—hold on—everything's going to be all right—you just hold on," he implored her.

A man in a ski cap ran across the road from the southbound lanes of the highway with a cell phone in his hand, and yelled excitedly, "I just called 911; an ambulance is on the way. They'll be here any minute."

Paul stayed with Kate as the man ran over to Gallagher, lying on the side of the embankment, and tried to offer some first-aid.

Fortunately, the man was correct; within minutes, the New Hampshire State Police, a fire truck, and an ambulance arrived. The three EMTs worked quickly to immobilize Gallagher and Kate on emergency carts and then hoisted them into the ambulance and prepared to take them to the hospital. The men worked frantically on Kate, trying to stabilize her breathing, stop her bleeding, start an intravenous drip, and keep her warm. In a few minutes, the rear doors closed. The ambulance drove off, sirens blaring and lights flashing, with a police cruiser as an escort.

Paul Slobozien leaned against the side of his SUV and watched the firemen extinguish the fire in the badly damaged car. It took them less than a minute to totally squelch the blaze that had erupted a short time after he pulled both of the victims out of the car. A state police trooper walked over, carrying the coat Paul had wrapped around Kate, and offered it to him.

"You okay, buddy?" the officer asked.

"Yeah—I'm all right; just tryin' to catch my breath," he said. "Haven't had a workout like that in a long time."

"Did you see how the accident happened?"

"No. I was just driving up the highway and saw the smoke. Looks like he had a blowout, lost control, then spun off into that ditch and hit the tree." He paused for a few seconds and then looked at the police officer. "Are they going to make it?"

"The guy should be all right, but the lady looked like she was in rough shape. She lost a lot of blood and might have internal injuries. They were lucky you got them out. They had no chance if they stayed in that car. For a man of your age that's pretty amazing. I'll be sure to give them your name if they pull through. They owe you a big 'thank you.'"

Paul gave his driver's license to the officer, who wrote down the information, in case there were any other questions in the future. About fifteen minutes later, a large flatbed tow truck arrived. The charred, almost unrecognizable BMW was pulled off the embankment and loaded onto the back of the truck. The truck and the last of the police cruisers drove away, leaving Paul alone at the scene, contemplating all that had transpired in the past hour.

Still somewhat shaken by the stress of the event but, except for a sore ankle, fully recovered from a physical standpoint, Paul got into his car and resumed his trip north toward Duxbury.

*God, I hope they make it!*

# Chapter 65

At first, the news from the phone call made Randi shudder—as if she had just received an electric shock from an exposed wire. She had to sit down because the next feelings that overcame her were those of weakness and nausea. The call had come from Suzanne Becker who had heard the news from Diane Beane after she was notified by the hospital in Concord, New Hampshire. Gallagher and a female companion were seriously hurt in an automobile accident. The car was totaled, and they were both in the hospital with significant injuries.

Randi Stockdale tried to deal with the waves of emotions that were coursing through her: shock, disbelief, regret, and now anger. She had to do something to put an end to this. Suzanne had said that Gallagher had been in an accident, but Randi knew better.

Someone had tried to kill him.

Initially, she had been afraid to divulge everything to the police and then, later, she hesitated to fully inform Gallagher. She feared being implicated in a scandal and was worried that she would be drawn into some type of legal jeopardy, possibly viewed as someone who was obstructing justice or, at worst, an accessory to murder. She couldn't risk going to jail for a criminal act in which she really had no part. So she tried to hide as much as possible without making her deception obvious.

In the beginning, she deluded herself with the thought that the murders of Jonathan and Dick were the work of some lunatic—a crazy person who had it in for the health professions or the doctors in the building. But after Phil's murder in Vermont and the arrest of Mickey Ryan, she realized that she had been used and preyed upon to provide the information needed to carry out ruthless plans. She knew that the people who had come to visit her had lied. They had threatened and scared her just to find out about the partners. Then that information was used to kill three of them and frame Mickey.

Now they were going after Gallagher. He must be close to discovering who they were and how they conspired together to keep the partners quiet and fool the police. She knew he was smart that eventually he might figure it all out. She had hoped that he would do it without involving her, sparing her the embarrassment of having to explain why she had not come forward sooner. That's why she had tried to feed him as much information as possible to keep him on the trail without ever implicating herself.

But now, all of those plans seemed misguided. She sat at her desk with her head in her hands.

*I've been so stupid!*

She may have put him at higher risk by not telling him everything; she was resolved to reveal everything now; to hold back nothing in the future and to help him get all the facts so he could find these vicious people and stop them from killing anyone else.

*I've got to speak to Gallagher—as soon as possible.*

# Chapter 66

The plastic bracelet that hung loosely around his wrist read "Daniel C. Gallagher Jr.," but the person lying in the bed hardly resembled the handsome forty-five-year-old private detective on his way to a relaxing weekend just twenty-four hours earlier with the woman he loved. His head was wrapped in gauze; his eyes were puffy and swollen, with black and blue marks below them; the scratches and cuts on his face were either covered with bandages or coated with a brown-colored ointment; his left arm was strapped to a board to prevent the intravenous line that was inserted into the back of his wrist from shifting; plastic-coated wires led from various points on his chest and abdomen to a group of monitors stationed to the right of his bed.

As Gallagher slowly opened his eyes, his first glance caught the rhythmical bouncing graph of the EKG monitor. Above it, the numbers"72" and "120/76" appeared on the digital readout.

*Considering the fact that I feel like I was just hit with a sledge hammer, it's good to see that my pulse and blood pressure are normal.*

He looked around at the rest of the semi-private room. The bed next to his was empty. The sight of the empty bed shocked his brain into reality. Now fully alert, he pressed the red rubber button that was attached to a long cord lying on his bed near his right arm. He noticed that a red light went on immediately above the door that was open to the corridor. In a few seconds, a nurse appeared at his doorway.

"Oh—Mr. Gallagher. I'm glad to see that you're awake. Are you feeling all right?"

Gallagher ignored her question and simply asked, "Kate—where's Kate?"

The nurse moved closer to his bed and leaned over near his face, speaking softly, "She's had a lot of surgery and blood transfusions, so they're keeping her in intensive care for awhile."

"I need to see her. When can I see her?" he asked, almost frantic to get a positive answer.

"Oh, you're not ready to be moved anywhere; besides she had quite a serious concussion on top of everything else, so she's still a bit out of it. The best thing for you is to rest up, regain your strength, and then we can take you over to visit her."

Gallagher reached out with his right hand. His fingers clutched the sleeve of the nurse's jacket. He pulled her even closer to him.

"Is she going to be all right? Is Kate going to be all right?" he asked, his tone demanding a direct response.

"From what I've heard, she's going to be fine; she just needs some time to recover. That was a serious accident you had out there on Route 89."

Gallagher relaxed his grip on her sleeve and leaned back on his pillow. His eyes welled up with tears from the report about Kate.

*Thank God she's still alive! But look what I've done to her!*

He stared up at the ceiling, unable to make eye contact with the nurse.

"Yes," he said, "It was a bad accident."

His thoughts went back to the events of yesterday afternoon. The face of the passenger who pulled up next to his car was fixed in his memory—the brown wavy hair, tanned face, and dark eyes. He remembered every detail of the sequence as the window of the blue Mercedes lowered, the man's arm extended out of the car, holding a gun and pointing it directly at his car. His recalled the adept way the man brought his left arm around to grip the gun with both hands, stabilizing it against the wind to ensure a straight shot at the target—a shot that Gallagher was unable to avoid.

The man could have easily fired directly at him instead of his tire and most likely could have killed him instantly. However, it seemed like he was more interested in causing the car to crash and to eliminate Gallagher without traceable bullets to the body by means of a violent collision from which there would be no escape.

*It was the guy who killed the West Castle partners.*

Just days after he had announced his presence in Washington and specifically questioned Congressman Prendergast's knowledge of the partners' loan payoff, a professional hit man had followed him toward Vermont to "arrange" a tragic accident. The timing of these events was too much of a coincidence to believe otherwise.

The orders to do away with him must have been hatched during the dinner meeting of Prendergast and Lan Tauber—two men with an apparent insatiable desire for wealth and no limits on the measures they would take to achieve it.

*I'm going to put those bastards away for life—especially for what they did to Kate.*

As Gallagher lay in his hospital bed, he continued to think back to the details of the crash. Surely, sometime in the next few days, the New Hampshire state police would be coming by to question him about the accident. How did it happen? What made him lose control of his car?

*Control. Yes—control. This is all about keeping control. If I tell them that some gunman shot out my front tire trying to kill me and make it look like an accident, then I lose control of this entire investigation; too many people will get involved and the whole thing will get botched.*

Gallagher knew that he was the only person who could bring an end to this case, the only person with the motivation and determination to see it through until all the guilty parties were arrested.

*When they ask, I'll just claim memory loss. I'll tell them nothing about the man in the other car. I'll say that I only remember trying to keep the car from spinning off the road. Next thing I knew, I woke up in the hospital. No—no one else is going to take over this case. That guy missed his chance to kill me, and he almost killed Kate. The next time I see him, I'll show him how to handle a gun.*

# Chapter 67

Five days later, Gallagher and Kate were still in Concord Hospital. Remarkably, their physical and medical condition had decidedly improved. Gallagher, in fact, was near ready for discharge, and his head was now completely cleared after his concussion. His variety of cuts and lacerations were well on the way to healing.

Kate, however, needed a few more days to recover from her more serious injuries. The force of the impact on the passenger side of the car had caused trauma to her spleen that resulted in internal bleeding. Combined with the bleeding from her other superficial and head injuries, she had significant blood loss. She required several transfusions followed by emergency surgery to remove her damaged spleen. Despite the scope of the trauma, her prognosis for an uncomplicated, long-term recovery was excellent.

Their first reunion since the accident occurred in the intensive care unit, when Gallagher, still somewhat unsteady on his feet, was brought over to see Kate by one of the nurses. Although weakened by all that she had gone through in the past three days, Kate clasped his hand firmly as if she never wanted to let it go. He realized that she had shared a similar fear—not knowing if he had survived and wondering if she would ever see him again.

"I'm so glad that you're alive," she said, as tears streamed down her face. "The nurses kept telling me you were okay, but I was afraid they were just saying that until I got better."

"Don't worry. I'm here, and we're going to stay together for a long time," he said, returning her firm grip on his hand, and leaning over to kiss her tenderly. All the trauma and anxiety of the past five days poured out as their emotions took over. They were two people united again with bright hopes for the future rather than facing the pain of trying to endure life without the other.

She looked up at him after a few minutes and asked, "What happened? I remember the car coming up next to us; then you were turning the steering wheel away. I remember putting my hands in front of my face because I could see us spinning toward the tree. I was so scared."

The horror of recalling these events sparked a new outburst of emotions. She began crying again.

He bent down, kissed her forehead, stroked her cheek gently, and tried to comfort her as much as possible. He could tell from her question that she had not seen the gun and did not know that the accident was actually an attempt on his life. He also thought it would be best, at least for the time being, not to tell her what really had happened. She would be too fearful for his safety and want to inform the police; certainly that could only hinder the work he had to do.

He answered her question by simply saying, "That car began drifting to the right. I turned the wheel trying to avoid a collision. But we got into a spinout, and I couldn't control it. The guy never even stopped to see what happened or to help us. I wish I could remember more about his car so I could report it to the police."

Fortunately, Kate accepted his explanation and continued to clutch his hand, happy to be united with him once again now and, hopefully, forever. Later in the day, he told the same story to the trooper from the New Hampshire State Police who came to the hospital to interview him about the accident.

It went against his grain to be less than truthful about the events on the highway three days ago, but there were too many issues that he had to resolve by himself. He couldn't allow anything to deter him from his goal.

Eventually, the truth would be told, but only after Gallagher discovered the identity of the man who had tried to kill him.

And most importantly, who had hired him to do it.

# CHAPTER 68

Several days later, Gallagher drove back to his office in Boston in a Ford Taurus that he had rented until he settled with his insurance company and found time to buy a new car.

Diane greeted him as he walked through the door. She hugged him warmly. Her eyes grew misty.

"What a relief to see you! I've been so worried. Are you all right now?" she asked.

"I'm fine, Diane. Don't worry," he replied, trying to reassure her. "It was just an unfortunate accident. Kate's going to be fine. We were both lucky. It could have been a lot worse."

He treated Diane like a member of his family. At this point he'd rather spare her from the rest of the sordid details.

He poured a cup of coffee and walked back to his private office. Diane had a stack of mail and messages waiting for him and, in her usual manner, had them piled according to the priority she established. Interestingly enough, she always seemed to be right about the relative urgency of things.

Conspicuously at the top of the stack was a message from Randi Stockdale: "Call me as soon as you're well enough to speak. Important."

Just below it was a message from David Gorkin: "Hope you're recovering; call me when you can. I've got some news from Jimmy Galdieri."

Diane called Randi. She agreed to drive down to the office

without delay. Less than a half-hour later, she was in Gallagher's office with a paper cup of coffee in one hand and a brown leather notebook in the other. Diane escorted her back to Gallagher's private office where he sat behind his desk. Randi slipped off her coat and put her coffee and notebook on the desk. She looked concerned.

"Are you all right?" she asked. "It must have been pretty scary."

"Yeah, it was an unexpected turn of events, to say the least," said Gallagher, wondering what had prompted her to drop everything and so urgently request to see him.

"I guess we can both assume that it was no accident," she said.

Gallagher looked at her, trying to measure her intent. At first, he did not want to acknowledge her assumption and let her be the first person in on his secret. But he recognized that she was finally about to open up to him. He replied with an emphatic nod.

"Yes, it was no accident. In fact, I believe quite a bit of thought went into it."

Randi moved to the edge of her seat and leaned toward him. Her eyes filled with tears.

"Listen, Gallagher, there is a lot I haven't told you or anyone else. It's time I came clean on this whole thing. Five months ago, two guys came to my office without any warning. Said they were from Washington and were investigating a case involving the partnership and their loan payoff years ago to the FDIC. They also said they had uncovered some serious improprieties about the way the loan was handled and that the partners were going to be indicted under federal racketeering statutes. They told me if I cooperated with them, they would make sure that I received immunity from any charges. As the business manager of the group, they said I could be implicated as a co-conspirator. I was really shocked. They caught me totally off guard, and I was afraid not to cooperate."

She stopped for a few seconds to take a sip from her coffee. Her hand trembled slightly, but she exhaled deeply after she swallowed. She appeared relieved to be finally getting this story off her chest.

Anxious to hear more, he asked her, "So then what happened?"

"I told them everything I knew about the partnership and how it operated. They wanted to know when it was formed, how the partners acquired the land, where they lived—a lot of the same stuff I told you when you first came to my office."

"Did you happen to tell them about Mickey Ryan and his old dispute with the partners?" he asked with a knowing look, fully expecting the answer to be "yes."

Randi put her head down and nodded.

"Yes, I did. That must be how they got the information to set him up as the fall guy for the murders. I knew it when he got brought in by the West Castle police. I felt so stupid for having fallen for their act. When they were in my office, I panicked, and I never even asked them for any identification. They just looked so official and scary; I fell for it."

"Then what?"

"After they left my office, I didn't say anything to anyone. I knew the partners had been having those secret meetings and figured they were deciding how to handle their problems. One night, at the end of one of the meetings, I went into their conference room to discuss some business with the group. I overheard Barry saying to Jonathan, 'Maybe the immunity deal isn't such a bad play for us after all.'"

"Did they know you overheard that?"

"Yes. Jonathan stared at Barry with a look that would kill and waved him off as if to say 'Shut up!' So I assumed they were wrestling with some decision about how to proceed and didn't want anybody to know about the problem, including me."

"And you never pressed the issue?"

"No. After Jonathan's murder and then Dick's, I was so stunned that I didn't relate their murders to the meetings or the visit by those two characters to my office. Like everyone else, I thought some lunatic was responsible."

She paused, then took another sip from her coffee.

"But when Phil was murdered in Vermont, you knew that someone was trying to systematically eliminate the partners," said Gallagher.

"Yes, I was sick about it. I hoped you would be able to figure out who was responsible, and maybe I could stay out of it and never be connected to what happened. It was so dumb. I should have told you and the police everything I knew from the start."

Her voice trailed off as she considered the alternatives and shook her head.

"Do you remember what the two guys looked like? Could you identify them in a police lineup?"

"Oh, yeah! I could never forget those two! One of them was a tall, husky guy—dark hair, combed forward, and down toward his eyes. He didn't say very much. The other guy did most of the talking. He had brown wavy hair, about five feet ten inches tall. Now that I think of it, he had a pretty good tan for a guy from Washington. They told me their names were Jess Kane and Butch Tesini; I wrote them down as soon as they left my office, but now I'm sure they were bogus."

Gallagher jotted the names down on his notepad, but agreed that they were probably phony. He focused strictly on the description of the second man, who was apparently the same man who had tried to kill him on the highway.

"So where do we go from here?" he asked, almost rhetorically.

Randi was quick to answer.

"I know the remaining partners have refused to talk to you, but I spoke to Dan Oblas in Florida and explained the whole situation to him. He's willing to see you and to tell you about their meetings. He agrees that this has to end. Too many people have been killed or hurt. We can't let this go on any more. If you can fly down to his place in Florida, he can spend as much time as necessary to give you the information you need. He insists on seeing you in person."

There was no hesitation in Gallagher's response.

"Tell Dr. Oblas I'll be on the first flight out of here tomorrow morning; I'll be there by early afternoon."

Gallagher could picture a noose around Congressman William J. Prendergast's neck, and he had just pulled it a little tighter.

# Chapter 69

Randi Stockdale had only been out of his office for less than a minute when Gallagher was on the phone with attorney David Gorkin.

"David? It's Gallagher, I got your message. What's up with Jimmy Galdieri?" he asked, not wasting any time on friendly banter.

Gorkin, however, with his usual unfazed approach, was not interested in rushing into anything without satisfying his own curiosity about the recent travails of his new friend.

"First, tell me about yourself. How are you doing? Was that an accident up north, or were the 'big boys' we talked about a few weeks ago trying to silence another critic?" he asked.

Gallagher could picture the twinkle in the old guy's eyes as he asked the question to which he already knew the answer.

"I'm okay now, and, you're right—it was not a spinout on a patch of ice. But that's between us. Officially, at this time, it's considered a motor-vehicle accident caused by an unidentified passing car that cut me off the road. I'll provide all the details at some time in the future."

Gorkin laughed.

"I can't wait," he said.

"More importantly," asked Gallagher, "what's the deal on Jimmy Galdieri? Did he talk to you?"

"Yes, it took some time, but he eventually met with me. We had a very pleasant conversation until I brought up the name of Lan Tauber. Then he got sullen, very defensive, and didn't want to say very much. I told him that this guy was the key to getting his friend

Mickey out of jail and off the hook for murders he didn't commit. He came around a little, but emphasized that he was never to be quoted or cited as the source of this information."

"You know it's safe with me."

"I do. Jimmy said Lan Tauber is in charge of special operations for the casino syndicate in Las Vegas. No one quite knows what that title means, but certainly nobody ever wants to cross the guy. He didn't know how to reach him or where his office in Vegas is located. He thinks the guy tries to keep a pretty low profile and only surfaces to deal with something referred to as 'special problems.' He has never spoken to him, but one of Jimmy Gal's gambling associates out there told him that 'LT' was making inquiries about a guy in Massachusetts named Mickey Ryan. That's when he heard the question about whether Mickey was known to carry a gun."

"Will it do any good for me to talk to him?"

"I doubt it. I believe he told me everything he could. I think it's enough information for an agency like the FBI to locate this guy without any problem. I'm sure he's not listed in the phone book, but they'll get to him in a hurry if they want to."

"Okay, David. Thanks for the update. I'm on my way to Florida."

"Florida? What for?"

"One of the tight-lipped partners has decided to speak to me."

"It's about time."

"Yes. Should be interesting. I expect to be back in Boston in a couple of days with enough information for the Feds to indict Prendergast."

"Ahh—maybe then we'll know the real murderer?"

"Right."

Gorkin paused. A long silence. Then he spoke in a slow measured tone.

"Now keep your eyes open. These guys already tried to kill you and make it look like an accident. Next time, they'll just try to kill you straight up with no fooling around. So don't take any chances."

"Thanks, David. I always appreciate your concern for my well-being. I'll be in touch when I get back from Florida. Tell Mickey to hang in there a little longer. I've got an expensive dinner riding on his early release," he laughed as he put down the phone.

Gallagher got up from his desk and stood by the window in his office looking out at Boston harbor. The water was calm and peaceful—unlike the events he expected to unfold in the very near future. He knew that Gorkin was right. The people who wanted him to die in the accident were probably aware by now that their plan did not succeed. They would be coming after him again to finish the job and to make sure that he did not reveal any of the facts he had uncovered and to keep the lid on a story they wanted no one to know.

Gallagher was confident that this time would be different; the man he could picture so clearly in the passenger seat of that car—the man with the wavy brown hair, tanned face, and dark eyes; the man who tried to kill him and injured Kate—that man was in for a surprise of his own.

# Chapter 70

The beautiful, young woman rolled over in bed. The sheets barely covered her legs as she moved, exposing most of her naked body. Eight o'clock in the morning—too early to get up after a long night of work, so she wanted to continue to sleep until she would be forced to leave. The man close beside her was wide awake and, lying on his back, lit another cigarette while occasionally admiring the natural beauty cuddled up next to him.

This seemed to be the perfect start to another great day for Johnny Nicoletti, who thought to himself that this woman had definitely earned a repeat performance. She would be at the top of his list the next time he was in the mood for a little night music.

The telephone rang and interrupted his daydream. He almost chose to ignore it, but realizing that the price he paid for this luxurious life was being on-call 24/7, he reached over the buxom beauty beside him and picked up the phone. The brief pause at the other end of the line told him immediately who was calling.

"Johnny, are you alone?" the voice asked.

"No, I've got a little company," he replied.

"Well, get rid of her fast," the voice demanded impatiently. "I'm coming over in an hour."

Johnny knew the basic rule imposed by Jerry Murray: he must always meet him alone and he demanded complete privacy. No one else could be present to hear any of their conversation, or, for that matter, even get a look at Jerry. He insisted on being a nonentity to everyone except Johnny. Frankly, from Johnny's standpoint, it didn't matter. Whatever Jerry Murray wanted was fine with him.

Johnny nudged the sleeping beauty beside him.

"Time to leave, Sugar."

She rolled over and opened her groggy eyes.

"What?"

"Time to leave."

"Why?"

"Important business. Have to get ready for a meeting. You've gotta be out of here."

"You just don't appreciate me," she mumbled.

Nevertheless, she got out of bed and began to put on her clothes. Johnny lay back on his pillow and took in the sight. Within ten minutes she had left.

Johnny got dressed, drank a cup of coffee, and waited for Jerry Murray's arrival. His doorbell rang almost exactly an hour after Johnny had received the phone call. Jerry came in and walked from the door to his usual seat in the swivel chair near the couch, looking back only to be sure that Johnny had closed and locked the door.

He was all business today.

He did not look happy.

He stared harshly at Johnny for a few seconds and then finally spoke, "What's the matter, Johnny? Are you losing your touch?"

Johnny was taken aback by the question.

"Whaddya' mean, Jerry? What's the problem?"

"That last job I gave you—the private eye in Boston—I told you to take care of that guy, didn't I?"

Johnny blinked rapidly, becoming more defensive at this point, not knowing where his employer was leading with his questions.

"I did it just the way you asked, Jerry. I arranged an accident for him on the interstate. I saw his car burning on the side of the road after he hit a tree. Nobody came out of that crash alive. I'm sure of it."

Jerry mocked Johnny's last sentence by raising his eyebrows and inhaling forcibly, “So, you’re sure of it? Did you go back to see the dead body? To see that guy burned to a crisp!” he yelled.

His voice reached a higher decibel with each spoken word.

“No, Jerry. We had to get the hell out of there before someone got our plates. That guy had to be dead,” protested Johnny, pleading his case.

“Well, he’s still alive, and I’ll bet he’s asking more questions than ever.”

Jerry stood up from his seat and walked over to Johnny, who rose to meet him eye to eye. Jerry’s demanding voice bellowed through the room as he raised his right hand—the hand with the distinctive blue sapphire ring—and pointed his index finger into Johnny’s face in a threatening gesture.

“Look! I want that guy out of the picture for good. No excuses. If you want to keep this nice place you have here and all the girls that come with it, you better not mess this up again. Hear me?”

With that final admonition, the white-haired man walked over to the door, unbolted the lock, and left the room. Johnny Nicoletti’s demeanor quickly changed from stunned surprise to one of anger. No two-bit private eye would be the cause of losing this wonderful life he had in Las Vegas. He wouldn’t allow it.

*No—no way. That son of a bitch may have survived the car crash, but he won’t live to see another Christmas.*

# CHAPTER 71

As Gallagher turned into the main entrance of Bonita Bay, the combination of nature and man-made beauty made a strong impression. Having left the cold and December dreariness of the Northeast just hours before, the lush green fairways of the golf courses and palm trees lining the roadway of this all-inclusive retirement community were a refreshing change of scenery. After he checked in at the security gate, he thought he had arrived at his destination; however, the high-rise towers were almost three miles away. As he drove down the winding road that led back toward the beach, he marveled at the beautiful complex surrounding him: five championship golf courses, restaurants, magnificent homes, a marina and private beach, and a health and fitness center.

He pulled into the parking lot in front of the high-rise towers and, after entering the outer lobby, pressed the button next to the name Oblas.

A few seconds later, a woman's voice answered, "Mr. Gallagher? I'll be right down."

While he waited, Gallagher looked through the outer glass panels at the main lobby of the building. He was certain it would take a lot of cases for a private investigator to pay for a place like this. The elevator door opened after a few minutes, and a thin woman wearing a white warm-up suit and gold jewelry walked over to the outer lobby door and opened it.

"You must be Gallagher," she said, "My husband is waiting for you."

He was surprised at the familiar greeting but assumed that Randi Stockdale had prepared them very well for his arrival.

They rode the elevator to the twenty-first floor, exchanging small talk about his flight and the weather in New England. She opened the door to the condominium and escorted him into a beautiful living room with a ten-foot high ceiling and a Tommy Bahama décor. The room was also decorated with artificial green ferns of various sizes, all planted in coordinated ceramic pots, a white, semi-circular sectional couch with large, inviting soft pillows, and a colorful, patterned green rug that all combined to create a wonderful tropical atmosphere. The furthest wall in the room consisted of large glass windows with views of the Bonita Bay community, a golf course, Estero Bay, the beach, and the Gulf of Mexico.

"Pretty impressive view," said Gallagher. He looked all around. "In fact, it's breathtaking."

"Glad you like it," observed the man in a reclining chair to the right of the room.

Gallagher had missed seeing him when he walked in. Now, almost embarrassed by the oversight, he walked over to him.

"You must be Dr. Oblas," he said extending his hand. "I really appreciate your offer to talk to me."

"No problem; welcome to sunny Florida. Just call me Dan. I'd get up, but I'm still recovering from my hip-replacement surgery. The surgeon tells me it should be completely healed by now, but he forgets how old I am. I used to be young like you, but now, as you can see, I'm on the back nine."

Gallagher welcomed the opportunity to engage in some friendly banter.

"Hey, you don't look so old to me, and I hate to tell you but I'm not as young as you think."

"Well, you look to be middle aged to me, and that's not so bad; the only problem with middle age is that you outgrow it," he said.

Then he laughed at his own wit.

Gallagher immediately liked his self-deprecating, friendly host and took a seat across from him so they could begin their conversation. Dan Oblas was in his early seventies with thinning gray hair— a retired radiologist and one of the original partners in the development of the Parker Hill Medical Building. Although he stopped practicing medicine five years ago, he maintained his share in the real-estate holdings of the group and often flew to Boston for business meetings with his partners. He started their discussion by letting Gallagher know he had been given some background information.

"Randi told me about your accident. Very unfortunate. You're lucky you came out of it alive. And your passenger? Was that your wife?"

"No, not my wife yet, but I hope soon," he said.

"I hope you get your wish on that. Is she alright?"

"Yes, thanks; she's still in the hospital, but getting better every day. Her parents are with her now. I expect she'll be coming home in a few days."

Oblas' wife, Phyllis, entered the room carrying a tray with iced tea and a small collection of delicious looking pastries. Famished from not having eaten lunch, but embarrassed to say so, Gallagher was grateful for the hospitality and immediately reached for the chocolate covered delicacy in the middle. "Thank you," he said, "these look wonderful."

"You've had a long trip," she said. "You need a little something."

She then excused herself, stating that she was going down to the club for a tennis lesson.

"You guys have a lot to discuss; you don't need me around."

Dan waved to her and then squirmed carefully in his chair, trying to find a comfortable position for his hip. He exhaled deeply as he began to speak.

"This whole thing has been unbelievable and taken on a life of its own. Who could have ever predicted that these things could happen? All because of an overdue loan? Isn't that incredible? A goddamned overdue loan!" he exclaimed, shaking his head in disbelief. "And three people end up dead; others get hurt. Who could have known?"

He held out his arms and then dropped them into his lap in despair.

Gallagher sat back in his chair, knowing that he was about to learn the answers to the questions that had been dogging him for weeks.

"Why don't you take me back to the beginning? How did all of this get started?" he asked, taking out a small notepad so he could keep track of every detail.

Dan proceeded to relate the entire history of the partnership, most of which Gallagher already knew. But he was not about to stop Oblas; he wanted to hear everything.

When the building was nearly completed, the savings bank that loaned the partnership the money for the construction went into receivership—a type of bankruptcy where all the bank's loans were taken over by the FDIC. Oblas explained how the partnership asked Randi Stockdale to find out where the payments were to be sent and who they could contact regarding their loan balance. However, the FDIC appeared to be in chaos, and no one could give her the information. No mortgage bills arrived. Phone calls to the FDIC went unanswered.

"We wanted to stay current with our payments," he went on, "but there was no place to send them. No one was available to give us the status of our loan. So we just finished the building, sold off the condos, and banked the money, knowing that eventually we would be contacted to settle the loan."

"But it took quite a while," said Gallagher.

"More than three years. When that notice came from the FDIC, it was a bombshell."

"How much was the damage?"

"We were shocked. Those idiots had ignored all our calls and letters and then had the gall to charge us $1.5 million dollars in interest and penalties."

"Ouch!"

"It was totally unfair, but it appeared that there was nothing we could do about it. That would have completely sucked up the profit we made on the building."

"So what did you do?"

"I had a friend from my days in the military service. He worked at the Federal Reserve. He told me that a young congressman from Pennsylvania was on the Banking Committee and had a reputation for being very helpful to businesses that were having trouble with the FDIC. He got word to the congressman. One day, Jonathan received a call from Congressman William J. Prendergast. Ever hear of him?"

"Yes, I've come to learn a lot about Congressman Prendergast."

"I'm sure."

Oblas flashed a look of disgust and nodded his head. Then, he shifted in his chair and continued.

"Prendergast told Jonathan that he had a lot of connections at the FDIC and that he could help us dismiss the interest and penalties. He said we would have to come up with some cash that he would use to pay for the recording fees and background work. He would also need some money to convince other representatives on the committee to be sympathetic to our cause by making a few contributions to their reelection campaigns—to host some coffee klatches for voters in their districts and help defray some other campaign expenses."

"Did it sound a bit fishy to you?" asked Gallagher.

"Sure, but we only had to come up with thirty thousand dollars apiece, a total of $180,000. He claimed that's all he would need to eliminate all the interest and penalties."

"So you would save more than $1.3 million dollars," said Gallagher.

Oblas poured another glass of ice tea for himself and picked up one of the pastries from the tray resting on the table next to him.

"Yes, and it was $1.3 million that we didn't feel we rightfully owed. So when it came to a vote, we all agreed that it was the way to go. We each put the cash together, and then Jonathan and Dick flew down to Washington to deliver it to Prendergast."

"How did that go?"

"Everything went as expected. Within two weeks, we settled our obligation to the FDIC for two million and continued on our merry way. We never once thought there would be a problem. We just figured that's how things worked in Washington: we made some donations, paid off our loan, and that was it," he said as he wiped his hands together.

"Then what happened?" asked Gallagher.

"Sixteen years later, we get a call from a guy who claimed to be an investigator for the Democrat National Party. Says he wanted to meet with us regarding possible violations of congressional ethics codes. We didn't know what the hell it was all about, so we agreed to at least talk to this guy with no obligation or admission of wrongdoing on our part."

Gallagher simply nodded, took a drink from his glass of iced tea, and waited for more facts to come out.

Dan continued.

"So this young man shows up and tells us his company had been reviewing old loans from the FDIC. Says he was checking on how the final payment was handled. Then he says that our loan payoff looked suspicious."

"I'll bet that didn't go over very well."

"Damn right."

"Then what?" asked Gallagher.

Oblas's annoyance level had risen near the boiling point.

"The little brat actually had the nerve to ask us if we had bribed a member of the Banking Committee to help reduce the loan obligation. We were furious!"

"Did he accept your negative answer?"

"He ignored it. He just told us that, if we agreed to cooperate and testify against a member of the committee, he would recommend that we receive immunity from any federal prosecution. However, we would have to admit to bribery!" he exclaimed, becoming incensed at the very notion. "We were really pissed and virtually told the guy to get lost."

Gallagher continued taking notes, not wanting to interrupt, recognizing that his host was about to get to the crux of the story.

Oblas revealed that, as the weeks went by, the partners continued to meet privately to discuss the pros and cons of the legal bind in which they had become entangled.

"We knew we just couldn't dismiss this investigation. If something came up, or if someone misinterpreted our actions, we could all go to jail. We knew we had to come up with a logical plan. So, Jonathan decided to contact Prendergast to see what he knew about this investigation and whether he could give us any advice about how to respond."

"And what did Prendergast say?" asked Gallagher.

"According to Jonathan, the guy blew a gasket! Told Jonathan to sit tight, deny everything, and never let on that we had any contact with him. It suddenly became clear to us that Prendergast had a lot to hide. We knew that all that bullshit about other members of the committee and campaign contributions was simply that: unadulterated bullshit! We had been naïve and fooled by this bastard who was really out to make a pile of cash for himself," he fumed, becoming more animated and upset with each phrase.

He shifted his weight in his chair, wincing at times. Obviously, the feeling of discomfort in his hip seemed to escalate with his level of annoyance with the congressman.

"We met for several more weeks, trying to decide how to handle this. Finally, we agreed that we had to reveal the truth and tell our story, in the hope that the government, our friends, patients, and most of all, our families, would understand what happened."

He looked down, seemingly distraught by reliving the experience.

"But then, something happened?"

"Yes. Jonathan felt strongly that he should advise Prendergast of our decision. He wanted to call him and let him know that we were prepared to tell the story of how we gave him $180,000 in cash, expecting that it would be used as he promised. Jonathan thought that perhaps Prendergast could come up with some reasonable explanation of where the money went and provide verification of the fees and background expenses involved or show some accounting of the legitimate campaign contributions that were made. All we were asking was some proof that Prendergast hadn't kept all the money for himself. I loved Jonathan, but he had a Pollyanna view of this matter and gave Prendergast more trust than he deserved."

"What did Prendergast say when he heard that you were going to testify against him?"

"Surprisingly, Jonathan said Prendergast was pretty calm about it and just asked for a little time to put together some paperwork. He said he would contact us in about a month. He was not confrontational in the least. Jonathan felt that we may have weathered the storm. Meanwhile, we had heard nothing else from that investigator, so we didn't feel any urgency to act. We were lulled into a false sense of security that we had gotten through the crisis, and everything would be okay."

"Then what happened?" Gallagher pressed on.

"One of the worst days of my life. Jonathan was murdered in his car. When I first got the call, I became numb and couldn't believe it. I thought, 'Who could do such a terrible thing?' I know you probably think that we should have known immediately that Prendergast was involved. But imagine our position. We could never in our wildest dreams imagine that someone would kill one of us over this stupid loan payment. It seemed too trivial for such drastic action. And then, a couple of weeks later, Dick was shot in the elevator. Again, we bought the prevailing theory and the rumors from the police that some lunatic with a vendetta against doctors was loose in the town. In retrospect, we were blind to the facts that were right before our eyes."

He put his head down and shook it slowly, bothered by his last thought.

Gallagher could sense that Oblas' emotions were fragile and asked him if he needed to take a break.

"No, I'm okay," he shrugged. "Sometimes it's a little difficult to fathom all that has happened. Those guys were not just partners; we were friends."

After a brief pause, Dan continued by stating how everything changed when Phil Lombardo was murdered in Vermont.

"When that happened, the rest of us knew what was going on. We didn't know why such extremes had been necessary, but figured Prendergast must be involved in some major project in Washington and couldn't afford the risk of a bribery scandal. So Barry, Tony, and I got together and talked. We knew why Jonathan and Dick were the first ones killed: they had delivered the money. So they were the ones who could truly put that bastard behind bars. Phil was next because he handled most of our business affairs and had intimate knowledge of Jonathan's phone calls to Prendergast. In fact, I think Phil even spoke to Prendergast a few times."

He leaned back in his chair, gesturing with his hands held apart.

"The three of us who remained were really peripherally involved in the business functions of the partnership. None of us had ever spoken to or seen Prendergast. Technically, we only had hearsay knowledge about the money that was delivered. Barry and Tony were really scared and begged me to go along with them; they decided to say nothing to anyone, and let the police conduct their investigation."

"Then, out of the blue, a name from the past appeared in the news. Mickey Ryan was arrested and his gun matched the weapon that was used in the murders. That threw all the theories out the window and created more doubt in the minds of Barry and Tony. They were now convinced, more than ever, that keeping quiet was the best course of action until all this madness sorted itself out."

Gallagher was so engrossed in hearing the story that he was practically speechless. Then Oblas continued with a question for him.

"Tell me, Gallagher, do you think Mickey Ryan killed my partners?"

"No, I don't. I think he was set up."

Oblas heaved a deep breath and sighed, "So do I. Mickey was a hard-nosed guy to deal with, and we used the old straw-buyer trick to get him to sell that piece of frontage to us. But he would never retaliate like that. No, he was the fall guy in a clever plot to keep Congressman Prendergast in power."

Gallagher felt that he had heard the whole story and now asked the question that he had held back from the time he walked in the door.

"Are you willing to tell this story to the FBI? To bring Prendergast down, and, in the process, find out who killed your partners?"

Oblas looked up at Gallagher. His face sagged.

"Yes, I am. I wasn't willing before, but now I am," he answered, seemingly drained of his emotional energy. "This has to stop; we can't let that power-hungry son of a bitch get away with this. I'm even willing to go back to Boston to convince my remaining partners, Tony and Barry, that this is the right thing—the only thing—to do. I'll talk to Randi; she'll set it up for us. I'd like you to be there as well; after all, they tried to kill you, didn't they?"

Gallagher spent the next hour talking to Dan about his trips to Washington, his theory about a Las Vegas connection and the evening he saw Prendergast coming out of Gerard's Place after meeting with the mysterious Lan Tauber. Oblas listened with fascination, agreeing with Gallagher's premise that money was the factor that precipitated all the untoward events that had transpired.

By the end of their conversation, Oblas had finally cleared up most of the issues that Gallagher had been struggling with for weeks. However, Gallagher couldn't visit with him any longer—he wanted to get to the airport in time to catch an early evening flight back to Boston. He couldn't wait to drive up to Concord to see Kate in the morning and begin to make plans to bring her home and resume their life together.

There were now very few questions remaining. The secret meetings; the loan payment; the partners' relationship to Prendergast; Randi's hesitancy to tell him everything she knew. These troublesome questions had been answered. All that remained was to identify the murderer and determine who gave him the orders. And how did the murderer manage to steal Mickey Ryan's gun and then place it where it could be so easily found by the police?

Gallagher felt confident that these final few answers would be revealed in a short time and was buoyed with a new level of excitement and expectation as he drove to the airport. It was almost over—the case that had practically consumed his every waking moment for the past two months and had almost gotten him killed was almost over.

# CHAPTER 72

Three days later, Gallagher brought Kate home from the hospital. A few more weeks were needed to completely regain her strength. But her recovery had been remarkable. She planned to stay in Gallagher's condominium at BayView Towers where she could rest and do some work via the telephone and computer. If there was one positive outcome of the near fatal events almost two weeks ago, it was their mutual resolve to be together—forever.

Gallagher had adopted a cautiously protective attitude toward Kate, feeling guilty that this investigation had directly resulted in her injuries. He feared that the men who had tried to kill him on the highway would involve her again. Keeping her safe became his top priority. He was relieved when she agreed to stay at BayView Towers where the entrance to the building was protected by a security guard twenty-four hours a day. The condo also had an alarm system and a double dead-bolt lock to discourage any intruders from entering.

The doctors had told her that she couldn't drive a car for at least three more weeks, so Gallagher was confident that she would be out of danger by staying at home. He cautioned her not to open the door for anyone she didn't know.

Gallagher had taken some additional precautions for his own protection. In addition to his .38 Special snubbed-nose revolver, which he now carried in a belt holster so it could be concealed under a sweater, he had purchased a Smith & Wesson Model 642 revolver. This .38 Special caliber gun was only 6-3/8 inches long, weighed less than fifteen ounces, and had a barrel size of less than two inches. He placed it in an ankle holster on his left leg. When he wore a pair of loose fitting slacks, this weapon was virtually undetectable and offered him some extra firepower in an emergency.

Gallagher didn't know how or where the gunmen would come after him, but he knew they wouldn't delay much longer. He was in the final stages of piecing together the information that would put them behind bars. These men had followed him before, willing to wait for the perfect opportunity to dispose of him and keep him from divulging the facts he had gathered. They had proven their ability to track his every movement—to know his routines, where he traveled, and how he got there. He doubted they would risk attacking him in a public place where there would be too great a chance of being stopped or identified. He had to be cautious, therefore, of those times when he was alone, such as when entering and leaving his office or his condo at BayView Towers; on an elevator or a staircase; and especially while driving in his car.

The next time he would see the tanned face of the man who shot at his car—an image that was indelibly fixed in his mind, a face he could never forget—he could not hesitate to react; to do so would be a fatal error, a mistake from which there would be no recovery.

Gallagher knew that he was near the end of this game but, when it ended, whose gun would be firing the final shot?

# CHAPTER 73

The meeting in Gallagher's office went more smoothly than he expected. Dan Oblas had flown up from Florida to present his case to his partners, Barry Nickerson and Tony Cognetti, trying to convince them to turn state's evidence against Congressman William J. Prendergast. Randi Stockdale sat in on the meeting; only this time she took notes and recorded the proceedings that discussed a topic that had been kept secret from her in the past.

Dan presented a compelling argument. The partners no longer had any doubts about the origin of the deadly attacks on Jonathan Becker, Dick Evans, and Phil Lombardo and the near-fatal attempt on the life of Gallagher. Something had to be done to stop the perpetrators of this violence; otherwise the remaining partners would eventually become targets in order to guarantee their silence. Congressman Prendergast didn't commit the murders, but certainly he could lead the FBI to the individuals who did.

Barry and Tony acknowledged that they had previously acted out of fear and uncertainty. When the police arrested Mickey Ryan and announced that his gun was the murder weapon, the partners' suspicions of a conspiracy emanating from their contacts with Prendergast began to fade. Why come forward with a self-indicting confession in the absence of a perceived need or threat to their safety? Now, however, they had to agree with Dan; the time had come to go after the man responsible for the murder of their partners, no matter of the personal consequences.

The plan was logical. Gallagher would contact Jack McKissock in Washington to obtain the name of an agent within the FBI to whom the partners could make their depositions. Armed with that incriminating information, the pursuing investigation should cause Prendergast to seek a deal to save himself—to cop a plea that would implicate the criminal element in Las Vegas, which had orchestrated the murders, and, hopefully, identify the men who carried out the orders.

Lan Tauber, the evanescent LT, had to be a major player in the whole scheme and would ultimately become a key witness in uncovering the truth. As far as Congressman Prendergast was concerned, the three partners and Gallagher agreed that they couldn't wait to see the corrupt politician scrambling to save his own skin, all the while pointing fingers at everyone else.

The partners finished their meeting with a collective feeling of satisfaction. They were prepared to make their depositions, knowing they were embarking on a course that would seek justice, not only for their deceased partners but for an old nemesis who had been unjustly charged with their murders.

After the partners and Randi left, Gallagher called Suzanne Becker to inform her of the meeting and assure her that the case was in its final phases. Ever since the car accident, she had been worried about his safety and expressed her relief that the nightmarish ordeal was close to an end.

As he left his office, he exercised the cautious routine to which he had grown accustomed in the past several days. He carefully surveyed the corridor to the elevator prior to entering it and stood to the side before the elevator door opened. Simple things, yes, but designed to give him that split second of extra time he might need to defend himself and react to an emergency situation. He had even parked his car at the end of an aisle in the garage where he could more easily see if anyone was hiding from view, waiting to attack him without warning.

*They caught me off guard once. I'm not going to let them do it again.*

# Chapter 74

The daytime security officer at Tower II of BayView Towers was trying to concentrate on the sports page of the *Boston Globe* that featured a story about the New England Patriots and the upcoming playoffs. Wearing a white shirt and a black tie, he sat behind the curved desk near the entrance to this landmark apartment complex consisting of two forty-story buildings in downtown Boston.

Late afternoon.

The outer lobby bustled with activity as the occupants of the building rushed past the desk and flashed their entrance cards in front of the electronic card reader to gain access to the main lobby and the elevators. The security guard looked over occasionally; nodded to the occupants he recognized and made a casual effort to verify that everyone passing the card reader had a proper access card.

A man in a black leather jacket, with a brief case in one hand, approached the security guard.

"Excuse me. I'm trying to reach Bruce Butler; he gave me his address as BayView Towers."

Reaching over to the side of the desk, the security guard opened a large blue binder that had a long list of names with unit and phone numbers next to them.

"Doesn't sound familiar," he muttered as he scanned down the list. "Are you sure you've got the right place?"

"I'm positive 65 East Harbor Row, BayView Towers," the man insisted, now leaning down on the desk, partially obscuring the people who passed by—in particular a husky man in a black ski jacket. The security guard kept browsing through the list, shaking his head slowly as he couldn't come up with the name, unaware of the husky man who had just slipped by his watch and entered the lobby with several residents who clicked their access card on the card reader.

"Does he live with someone else who might be the owner?" the guard asked, trying his best to accommodate the visitor.

"Yeah, his girlfriend is Gina, but I only met her once. Sorry, but I don't know her last name," the man apologized.

Just then, the loud reverberation of a fire alarm punctuated the clamor of people walking by. The security guard shook his head and annoyingly slammed his pen on the desk.

"Oh, shit, not again!" he exclaimed as he got to his feet. "I'll be right back; I've got to check that out. Damn thing has been going off for a week."

Despite the blare of the alarm, the residents kept walking into the building, ignoring the sound that apparently had become all too commonplace. The small crowd was forced to mull around the lobby until the elevators were working again.

The guard swung a set of keys from a long chain on his belt as he walked through the lobby, past the elevators and entered the control room labeled "Private" at the far end of the corridor. The man who had been standing at the desk moved quickly, wasting no time getting to the staircase door that was located across from the elevators. When he opened the door, he was greeted by the husky man in the black ski jacket who gave him a smile of acknowledgement as they both made their way up the stairs.

"Good job, Nick," said Johnny, "You tripped that alarm just in time; I was runnin' out of excuses."

The two men slowly made their way up to the eighth floor. The fire alarm abruptly became silent. It had only taken the security guard about ten minutes to reset the alarm and return the elevators to normal operation. On the eighth floor, the men waited for an "Up' elevator. When the elevator door opened, there were ten other passengers. By luck, none had pressed "17." If they had, Johnny's plan was to get off at any other upper floor and wait in the stairwell for a few minutes before walking to the seventeenth. This was much easier; getting to his destination sooner while the commotion of the ringing alarm and the flashing lights of the fire trucks were still fresh in everyone's mind.

When they arrived on the seventeenth floor, Johnny looked down at the street from the elevator lobby window and could see the fire trucks assembled below.

"Beautiful," he said, "They're right on schedule."

He knew the "all clear" signal would be coming over the loudspeaker system in a few minutes, once the firefighters verified that this was a false alarm. His plan of deception had to be implemented without delay.

He stepped up to the door labeled "17C" and rapped firmly with the base of his key.

"Security!" he called loudly into the door, "Security! We're evacuating the building."

In a few seconds, a woman's voice answered, "Just a minute."

Four quick beeping noises signaled the disarming of the internal alarm system. Then, the sounds of the two dead-bolts sliding open and the doorknob turning could be heard in the hallway. When the first crack of light emanated from within the apartment, the two men forced the door open with a burst of muscle power. They pushed the woman off balance, and she tumbled to the floor. She started to scream for help, but the door was quickly closed.

Nick leaped down on her. He pinned her shoulders to the floor and placed his large hand over her mouth to muffle any further sounds, covering her nose in the process, making it difficult for her to breathe.

In the meantime, Johnny calmly secured the door by resetting the dead bolts. Then he assisted his partner in tying the woman's hands and feet with several small cords that he took from his briefcase.

They dragged her to an armchair that faced the entrance door to the apartment. The chair was positioned next to the sectional couch in front of the large glass window overlooking the harbor. Johnny took out a cloth resembling a long handkerchief and tied it around the woman's head, between her upper and lower teeth, forcing her tongue to the back of her mouth making it impossible to utter a sound without gagging herself.

She became panicky and gasped for breath.

Her eyes darted wildly around the room seeking help or hoping for mercy from her vicious attackers.

The tightly tied cloth began to cut the corners of her lips.

She could do nothing about it.

Then, Johnny wrapped a six-inch wide, dark-blue elastic band around the woman's body just below her shoulders and around the chair to secure her firmly. The efficiency with which the now immobilized woman had been overpowered and restrained was an indication of the experience of her intruders.

Kate McSurdy, just days after her discharge from the hospital, trembled in the chair, terrorized by these two men who had boldly forced their way into the apartment. She watched helplessly as they took two guns from the briefcase and methodically screwed on silencers to the ends of the barrels.

She instantly recognized their purpose, fully aware that she had not been their primary target. Their motive was not robbery or assault on a defenseless woman. Her worst fears had been realized—the premonition of danger that she had expressed in Rossetti's restaurant only a few weeks ago had come true.

*They've come to kill Gallagher, and I'll be forced to witness it.*

# Chapter 75

Six o'clock in the evening.

The excitement of the approaching Christmas holiday, just four days away, could be felt in the air. Pedestrians, carrying more packages than usual, entered BayView Towers after a day that apparently combined some work and a lot of shopping. Gallagher walked from the street into the lobby, glad to be inside, away from the cold. He turned down the collar of his top coat and took off his gloves before reaching for his access card to pass through the security area.

Joe, the friendly night-time security guard who came on duty at five o'clock, gave him his usual celebrity-type welcome, lowering his voice to a guttural tone and slowly calling out "Gaaalllll..a.. gher!," emphasizing the first syllable as if he were the public address announcer at a Celtics basketball game.

Gallagher acknowledged Joe's familiar teasing act with a smile and continued through the lobby to the elevators for Tower II. He pressed the "Up" button for the elevator and entered the cabin with several other residents who had just come into the lobby. As was his habit for the past few days, he stood to the back of the elevator and looked intently at each passenger to ensure that no strangers made any sudden movements toward him. He was cautious about everything and everyone around him. Until this case was completely over and all the parties involved were arrested, he knew he would have to dedicate himself to being vigilant and not let himself become vulnerable to a surprise attack.

When the elevator stopped at the seventeenth floor, he walked out into the small lobby and stood in front of the door to his condominium, Unit 17-C. He could hear the stereo sound of his fifty-four inch LCD television set and assumed that Kate was watching the early evening news. He took out his keys and unlocked the two deadbolts, located one above the other on the right side of the door.

As the door opened, he expected to hear the high-pitched signal of the interior alarm system; he expected that he would then turn to the keypad to disarm the alarm. But the only sound came from the television set playing loudly in the background.

He stepped into the small foyer.

The absence of the alarm signal made him reach for the gun in his shoulder holster.

Too late.

He looked across the living room—confronted by a scene so dreadfully frightening that his heart sunk into his stomach. He was forced to withdraw his empty hand from the inside of his coat.

Kate was seated in the arm chair to the left of the couch, her arms and legs tied, her mouth gagged, and a blue elastic band wrapped around her chest. Next to her on her right stood a man of medium height with brown wavy hair, deep set, dark eyes, and a tanned complexion—the man Gallagher recognized as the gunman from the highway. He held a gun with a silencer on the barrel and pushed it firmly into the side of Kate's head as she struggled to lean to her left, away from the weapon.

She could not speak, but the look of terror in her eyes said everything.

Before he could react to the horrific scene in front of him, there was immediate movement to his left, as another man stepped behind him, closing the door as he slid by, all the while pointing his gun directly at Gallagher's head. Nick Roberto bolted the door, then moved around to Gallagher's right, pulled his coat open, and removed the gun from Gallagher's shoulder holster. Nick's gun remained fixed on his target's head.

Gallagher remained motionless, afraid to resist, fearing that any defensive action on his part could cause both men to pull their triggers, immediately ending his life and Kate's. Nick stuffed Gallagher's gun between his own belt and shirt, then retreated slightly to the right, his back to the small hallway that led to the bedroom. He continued to hold his gun less than six inches from Gallagher's right temple.

"Welcome home, Mr. Private Investigator. We've been waiting for you to join our little party," said Johnny, obviously taking pleasure in the dominant position he enjoyed over his opponent. "You're gonna be sorry you walked away from that car accident in New Hampshire," he said with a sneer. "Some of you guys just never know when to quit and to stop stickin' your fuckin' nose where it don't belong."

Gallagher looked at Kate, who still trembled with fear but was now able to make direct eye contact with him. His mind rippled with thoughts and possible actions.

*I've got to do something to stop them. They're going to kill both of us in a matter of seconds. I can't let them do anything to Kate.*

He cursed his job as a private investigator for what it was doing to her, this woman who deserved a fate far better than this. He was willing to sacrifice his own life if it meant saving hers, but there was no way that these two gunmen would allow any living witnesses to the crimes they were about to commit.

Johnny moved his gun away from Kate's head and pointed it at Gallagher, who now had both drawn weapons trained directly on him.

One shot from each gun meant death.

Gallagher tried to prolong the moment—to give himself more time to come up with a plan, to see an opening that would allow him to reverse the odds that were so heavily stacked against them.

"Who sent you here? Who are you working for?" he asked, almost demanding an answer.

Johnny, still standing at Kate's side with his left arm behind the chair, took a small step forward and grinned at his prey, "That's something you're never gonna find out."

He raised his gun toward Gallagher's head.

This was Johnny's chance to execute his target and eliminate the source of his recent embarrassment.

"No one stops me, pal. Anyone who stands in my way has to pay the price."

He always enjoyed these final seconds, when his mark looked into his eyes and knew the end was coming. For Johnny, this one felt particularly sweet.

"Goodbye, wise guy!"

Johnny started to squeeze the trigger. Kate, watching the scene in horror, pushed her heels deeply into the carpet and thrust her body and the chair sharply to the right. Her head pounded against Johnny's right arm and pushed him off balance. He fired a shot wildly into the wall above Gallagher's head.

For a nanosecond, Nick took his eyes off Gallagher to view his partner, who now stumbled on the carpet and tried to regain his aim and balance. Gallagher seized the opportunity and instantly delivered a violent, upward blow with the base of his right hand. The thrust was directed obliquely and powerfully to Nick's throat and caught him squarely in his Adam's apple.

Nick let out a painful groan, as he lunged backward and gasped for air.

His gun rolled out of his hand onto the living room carpet ahead of him.

Gallagher pitched downward to his left, directly behind the swivel-based chair at the entrance to the living room. With one clean motion, he lifted his left pants leg and removed the small .38 revolver from his ankle holster.

Johnny had stopped to push Kate to the side, toppling her chair onto the coffee table, exclaiming in the process, "You bitch!"

He now moved quickly across the room in three short steps and pointed his gun downward, ready to finish Gallagher, lying on his left side on the floor. Nick slowly regained his breath and crawled forward on his knees to retrieve his lost weapon with its silencer attached. He ignored the gun he had removed from Gallagher's shoulder holster to avoid the noise of a gun blast.

Gallagher could feel his reflexes rapidly gaining control of the situation. He viewed the action swirling around him as if it were in slow motion. He began to respond as he had in the convenience store years earlier when he saved the life of his partner from an armed robber who was about to kill him.

Gallagher's hands steadied.

His pulse rate stabilized.

His reflexes were acute and intense.

He rolled back on his right side.

His quick movement surprised his approaching attacker, forcing him to shoot and miss with his next round. The bullet ricocheted off the ceramic tile in the foyer and lodged in the wall with a thud.

Now in position to squarely face his onrushing adversary, Gallagher extended his arm upward and took dead aim at the tanned-face man.

His index finger squeezed the trigger smoothly.

Two shots fired in rapid succession.

The bullets struck Johnny squarely in the middle of his rib cage with powerful force.

His forward momentum reversed.

He reeled backwards.

His eyes widened.

He clutched his chest with his left hand and fired another shot randomly into the ceiling. Now out of control, he fell onto the coffee table and crashed down on top of Kate, who was lying on her side on the floor, still tied to the small armchair.

Gallagher quickly directed his attention to Nick who had reached his gun and, from a kneeling position, was turning toward him ready to shoot. Gallagher's reactions were much faster than his hulking opponent.

Gallagher aimed and fired twice—the first a precise shot that struck Nick in his right hand, blowing the gun out of his hand—the second, a disabling round into his left shoulder that left him writhing in pain, bleeding profusely, and unable to get to his feet.

Gallagher, however, had no trouble standing up. Without a second's delay, he removed his .38 revolver from Nick's waistband. He pointed his gun down at the large-framed man lying against the living room wall, half-tempted to finish him now and prevent the possibility of a retaliatory attack. But he knew that this stranger, who had not spoken a word since he entered, would ultimately provide the answers to the final questions in this case. Keeping him alive as a witness was worth more to Gallagher than the satisfaction of seeing him dead.

Rather than shoot, he simply immobilized the wounded man with a chilling threat.

"If you make a move, the next bullet goes into your head."

Nick stared up at him without saying anything. He acknowledged the command with a nod and a painful expression on his face that told Gallagher he surrendered, preferring to live instead of attempting any further aggression.

Gallagher backed away.

He kept his eyes focused on the man, darting an occasional glance at the dead body, lying on its back and straddled over the coffee table. Kate lay on her side, unable to free herself from the chair.

The man's empty, dark eyes were wide open and fixed on the ceiling.

His chest was motionless.

A small pool of blood accumulated on the carpet below him.

Gallagher pulled the body away from Kate and let it drop down to the floor with a thud. He untied her hands and legs, removed the long cloth from around her mouth, and slipped off the blue elastic band that had held her to the chair. She stood up and hugged him, crying almost hysterically, as her emotions took over and relief set in after the events of the past hour. He returned her hug with only his left arm, as he continued to look toward wounded aggressor, who held his shoulder and tried to stem the flow of blood that soaked through his clothing and trickled down onto the carpet.

"Kate," he said tenderly, rubbing her shoulder with his hand. "It's over—it's all over. Everything is going to be all right now."

He would have preferred to take more time to comfort her, but recognized the potential threat of the imposing man across the room whose lower body was uninjured, allowing him to be mobile and still dangerous.

"We need some help; call 911 and get the police; I'll keep an eye on this guy until they get here."

As Kate picked up the phone and spoke to the police, Gallagher looked down at the fixed stare of the dead man lying on the floor next to him. By the end of the night, he would know his identity, and hopefully in the near future, the name of the person who had sent him on this death mission that had resulted in his own demise.

# Chapter 76

When the Boston police responded to the 911 call, they walked into a residence that looked like the scene of a mini-war.

One man lay motionless on the floor.

Another man, covered with blood, had two bullet wounds and lay on the floor with his upper body against a wall. He looked as if he were about to go into shock from acute blood loss. Arriving just minutes after the police, the team of EMTs wasted no time administering to Nick Roberto. They placed an oxygen mask over his nose and mouth, stripped off his shirt, placed him on a stretcher, and started an intravenous line. They applied bandages to his open wounds to control the bleeding. Five minutes later, they wheeled him out of the apartment, on his way to the emergency room of Boston Medical Center.

The EMTs also attended to Johnny Nicoletti, but there was nothing they could do for him. They left his lifeless body lying on the floor until the crime scene investigators and the medical examiner arrived on the scene.

Kate was visibly shaken but had sustained no injuries that would require hospitalization. The ordeal had taken a much more emotional toll than physical. She just needed a few days of rest to recover. The emergency technicians offered to take her to the hospital for observation, but she declined, preferring to stay with Gallagher.

The police had many questions. They had immediately disarmed Gallagher upon entering the apartment. Now they asked him to provide an explanation of the other guns, with silencers attached, that were found on the floor. Gallagher gave them precise details of the events, including the exact location of everyone in the room during the gun battle. He also told the police about the attempt on his life in New Hampshire—how the dead gunman had tried to kill him and Kate by causing a fatal car accident.

Kate described how the two men had broken into the apartment, tied her up, and then waited for more than an hour for Gallagher to return home. She gave a vivid, emotional summary of the way the men prepared for Gallagher's assassination and explained how they mounted the silencers and never uttered a word until he walked through the door.

On the ride to the police station to make their sworn statements, Gallagher and Kate sat in the back seat of a Boston police cruiser. She leaned close to him, to feel the warmth of his body and shield herself from the cold night air. He kissed her forehead and hugged her firmly, as if he never wanted to let her go.

"It's over—now for sure it's all over," he said, as the police car drove them away.

# Chapter 77

Two days later, from his hospital bed at Boston Medical Center, Nick Roberto made the logical decision. His choices were life in prison without the possibility of parole for kidnapping and attempted murder, or he could sing like a bird and tell everything he knew to the police. His full cooperation would result in a reduced sentence: twenty-five years with time off for good behavior. For a man in his early fifties, it represented a chance to get on with his life for whatever years he would have left.

So Nick talked, and everyone listened. Several homicide detectives from the Boston Police Department as well as Chief Tom Tackage and Detective Jack Hoskins from the West Castle PD gathered around his bed as he spoke. He described how his old acquaintance from New York, Johnny Nicoletti, had contacted him in early September to obtain his help with a major job in the Boston area. Johnny's boss in Las Vegas was a guy named Jerry Murray, whom Nick had neither spoken to nor met. Jerry wanted them to impersonate two private detectives in order to obtain information about the real-estate partnership that had built the Parker Hill Medical Building.

Later, Jerry Murray instructed Johnny to steal a gun from the home of a small-time bookie in Everett named Mickey Ryan. The gun was to be used to murder two doctors in West Castle; Johnny was ordered to stage the murders in and around the same medical building.

"Who pulled the trigger on the two doctors in West Castle?" asked Tackage.

"Johnny. Always Johnny. He was in charge. He was a real professional. I was just there to drive the car," explained Nick.

"What about the third doctor up in Vermont?" Tackage continued.

"He never came to the building in West Castle. So we found out where he lived and went up to Vermont. We staked out his house and followed him. Then Johnny arranged for an 'accident' while he took a walk one morning."

"Why these guys, Nick? Did Johnny ever tell you why they were targets?" chimed in Hoskins.

"No idea. Didn't matter to me. I knew they were doctors, but that was it. I drove the car 'cause I knew the area and Johnny paid me cash—plenty of cash. He got a big charge out of puttin' on a Red Sox cap, a pair of jeans and some runnin' shoes as a disguise when he hit that second doctor."

Then, Nick looked up at Hoskins and smiled.

"Johnny was a beauty. He always said there was no match for him."

"Looks like he was wrong about that," quipped Hoskins.

Nick ignored the comeback and volunteered more information about his work with Johnny. After the murders, they stole a car from Mickey Ryan's used car lot. A few days later, they dumped the car in Dorchester, leaving the murder weapon in the glove compartment. From what Nick had seen in the newspapers, the police had fallen for their plan of deception. Mickey Ryan was arrested and charged with the murders.

The police had many questions about Jerry Murray, the man who gave the orders to Johnny Nicoletti. Nick, however, could not offer very much help. Murray was somewhere in Las Vegas.

"I was never with Johnny when he got a call from Murray. And I never heard Johnny call him. Once in a while he would mention his name. I knew Murray was calling the shots. That's all. But, the guy must have had a lot of dough. He paid real good for those hits."

While this confession took place, Gallagher sat in on the deposition of the three remaining West Castle real-estate partners. He had converted his office into a make-shift conference room and listened intently as Dan Oblas, Barry Nickerson, and Tony Cognetti reiterated their stories to a young FBI agent who recorded their statements on tape. It was the same story Gallagher had heard before, but he didn't mind listening to the facts again. The partners were represented by their lawyer who sat by quietly and never raised an objection. The partners provided the details about their relationship with Congressman William J. Prendergast and the money they had sent to Washington in exchange for his help with their loan.

This information was highly incriminating. Prendergast's days as a powerful committee chairman were numbered, and his career as a United States congressman would soon be over.

The very thought of this conclusion brought a smile to Gallagher's face. He also looked forward to meeting with Suzanne Becker—to see the proud look on her face. She would finally know that, before his murder, her husband and his partners had tried to do the right thing, and that the greedy, corrupt person who instigated this tragedy was being brought to justice.

As he continued listening, Diane entered the room and whispered quietly into Gallagher's ear. He excused himself from the proceedings and walked to the outer office to take a telephone call from Attorney David Gorkin.

"Gallagher? I have great news. Mickey Ryan has just been released from jail. All charges against him have been dropped. You just delivered the best Christmas present Mickey could ever receive!"

*Christmas?* Gallagher thought, savoring the satisfaction of this entire day. *Best present? No—being with Kate, keeping her alive, that's the best present a man could ever receive.*

# EPILOGUE

Six weeks later, in Washington, D.C., facing congressional censure and criminal charges after an intensive investigation by the FBI, Congressman William J. Prendergast stood before the microphones at a hastily called press conference and announced his resignation. Although he admitted accepting money for illegally helping to reduce loans while a member of the banking committee, he steadfastly denied the rumors about his part in the West Castle murders.

In Bedford, Massachusetts, Suzanne Becker, secure in the knowledge that her husband's reputation was not tainted, followed the government's case against Congressman Prendergast with great interest.

In Las Vegas, Lan Tauber was questioned extensively by the FBI, but would only acknowledge that he had visited Congressman Prendergast to recommend voting against the bill that would establish resort casinos on federally owned property. He disavowed any involvement in the West Castle murders, and, in particular, denied ever meeting or knowing a man named Johnny Nicoletti. The investigation into his activities was officially considered "ongoing."

In Boston, Nick Roberto, confined to a prison hospital, continued to recover from his gunshot wounds, but would soon begin his twenty-five year sentence for kidnapping and attempted murder.

In Somerville, Massachusetts, Jimmy Nolan, in custody and suffering from delirium tremors, entered a court-ordered alcohol treatment facility. Following his therapy, he was expected to receive a suspended sentence and be placed on probation.

In Everett, Massachusetts, Mickey Ryan, a free man once again, was busy tabulating his take from betting sheets on the recent Super Bowl.

In Boston, Detective Jack Hoskins, never one to welch on a bet, reluctantly purchased a gift certificate for dinner for two at the Aujourd'hui Restaurant of the Four Seasons Hotel.

In Washington, D.C., Stu Tane, on the recommendation of his friend, Tony Macmillan, accepted a position as an administrator for the Democrat National Party.

In Brewster, Massachusetts, Kathryn Daisy McSurdy made plans for a September wedding at her parents' home, overlooking Cape Cod Bay, in which she would become Mrs. Daniel C. Gallagher Jr.

In Las Vegas, the FBI pursued the investigation of an enigmatic man named Jerry Murray, but the trail had reached a dead end. There were no leads and no witnesses. No one they interviewed had ever heard of him.

In Boston, at his Commercial Street office, Daniel Cormac Gallagher Jr., reflecting on the events of the past three months, looked out at the harbor below, and pondered the possibilities of a new career.

# Acknowledgments

To my real estate partners: Giovanni Aurilio, Dan LaGatta, J. D. Murray, Dick Norberg, and Larry Tobiason, and our administrative assistant, Elizabeth Stockwood. Thank you for allowing me to fictionalize the story of how we built a professional office building. Fortunately, none of you ever considered bribing a congressman or had to duck for cover to avoid the bullets from a Las Vegas hit man. I hope you will have as much fun reading this work of fiction as I had writing it.

Thanks also to Diane Beane, Kristen Rzezuski, Britt Emery, and Marcia Stein who read the original manuscript as each chapter was written. Your enthusiasm and encouragement kept me going.

A special thank you to my cousin, Lan Tauber. No writer ever had a more enthusiastic supporter. His portrayal as a bad guy could not be further from the truth.

I also appreciate the technical assistance from Haig Soghigian, former Northeast Regional Director of Investigations, Treasury Department, U.S. Customs Services, and from Keith Kaplan of the Boston Police Department. And a very special thanks to PO Michael Del Peschio (Ret.) and Sergeant Pattiann Pavacic-Del Peschio of the City of Yonkers, New York Police Department for their advice and editing of the police scenes.

To my family members, friends, and colleagues who allowed me to use their names in this book: thank you for helping my characters to come alive.

To Mr. L. Edward Purcell for helping to bring my manuscript to its final form. No author ever had a better editor.

And special thanks to my wife, Ronney, who served as the main editor of the early drafts. Whenever there was a choice for a word or a phrase, I should have known—she was always right.

Printed in the United States
By Bookmasters